I0683870

NIGHT ANGEL

GARGOYLE NIGHT GUARDIANS BOOK 2

ROSALIE REDD

NIGHT ANGEL
Gargoyle Night Guardians
Book 2

By

Rosalie Redd

Copyright © March 2020 by Rosalie Redd

All rights reserved. The uploading, scanning, and distribution of this book in any form or by any means—including but not limited to electronic, mechanical, photocopying, recording, or otherwise—without the permission of the copyright holder is illegal and punishable by law.

This book is a work of fiction. All names, characters, locations, and incidents are products of the author's imagination, or have been used fictitiously. Any resemblance to actual persons living or dead, locales, or events is entirely coincidental.

For permissions contact: Rosalie@rosalieredd.com
Cover Design: Croco Designs
ISBN: 9781944419288
United States of America

To those who wear rose-colored glasses
and believe in the good in others, bless you.

CHAPTER 1

*S*unshine. Such beautiful torment.

Seth Denton squirmed inside his gargoyle, eager to break free from his unrelenting stone form, but the sun chained him to his daytime post atop Stuart Hall at the University of Chicago better than any manacles ever could.

A growl burned, hot and fevered, from the depths of his pitiful soul. Unable to move until the last rays of the setting sun plunged beneath the horizon, he hated the confinement. Even now the golden orb, descending slower-than-molasses, taunted him, but if sunlight brandished his tender flesh for more than a few minutes, he'd receive a sunburn from which he'd never recover. That wouldn't do.

In the library's shadow, darkness filtered between the newly budded limbs and over the expansive lawn. The tips of the branches swayed in a slight breeze, eerily similar to the claws of a predator. Come nightfall, as one of the goddess Rhiannon's Gargoyle Night Guardians, he'd hunt as well. Except his prey wasn't innocent. The dark fae were killers.

Created by Gwawl, a bitter, angry god of the Otherworld, after Rhiannon refused to wed him in favor of a human man, fae killed humans for his pleasure and his revenge, and he added corrupt and malevolent souls from recent human deaths to his burgeoning ranks.

Finn, Seth's best friend and one of his partners in this war against the fae, whistled through the gargoyle mind link. *"Seth, your lass, she's comin' this way."*

Irritation slipped along Seth's nerves.

"She's not my lass." Yet, his attention riveted to the library's steps.

Hannah McAllister tightened her grip around the collar of her pink jacket and raced down the stairs. Her exquisite blonde hair cascaded over her shoulders, bouncing with each step. Cheeks reddened from either exertion or cold accentuated her porcelain skin and her enchanting emerald green eyes.

Beautiful, pure, innocent.

Against his will, a warmth Seth had no business feeling expanded deep inside. As much as he longed to spend time with her, he didn't deserve anyone as fine as Hannah. He had a questionable soul, after all, and a job to do.

"Deny it all ya want, but I've seen ya pinin' over her many a time. It breaks my heart, muffin." Finn laughed.

"You're imagining things, partner." Despite his best friend's amicable taunt, Finn had hit the mark a little too close to home.

Seth had tried to forget her and failed. He'd earned a rare night off a couple of weeks ago and had spent it in one of the dance clubs, drowning his sorrow in Jim Beam and a welcoming woman, one as far away in innocence and purity from Hannah as one could get.

Seth tracked Hannah's movements as she strolled across the grass. There were no other students in the vicinity. Most had already left for vacation or returned home for spring break. Even at this distance, he had no trouble noting the twitch of a grin on her features. To him, her smile lit up his world.

"Grayson, Damian, Finn, Seth, I'm picking up signs of fae near the twelfth street beach. That's your first stop tonight." Drake, their follow-the-book squad leader, issued his command.

The last guy who disobeyed Drake's orders and took an unscheduled night off ended up grounded for a week. No one, absolutely no one, wanted that kind of break, especially Seth. Stuck in gargoyle form during daylight hours unable to move was bad enough, but to be submerged in total darkness and unable to see?

A chill rippled through him. That, he couldn't handle.

Better to fight the fae and follow Rhiannon's primary decree —*protect humans*. As with all her warriors, Seth had powerful strength, extraordinary speed, and extrasensory hearing and sight, along with the ability to shift and blend in with his surroundings.

At least he was on the right team in this war. He couldn't imagine what it would be like to be a fae in Gwawl's army.

Between the trees, wind swirled into a small dust storm, picking up a few bits of dirt and grass in the churn—the telltale sign of fae.

Adrenaline zipped along Seth's nerves. The distance between Hannah and the fae was far too close.

He glanced at the setting sun. A thin line of the golden orb remained.

Hurry, damn it!

It seemed the fae wanted an early start, pushing dusk to the limit. The dust storm whirled faster. A piece of paper caught in the undertow and rose into the air. A moment later, the roiling energy slowed. In its wake, stood a fae.

With short, dark hair, a blue button-down shirt, and a pair of designer jeans, he seemed as ordinary as any man except for the yellow glow around his eyes and his three-inch claws. He bolted after Hannah.

Seth's pulse skyrocketed. He yanked against his invisible bonds.

The sun slipped beyond the horizon.

"Single fae in the quad. I'm on it. See you at the meeting point." Seth didn't wait for a reply. He clicked off the mind link, dematerialized, and reformed on the grass into his human form.

The bitter metallic tang of fae coated the back of his throat, evidence his enemy remained close. He scanned the vicinity. Movement several yards away caught his attention. The fae slipped between two trees, stalking Hannah.

Rage, mixed with the tiniest bit of fear, surged through Seth's veins. His skin rippled, taking on the greenish hue of the nearby hedge and camouflaging him.

He drew his whip from the belt clip at his waist, and with the other hand, he yanked his dagger from its sheath. Seth really missed his old six-shooter, but bullets turned to mush when they hit a fae.

He bolted toward his enemy, boots silent over the lawn. His Stetson slid off his head and bounced against his back, the hat held in place by the strap under his chin.

The fae closed the distance to its target. A sharp hiss burst from its mouth.

Hannah spun around. A loud, terrified scream erupted from her lips.

The fae leapt into the air, claws extended.

A warlike cry burst from Seth as he uncloaked himself and cracked his whip. The barbed tips wound around the fae's torso. With a hard jerk, Seth yanked the fae off balance.

The evil creature fell to the ground. Blood oozed around the barbed tips and stained his blue shirt crimson.

Hannah stood frozen in place, her hands covering her mouth.

"Run, Hannah!" Seth barked.

Horror reflected in her beautiful eyes, but then a fire burned within their depths. She lowered her hands, turned, and bolted.

Relief swept through him so hard, his fingers shook.

"You cost me a nice kill." Whip still wrapped around his torso, the creature gripped the leather and yanked.

Seth dug in his heels, his snakeskin boots sinking into the soft grass. He hardened his skin, his flesh now solid as stone.

The taut rope strained under the force.

"I'll be doing the killin' tonight, not you." Seth jerked the whip, snapping the fae off his feet.

The whip uncoiled, and the barbed ends smacked the horrid creature in the face. A howl burst from his mouth.

Seth pounced on the guy.

The fae struggled under Seth's weight.

Seth raised his dagger and plunged the tip into the fae's eye. He buried the blade to the hilt. A familiar exhilaration swept through him. Damn, that never got old.

Fae died by one of three methods—piercing the eye, severing the jugular, or setting the fae on fire. Seth preferred to see the realization of impending death up close and personal. He twisted the blade and yanked it from the dying creature.

The fae stiffened. A blood bubble formed alongside the wound then popped. Droplets of blood splattered over the fae's cheeks and chin. On a slow exhale, the dark creature disintegrated into a swirl of dust, leaves, and twigs, leaving no trace behind.

Another fae down. Score one for team Rhiannon.

Seth rose to his feet, clipped his whip to his belt, and adjusted his hat on his head. He surveyed his surroundings. Muscles still tight with tension, he couldn't afford to relax. Where there was one fae, there could be more.

Several yards away, Marco Valentelli leaned against an oak tree. Seth sneered at the fae's signature designer suit and overcoat. With his short blond hair and model-like features, Marco had lured many an unsuspecting human to their death.

Seth clenched his jaw until his teeth audibly ground together. He'd encountered this particular fae several times over the years, but the guy always seemed to elude Seth's grasp. Not long ago, Marco had toyed with Hannah in a battle that hadn't ended well for the fae. It seemed too much of a coincidence that Marco was here now, within striking distance of her.

Hatred rose from deep inside, and the spark stone over Seth's heart, the one Rhiannon implanted in all her warriors and contained a small piece of his soul, burned hot and fevered. He didn't need to look to know the small gem had changed from its normal opaque white to a deep red. One of these days, he'd kill Marco or die in the process.

The dark fae's gaze drifted along Hannah's path.

Seth's stomach knotted. He couldn't allow the fae to pursue her.

"Marco!" Seth tightened his grip on his dagger and stepped into Marco's line of sight.

Marco pushed away from the tree and spread his hands wide. The edge of his coat billowed around his knees, and the handle of his cane rested over one elbow.

A mocking smile tugged at his lip. "Ah, Seth. So good to see you, *again*. I really don't appreciate you killing my minion."

Seth's fingers twitched with the urge to bury his blade in the fae's eye.

"You're next, you piece of..." He clamped his jaw tight.

"Tsk, tsk. Such a gentleman. Won't cuss in front of the lady, hmm? I know Hannah's here somewhere. Think I can catch her before you?" Marco glanced between the trees.

Seth's gut twisted in agony as if Marco had shoved a knife deep inside, but he couldn't show any sign of weakness in front of this fae.

With a jerk of his wrist, Seth unclipped his weapon from his belt and cracked his whip. The barbed end crackled loud in the night air. "You won't get that far."

Marco smirked, and his eyes glowed a putrid shade of yellow. He placed his palm over the handle of his cane. "Well, cowboy, I hate to burst your bubble, but I can't stick around. I have other matters that require my attention. Perhaps we'll meet up another time."

Bits of grass and dirt swirled around Marco in a large whirlwind.

Seth lunged toward the dark fae, but the fiend disappeared into the churning mass before Seth could wrap his fingers around his measly ass and kill him.

Irritation flicked along his nerves followed by an uncanny sense of urgency. He glanced toward the trees. Hannah was out there somewhere. Whip in one hand, dagger in the other, he turned to pursue her.

"Seth?" Hannah's shaky whisper carried along the breeze.

"Hannah..." He exhaled, the tension at his nape slipping into the night air.

She stepped from behind a nearby tree. Her shoulders shook, and her fingers clasped and unclasped the strap of her backpack.

Seth hooked his rope onto his belt, shoved his dagger in its sheath, and ran to her side. The urge to wrap her in his arms and cradle her close swept over him, but he stopped mere inches away. Even though there wasn't a single spot of the fae's blood on him, he didn't deserve to touch her with his dirty, filthy hands.

"Are you all right?" he asked.

A shiver wracked her shoulders, and her cheeks reddened to a delightful shade that accentuated her rosy lips. "I'm okay. Thank you for saving me, yet again."

Last summer, after the encounter with Marco, he'd taken an unconscious Hannah to Wynne. The witch had revived her and from that moment forward, Hannah's beauty and innocence, so like his deceased Emily's, had branded into his soul.

In the ensuing nine months he'd tried to forget Hannah, but as she was a student here, he'd spotted her on a regular basis during her trips to and from the library.

Bound by his stone griffin during the day, he'd watched her from afar. Now that she stood next to him, her clean, crisp-as-fresh-linen scent weaved its way into his senses, burrowing deep and setting him on fire.

He removed his Stetson, ran his hand through his hair, and dipped his head. "You shouldn't be out here at night, especially alone."

Only a few people knew about the gargoyles, the fae, and the war between them. Cernunnos, Lord of the Otherworld and Rhiannon and Gwawl's boss, had decreed that all involved remain hidden from humans. Better that way for everyone, but a handful of humans had stumbled across the truth, including Hannah and her sister, Sadie.

If Hannah died at the hands of a fae, it would shred Seth from the inside out. He hadn't been able to protect his Emily, but he'd guard Hannah and keep his distance at the same time.

"It took longer to finish the final paper for my intro to business class than I thought, and I forgot to check the time. I hadn't realized dusk had fallen, but when I came outside, I thought I could make it home before the fae came out." Her gaze roamed his features, and she flitted her gorgeous green eyes back and forth as she studied him. "The fae... I was so scared. Until I saw you."

The muscles in his shoulders stiffened. She drew him in like a

7

moth to a flame. Little did she know how dangerous he could be to her purity and innocence. If he wasn't careful, he might—

A distinct metallic odor, like an old copper penny, swept by on the breeze. *Fae.*

He stiffened and settled his hat on his head. "I should get you home. Safer if I take you."

She nodded, her bottom lip quivering. "Do you mean fly? Like before. When you brought me home after you saved me from Marco the first time?"

The hair on his scalp rose. *Fly? Oh hell no.*

He reminded himself she, along with everyone else he knew, had no idea of his unusual skill. When Rhiannon selected a questionable soul for her army, she infused each gargoyle with a special talent, unique to each one.

No way this side of the Otherworld would he show Hannah his embarrassing gift. She was referring to the gargoyles' ability to transport people by dematerializing through space.

A sense of urgency spiked in his veins. He glanced around, his awareness growing of their vulnerability out in the open. "Yeah, we'll take the dematerialization express. Ready?"

She bit her bottom lip, gnawing at the plump flesh and distracting him beyond measure. A slow nod followed.

He didn't want to touch her, not with his filthy, no-good hands, but he needed the physical contact to transport her. With moths fluttering in his gut, he held out his palm.

She studied him for a moment, but then she slipped her fingers against his.

A tingle of pure sensual energy rippled between them.

The need to drag her into his arms whipped through him with gale-force intensity. Instead, he dematerialized.

Moments later, they arrived on the wrap-around front porch of an old Victorian a few blocks away. Streetlights spotlighted cars parked along the curb. Music blared from a nearby resident's window. Several houses down, a dog barked.

No sign of fae.

Although none of the fae's blood had coated his skin, the need to remove his dirty, tainted palms from her swept over him in a wave. Seth exhaled and released Hannah's hand. The lack of contact left him cold.

He removed his hat then cleared his throat. "We're here, darlin.'"

"I'll never get used to that feeling, my body breaking up like that and reforming. Weird, but thank you for bringing me home. Fae are so..."

"Evil. Dark. Dangerous. It's a down-right blessing the fae don't emerge during the day, but I don't like you out at night." He fisted his hands at the thought of one of those creatures harming or even worse, killing Hannah.

Hannah shivered and slid her palms up her pink jacket's sleeves.

Every time he'd seen her, she'd worn something pink. This time it was her coat, sometimes it was a shirt, or even a piece of jewelry. The pure, feminine color added to her air of innocence.

She drew her brows together. "Do you know what today is?"

Seth compressed his lips and rubbed his chin. "March twentieth. It's the spring equinox. Is that what you mean?"

She smiled and shook her head. The soft glow from the porch light bounced off her golden hair. "I really didn't expect you to know, but it's my birthday today. I'm nineteen."

Nineteen seemed so young, but he'd been that age when he'd married Emily in 1880. He swallowed and removed his hat. "Nineteen, wow. Happy birthday."

"You know, if not for you, it would've been my last."

The look of reverence and adoration in her eyes just about brought him to his knees. He stepped back, putting space between them.

She closed the distance and brushed her fingertips over the bare flesh on his arm.

His skin tingled along their connection.

"Would you like to come in? I'm sure Beaumont and Sadie would love to see you, and..."

Beaumont, a former gargoyle who'd passed his test, fell in love with Sadie, the human pickpocket that had stolen his spark stone. She was also Hannah's sister. A lump formed in Seth's throat. He missed his former teammate and had visited a few times, but he didn't trust himself around Hannah. She tempted him far more than he cared to admit.

He squeezed her hand then released her. "I can't. Not tonight. I have a job to do."

Besides, Drake would notice his absence if he stayed here much longer. Seth valued his freedom even if he had to traipse through the dark alleys at night and kill fae to protect the humans. A fitting punishment for his deeds.

At least he didn't have to worry about a fae nabbing her here. The witches warded this house. *Thank you, Wynne.*

Her lips pursed into a perfect bow, Hannah drew away. "Okay, then. Maybe some other time."

She withdrew a key from her pocket, inserted the metal end in the latch, then met his gaze. "I've seen you a few times here, talking with Beaumont. Why don't you ever stay?"

A lump stuck in his throat. What was he supposed to say? There was no way he'd tell her she reminded him of his deceased love, both in appearance and in mannerism, or that he'd often watched her out of the corner of his eye when he'd stopped by to see his old friend.

Besides, she was far better off without him. A nice young man would come along sometime, probably sooner rather than later, and give her all the things he never could—love, devotion, a life together.

A lance of jealousy pierced his heart, and the spark stone nestled on his chest flared hot. If he ever saw her with another man, he might beat the guy to a pulp.

He placed his hat on his head and gave her a quick nod. "If only I could."

Not waiting for her reply, he dematerialized in search of Marco. If Lady Luck smiled on him, she'd send that rat bastard of a fae to him along with a whole platoon of the evil creatures to kill, enough to erase his desire for what he couldn't have—Hannah, soft and willing beneath him.

CHAPTER 2

*H*annah McAllister inhaled, catching Seth's lingering masculine scent deep into her lungs. Hand on the doorknob, she stared at the porch step. He'd stood right there not a moment ago but vanished before she'd even blinked.

Still, she recalled every detail in vivid color—from his dreamy blue eyes, to his short brown hair poking underneath his Stetson hat, and on down to his sculpted muscles rippling under his dark blue button-down shirt. He was her savior, and a dream come true, all rolled into one fine package.

Thank God, he'd appeared when he did. Otherwise, she'd be dead.

Her pulse spiked at the memory of the fae, sending a jolt of pain to her temple. Despite his human appearance, the yellow glow in the creature's eyes held a promise of death.

Her death.

Until she moved to Chicago last summer, she'd never known such evil existed in the world. Well, that wasn't entirely true. She'd seen wickedness up close and personal at the hands of her Uncle Frank.

Mother was long gone, and after her father died four years ago, Aunt Sally had taken her in. Why her aunt stayed married to the creep, boggled Hannah's mind. At least her aunt had held him off, distracting him enough he lost the urge to strike. Well, most of the time.

On the few times Hannah had tried to interfere, it always ended up worse for her aunt, so she did her best to keep her distance. Later, she'd learned her uncle had a healthy fear of God. She used that to her advantage. Who knew words could be so powerful?

A car drove past, the engine's rumble fading into the distance and reminding her she couldn't stay out on the porch all night. Iciness crested over her shoulders and down her spine. Although the wards around the house's perimeter protected her, even in this nice neighborhood, evil could pay a visit.

She twisted the key in the lock and opened the door.

"Happy birthday, sis!" Sadie rushed forward and wrapped her arms around Hannah's shoulders. The tips of her shoulder-length dark hair tickled Hannah's neck.

Hannah returned the squeeze from the one person that meant more to her than anyone. She couldn't bring herself to tell Sadie about the fae. Not tonight. Instead, she did what she'd always done, buried her pain behind a smile. "I'm nineteen. Can you believe it?"

Sadie drew back, and her familiar grin curled her lips. "I know, right? That's so exciting! I'm glad we found each other again."

"Me, too." Hannah stared into her sister's green eyes. Their shared eye color was one of the few things they had in common.

Sadie had left home after their father died and had become a street kid. Both physically strong and mentally tough, she carried a healthy dose of skepticism and was slow to trust.

Hannah, on the other hand, became a cheerleader, a straight-A student, and even belonged to the drama club. Where Sadie had run from her problems, Hannah had done everything she could to become self-reliant. Although she wasn't tough like Sadie, she was determined, and when she put her mind to a task, she gave it her all.

Sadie arched a brow. "Finish your final paper?"

"You bet. Sent the file hours before the deadline." Hannah dropped her backpack on the couch. The cushions bounced from the weight.

Beaumont, former gargoyle and now Sadie's husband, strode into the adjacent dining room. He carried a cake, his biceps stretching his dark T-shirt taut. Scrawled in barely legible white letters on top of the chocolate frosting were the words "Happy 19th Birthday!"

"Sadie made you a cake. I attempted to frost it." A chagrinned smile tugged at his lips. "You want a piece?"

Hannah's throat constricted at their effort to honor her birthday. "It looks fantastic!"

Sadie smirked. "Hold judgment until you try a slice."

Hannah removed her pink jacket and laid it over the back of the couch. Pink was Hannah's favorite color. Even now, her fingernails sported a raspberry cream polish that matched her lacy, fuchsia, V-neck T-shirt.

The few friends she had in high school often told her she was too optimistic for her own good. They knew her uncle was an abusive bastard. But who wanted to live life jaded and bitter? Hannah refused to let him steal any more of her joy than he already had.

"Let's eat." Beaumont set the cake on the table next to a stack of plates and lit the candles.

"Happy birthday to you..." Off-tune and out of synch, Beaumont and Sadie sang the familiar song.

Tears formed in Hannah's eyes. The warm display was in such sharp contrast to her last disastrous birthday. An image surfaced, taking her down memory lane.

Aunt Sally carried a cake, singing the tune. Uncle Frank stormed into the room, launched the cake at the wall, and backhanded Sally. "You're spoiling the rotten kid." His actions and words had lingered for months.

As Sadie and Beaumont finished the song, Hannah wiped the tears from her eyes, and they all settled into their seats around the dining table.

Hannah scooted forward, stared at the candles, and drew in a large breath.

"Wait!" Sadie placed her hand on Hannah's arm. "Did you make a wish?"

Hannah shook her head.

"Hurry, before you blow them out."

Hannah's mind raced. *What should I wish for?*

Beaumont leaned toward Sadie, his gaze filled with reverence, and placed a kiss behind her ear. Sadie giggled, and a sly smile formed on her lips.

Longing swelled in Hannah's chest. *I want to be loved like that.*

Given the male influences in her life, her father's drunken absences, her abusive uncle, and her high school boyfriend who just wanted to get in her pants, she'd never found anyone who'd proven he wasn't in it just for himself. Even so, a sliver of hope that someday she'd have a real adult relationship with someone worthy had kept her from giving herself to anyone.

Lungs burning from holding her breath, she exhaled hard and fast. The rush of air blew out every candle.

Hope and excitement, mixed with the tiniest bit of nervousness, rippled along her arms. Although her girlfriends had talked plenty about sex, Sadie had never contributed to the conversations since she was still a virgin.

Beaumont clapped.

Sadie touched Hannah's arm, warmth embedded in her gaze. "I saw that gleam in your eyes. You must've wished for something good. I'd ask what it was, but…"

"It wouldn't come true." Hannah twisted her fingers over her pursed lips, locking in her secret. "I'll never tell."

Sadie laughed. "Good."

Beaumont slid a knife through the cake, balanced a large slice on the blade, and dumped it onto a plate. He handed the piece to Hannah along with a fork.

A sense of fatigue crested over her shoulders, and a headache built behind her eyes. The final paper had taken a toll on her energy level, but she pushed past the pain and gripped the plate.

She slid the utensil through the baked confection and slipped a forkful into her mouth. The sugary sweetness barely registered for her gaze focused on the knife's glinting tip as Beaumont cut another piece.

Her mind returned to the night's earlier events. The fae's glowing eyes. His sharp claws. Fleeing, hiding, shivering with fear.

What would Sadie do if Hannah had died tonight? Hannah shook her head and shoved the gloomy thought away. She'd survived, like always, and would continue to do so as long as she made smart choices.

Sadie placed her hand on Hannah's shoulder. Her brows furrowed. "Sis? Did you hear me?"

Hannah blinked. "What?"

"Are you sure you don't want to come along?"

"Along where?"

Sadie sat back in her chair, crossed her arms, and studied Hannah. "On the cruise with us. I'm sure we could get an extra cot put in our suite and—"

Hannah held up her hand. "Sleeping on a cot in your room while on your Caribbean cruise honeymoon is one of the worst ideas, like ever. That's just weird."

"But we'd have so much fun and—"

"Little bandit." Beaumont brushed a stray hair behind Sadie's ear. "Hannah will be just fine. She's nineteen. Maybe she has her own plans for spring break. With some hot new boyfriend we know nothing about."

Beaumont winked at her.

"Um, there's no boyfriend, but you two don't need a third wheel." Besides, she wanted time to sketch her belated wedding gift to Beaumont and Sadie. They'd married over the winter holidays, and Hannah hadn't had time to create the piece.

Now that spring break was here and they had plans, she'd finish the sketch and give it to them when they returned. Sadie had always liked the pictures Hannah had made for her, and Hannah couldn't wait to make this special sketch for both her sister and Beaumont.

Pain blossomed behind her eyes, crashing over her in a wave of agony. She inhaled and held her breath until the ache receded.

"Hey, you okay?" Sadie trailed her fingers down Hannah's arm.

"I'm fine." Her stomach roiled. She couldn't get sick. Not now. But it was just like a flu bug to wait until all your classes and tests were done, then swoop in and slap you with a good one.

Sadie crossed her arms. "Nothing happened today at school, did it? You look pale."

"I'm perfectly fine." Hannah crossed her arms, mimicking Sadie's posture.

As much as Hannah longed to tell her sister and Beaumont about her brush with death, she refused to give Sadie a reason to cancel the trip. Sadie and Beaumont deserved their honeymoon.

Sadie blew out an exasperated breath then wrapped her arms around Hannah's shoulders. "All right. I just worry, you know? We've been back together now, what, nine months? I can't help it."

Love for her sister swelled inside. "I love you, too. You and Beaumont will have a great time. Can't wait to see you off tomorrow morning. Don't forget to send me pictures, okay?"

Sadie drew back, her eyes moist. "Of course. Oh, I almost forgot."

Sadie rose from her seat, hurried to the sideboard, and withdrew a package wrapped in blue and white striped paper. She returned and held it toward Hannah. "For you, from the both of us. Happy birthday."

Beaumont rose from his seat, strode to Sadie's side, and wrapped his arm around her waist. "We hope you like it."

Hannah scooted the chair back and stood. With trembling fingers, she accepted the gift. Gentle, at first, she tugged at the paper's edge.

"Rip it open." Beaumont's brown eyes sparked.

A laugh bubbled from deep within, chasing away her earlier gloom. She grabbed the paper and ripped it off the gift box. She lifted the lid and—

Her breath stalled. "It's beautiful."

Hannah withdrew the angel from its resting place. The tips of the angel's white wings flared at the ends, and its eyes seemed to project a fierce protectiveness.

She trailed her fingers over the palm-size wall hanging, enjoying how the cool ceramic eased the warm clamminess in her hands. "Thank you, thank you, thank you."

Not giving Sadie a chance to respond, Hannah hugged her sister. The bond between them warmed her heart.

After drawing away, Sadie smiled. "I remember when you broke the one Mom gave you a couple of weeks ago. You were so sad, and I know how much that piece meant to you."

Hannah sniffled. When she was six years old, Mom had given her the angel before she'd walked out the door never to return. Hannah had held on to the small memento ever since and had cried when she'd knocked it off its resting place over her bed. To have Sadie give her another, though, meant more to her than she could say.

She forced the lump in her throat down with a hard swallow. "This one is much nicer. You shouldn't have."

Sadie waved her hand in the air. "If you're worried about the money, don't. I wanted to get you something special to make up for all the birthdays I missed."

Hannah's chest tightened at Sadie's heartfelt words. She'd missed her sister so much over the last four years and they'd grown close again these past few months. Threatening tears burned her eyes. Refusing to cry, she straightened her back.

"I know right where to put this one. Goodnight, and thanks!" Before Sadie could see how much the gift had affected her, Hannah raced up the stairs and into her bedroom.

An empty picture hook rested over her single bed. She crawled onto her comforter and set the angel in its place. Here, he'd watch over her as she slept. Even as a sense of peace settled over her shoulders, her pounding headache resumed.

The cake soured in her stomach. Her mouth watered, the precursor to—

Hannah lurched off the bed and ran straight for the toilet. She'd caught a nasty bug after all. Her stomach roiled, and she slipped to the floor and wrapped her fingers around the cold rim, her face mere inches from the porcelain throne.

The sound of her quick breaths echoed from the bowl. *What a way to spend a birthday, right?* If not for the queasiness churning in her stomach, she'd laugh.

A few minutes passed without incident, and the nausea receded. Her arms weak and shaky, she pushed off the floor and rose to unsteady feet.

Her mirrored image caught her attention. Dark circles rimmed her eyes, her cheeks seemed flushed, and sweat beaded her upper lip. If today wasn't her nineteenth birthday, she'd swear she looked much older, and she couldn't attribute all of that to the illness. Had the pressure she placed on herself to succeed and beat the odds taken a toll?

A shudder rippled down her arms, leaving goose bumps in its wake. She rubbed the bristled flesh. The black lines of her tattoo peeked from beneath her shirt. She slid the fabric over her left shoulder and stared at the design of a small pair of white wings.

Memories assaulted her like an unwanted visitor. Uncle Frank's fist smashing against her back, her ribs, her shoulder, anyplace clothing could cover the bruises. That was the one time she'd arrived home from school before Aunt Sally, who'd ended up caught in traffic.

After the bruises healed and out of guilt, her aunt had given in to Hannah's request for a tattoo and taken her to Destination Ink, the local tattoo shop. Hannah had known right away what she'd wanted.

Somewhere out there she had a guardian angel. She believed it deep in her soul. That terrible day her uncle had seen the ceramic angel her mother had given her sitting on the picture hook over her bed. He'd ceased the beating, leaving her bruised, but not broken.

Hannah released the shirt. The fabric slid over her skin, covering the tattoo once again. She studied her reflection a moment longer, wondering at the young nineteen-year-old woman staring back at her. *Could a man ever love me?*

Doubt danced across her mind, unbidden and unwelcome, but she chased it away with a determination she'd honed to a fine point over her short life. After the negative way men in her life had treated her, she refused to rely on any man to survive.

Hell, that was the main reason she'd decided to major in business. A business degree was the smart thing to do, but it didn't feed her soul, not like her sketches.

Whenever she put charcoal to paper, her chest lightened. The world seemed as bright and beautiful as the sun shining off a waterfall, snow blanketing a forest under the full moon, or the colorful bloom of a meadow in springtime. Even now, just thinking about creating art warmed her on the inside, chasing away some of her headache.

Maybe, just maybe, if she received a decent night's sleep, the rest of her headache would be gone by morning. Yeah, that was it.

With an ease in her step counterpoint to the slight pounding behind her eyes, she flicked off the bathroom light and padded into her bedroom.

After the stress of finishing her school paper, her near-death encounter with the fae, the birthday surprise from Sadie and Beaumont, and seeing Seth again, no wonder her nerves had gone all haywire and she had become ill.

Hannah changed into a pair of pajamas with the words *"Let Me Sleep"* printed on the front and slipped between the covers.

Before she lay down, she glanced at her birthday present then drew her finger over the angel's magnificent wings. An image of Seth with his deep blue eyes and sexy smile flitted across her mind.

If anyone deserved the title of "guardian angel," it was him. He'd saved her yet again.

She flicked off the lamp on her nightstand and drew the comforter up to her chin. As her headache blended in with her exhaustion and tugged on her consciousness, her last thoughts centered around the sculpted, sexy gargoyle. Only in her dreams could she be with a guy like him.

CHAPTER 3

*S*eth dematerialized on the shore of Lake Michigan, along the twelfth street beach. Water lapped against the sand, the rhythmic cadence eerily chilling in its peacefulness. In this war, any fleeting sense of peace never lasted long.

As he inhaled, the metallic scent of fae burned the hairs inside his nose. He stifled a gag and unclipped his whip from his belt.

Several feet away, Finn, Damian, and Grayson surrounded one of the deadly creatures. Blood dripped from numerous gashes on the fae's arms, chest, and face. Even without his gargoyle senses, the scent of impending death was unmistakable.

Damian plunged his dagger into the fae's eye. The creature slid to the ground and his body disappeared into a small swirl of dust. Another dark soul banished from Earth.

After Beaumont, Seth and Finn's former partner, passed his test and became human once again, Rhiannon brought in two new team-mates. Grayson, a dark-haired guy with a gold ring in his ear and a red scarf around his neck, looked like a deranged pirate. Damian was a dark-skinned guy of African descent born soon after World War II.

Neither were as close to him as Finn. He and his best friend had battled fae together for over a century. Yet, Seth kept some secrets hidden even from his best buddy.

Seth rewound his whip and clipped his trusty weapon to his belt. "Good job, boys."

Ever-present black gloves hid Damian's hands from view as he wiped his blade across his dark jeans. "Where the hell you been?"

"Picked off a fae in the quad." *Rescued a sweet, innocent young lady.* "Then found a few more. Took me a while."

Indeed, after his time with Hannah, he'd returned to the University of Chicago in search of Marco and intent on purging any other fae in the vicinity. More than that, though, he'd needed the distraction.

He couldn't afford to spend too much time with that pretty young thing. She tortured him far too much. Although he hadn't run across his nemesis, he'd found several other fae. Nothing satisfied him more than dispatching those dark creatures to the ether, the space between space.

"Jaysus, why did ya turn the mind link off? We communicate that way for a reason." Finn raised a dark eyebrow over his piercing Irish green eyes. "Drake's been askin' about ya. Threatened ta track ya down if ya didn't show soon."

"And he's not happy. Sucks to be you." Grayson shook his head and the tips of his curly, dark mane bounced against his shoulders. "You itching to spend some R&R on top of Stuart Hall, or do you want us to cover for you?"

A groundswell of gratitude swept over Seth. Despite the razzing from his teammates, he knew without question the guys would have his back. "Drake's as irritating as a rock in my boot. I shut down the mind link for a few hours and it's like he's as nervous as a long-tailed cat in a room full of rocking chairs. He can check my kill record if he's of a mind to."

He touched the brim of his hat, turned on the mind link, and strode to the water's edge. His snakeskin boots sunk into the sand and small ripples washed over the tips.

Even above the glow from the city's lights, a purple tinge brightened the horizon. "Daylight soon. Need to—"

"Well shit, Seth, decided to link in, did you?" Drake's irritating voice filtered through Seth's mind. *"Glad we could be of service. You and I will chat later. For now, you and Finn sweep the beach for any remaining fae. Damian, Grayson. Need you to help squad Delta. Meet me at Wrigley Field."*

The mind link severed.

Seth ground his teeth so hard the cartilage in his jaw crackled. *Bite my ass, Drake.*

Drake oversaw several squads within the city. Even though Drake's hard-nosed, rule-abiding attitude slipped under Seth's skin, there were worse squad leaders out there. Seth had reported to a few in the past. Drake was one of several throughout the country and, for that matter, the world, but he could count on Drake's consistency. For that reason alone, Seth put up with him.

Damian clapped his large, gloved palm across Seth's shoulder. "Good luck, my man."

Grayson stroked his dark mustache and shrugged. "I had a feeling..."

"Don't ya two have someplace ta go?" Finn pursed his lips, and a tic pulsed to life in his jaw.

Seth's mouth dried, as if a desert wind had sucked all the moisture from the air. Over the past few months, Finn's temper had worsened. If his friend wasn't careful, he'd end up on Drake's short list or worse.

Grayson and Damian dematerialized, but not before Seth caught the smirks on their faces. Figures.

Finn glanced at him and narrowed his gaze. "Now, what were ya really up ta? Were ya with the lass?"

Seth raised his hands. "Don't go there. Just don't."

"So you were with the lass." Finn's features softened, and a chuckle eased from his lips. "My, that's sweet."

"Enough already." Seth ground his teeth. "Like I said, I took out a few fae in the central district—"

Finn stiffened, and his lip curled. "Shite. By yerself? Don't tell me ya were lured into someplace ya shouldn't be."

A few years ago, Seth had chased a fae through an old abandoned building and nearly into the dark depths of Chicago's underground tunnels. Memories of the old abandoned mine he'd fell into when he was five had swirled in his head—the numbing cold, the utter darkness, and his unanswered cries for help. Maybe it was karma the fae had escaped.

Finn knew about Seth's past and dagnab the guy for worrying. How pathetically sweet.

Seth shook his head. "No, of course not, and you better watch it, or your face'll freeze like that."

Finn placed his hand over his heart and feigned pain. "Oh, ow, it's stuck! Help me, mate. My face... Ahhh!"

"Your expression... Oh, man." Seth laughed and playfully shoved Finn. "Remember the time we ran into that guy outside the bar on Canal street?"

Finn righted himself, a grin on his face, then pointed at Seth. "You mean the one that saw us materialize next to his car and his eyes bulged?"

"Yeah, that one." Seth chuckled as they walked along the beach. "You looked just like him."

"I kind of felt for the guy, ya know. Too much ta drink and all." Finn bumped his shoulder into Seth and kicked up some sand.

Seth laughed at the memory. Although Finn had a great sense of humor, he often struggled with his internal demons. Finn had lost a sister to an abusive husband. They'd never spoken directly about it, but Seth suspected his path to becoming a gargoyle revolved around his sister's death.

Seth placed his palm on Finn's shoulder. "Yeah, but telling him we were figments of his imagination really pushed it too far, don't you think? Good thing we mind swept him, but we should've been more careful—"

A woman's shrill cry echoed through the night. "Stop! You're hurting me!"

The muscles in Seth's shoulders stiffened, his senses on high alert.

Bathrooms in a long building, part of the Chicago Park District, stood several yards away. Two different sized figures struggled outside one of the doors. The dim light from overhead fixtures cast their male and female features in a soft glow.

With his extrasensory vision, Seth noted the dark hair and the familiar three small teardrop tattoos on the large guy's cheek. *Gabriel Rhodes.* Last summer, he'd abducted Hannah in an effort to lure Sadie to him.

Anger-fed adrenaline ripped through Seth's veins. He bolted toward the couple. Caught in the breeze he'd created, his hat flipped off his head to its resting place on his back.

Gabriel punched the woman in the face, once, twice, three times.

The woman doubled over. Her knees hit the pavement, and her long, dark brown hair fell over her shoulders, obscuring her features.

A war cry erupted from Finn. Murderous intent etched lines around his thin lips. Even as Seth closed the distance, Finn dematerialized. A moment later, he reformed in front of the couple.

Seth's stomach tightened. Finn shouldn't appear in front of humans like that. Staying under the radar was a top priority. The less the humans knew about the war around them, the better.

"Take yer dirty hands off her." Finn gripped Gabriel's shoulders and flung him against the buildings outer wall.

The crunch of breaking bones echoed into the night.

Gabriel moaned.

Seth wrapped his arms around the woman and drew her to her feet. She trembled against him. "You're okay. He won't hurt you anym—"

"Ya piece of trash. Didn't yer ma teach ya not ta hit a lass?" Finn grabbed Gabriel by his jacket's collar and yanked him upward.

His feet dangled above the ground. Mere inches from Finn's face, Gabriel's mouth opened and closed, but no words emerged.

Seth's pulse spiked. With Finn's recent hair-trigger temper, this situation might spin out of control fast. "Finn, let him go. He's not the enemy."

"D...don't hurt him." A tear slipped over the woman's lashes and melded with the red snot seeping from her nose.

The coppery scent of human blood filtered through the air.

Finn's gaze riveted on the woman. A darkness Seth had never seen before sparked in Finn's eyes. "Ya bloodied her..."

A brisk cold raised the hair along Seth's nape.

Time seemed to slow.

Finn's grip tightened around Gabriel's collar to the point his knuckles crackled.

Gabriel clawed at Finn's arm.

Finn shoved Gabriel against the wall and wrapped his other hand around the guy's throat.

"No, Finn!" Seth lunged for Finn, but the woman in his grasp slowed him down. He bolted around her to—

Finn snapped Gabriel's neck.

The crisp pop echoed off the brick then dispersed amid the soft murmur of the lake's gentle wake.

The woman screamed and bolted.

Seth caught her around the waist and placed his hand over her mouth. With her in his arms, he glanced at his best friend, his eyes wide, his heart pounding. "Finn, what the hell did you do?"

Finn released Gabriel. The dead body slid down the brick wall and slumped onto the pavement. Gabriel's head rested at an odd angle, his glazed eyes staring into nothingness.

Finn backed up. He gawked at his hands. "This canna be real."

He glanced at Seth. Terror reflected in the depths of his eyes.

"Finn. Let me help you—"

A deranged laugh burst from Finn's lips. "There's nothin' ya can do. I've made a right bags of a mess. I donc killed a human."

Seth couldn't speak past the tightness in his throat. Finn had committed the ultimate crime for a gargoyle. The animalistic side of him, the one Rhiannon buried deep in all her warriors to match their hardened, daytime gargoyle forms, shrieked in outrage.

The molecules in Finn's fingers disintegrated, turning to a fine powder. He stared at Seth, shock etched in his features. The condition tracked up his arms and into his torso. A moment later, he disappeared in a whirlwind of dust and debris.

25

Finn, Seth's longest and best friend, was gone.

Helplessness like he'd experienced more than a century ago washed over him. Memories of Emily's illness and subsequent death triggered in his mind. He hadn't been able to save her either. The tiny bit of his spirit embedded in his spark stone ached with raw pain. A sorrowful cry erupted from his soul.

The woman struggled in Seth's grasp.

He pulled on the self-control he'd honed since he'd first joined Rhiannon's army and spoke to her. "It's okay. I'm not going to hurt you. When I remove my hand, don't scream."

He let her go.

She turned to face him, and her eyes widened. "W...what are you?"

"A nightmare you will soon forget." He placed his palm on her forehead and wiped her mind, implanting a fake memory that a shadow, a man she didn't get a good look at, had killed Gabriel.

After he removed his hand, he set his hat on his head then dematerialized to the one place that might give him a fraction of the relief he so desperately needed.

Seth's molecules reformed on the dome of the old, abandoned church not far from the university. The circular glass panes bore his physical weight which was far less than the heaviness he carried on his shoulders.

His skin rippled as he assumed the building's light gray color, blending in with his surroundings. Any human out for a pre-dawn walk on the street below would never know he existed.

He kneeled, removed his hat, and lowered his head. After the night's events, the lingering scent of fae seemed like a permanent burn in his nostrils.

"Dearest Rhiannon, have mercy on Finn's soul." Even as Seth said the words, he understood from countless years under Rhiannon's command that there was no leniency available.

In this war between fae and gargoyle, Rhiannon couldn't afford to show an ounce of compassion toward one of her warriors that failed his test. Gwawl would seize upon the opportunity and use it against her.

The weight on Seth's shoulders slid into his upper body becoming a full-on ache. He and Finn had become gargoyles within a year of each other, both joining Rhiannon's team in the mid-1880s. They had become an unbreakable pair, teaming up together and hunting fae with a dedication and commitment to rival even the best gargoyle hunters.

With an internal thought Seth hardened his fist, turning the flesh to stone. The urge to punch the glass and shatter the panes rippled through him so fierce his hand shook, but he wouldn't desecrate this holy place. Not that numerous humans hadn't already marred the abandoned church.

But that was the very reason he liked to come here. The neglected shrine reminded him of his prior human faith in God and, without humans, the empty building became his private sanctuary.

After he'd died and his soul had traveled to the Otherworld, he'd realized that all religions had common threads and that many of the gods and goddesses of the past still existed, side by side with current theology. Rhiannon had stepped forward, claimed him as a questionable soul, and he'd devoted his second chance to serve in her army.

Seth returned his hand to flesh. With the utmost care, he set his hat on one of the glass panes then wiped his brow with the back of his hand. He stared at the sky, his heart heavy. Pink tinged the clouds on the horizon, the first inkling of dawn.

"Why'd you do it, Finn?" Seth forced the words through clenched teeth. "Why, why, why?"

Presented with his test, Finn had failed. Tonight, tomorrow, no later than that, Finn would re-emerge at dusk as a fae. Seth prayed he never ran into his old friend. He wasn't sure he could plunge a dagger in his eye.

Seth brushed his fingers over the braided leather cord at his wrist, tracing the infinity symbol with his finger. The self-made design was a tribute to Rhiannon, a way to remember his infinite dedication to his goddess.

He longed to be human once again, to experience a love like the one he'd had with Emily, but unrelenting doubt over his ability to pass his test plagued him like a man in a desert seeking water. Out of reach and unattainable.

He didn't know what the test would entail, but he'd be forced to face his fears, his past, or both. Seth was caught in a never-ending cycle. He pivoted from dreading his test to inviting the challenge, switching from breaking out in a sweat to screaming at the top of his lungs. The roller coaster ride had no exit.

Rhiannon, though, had given him a chance by selecting him as one of her gargoyle night guardians. He wasn't sure if he'd have given himself the same opportunity, but he thanked her endlessly, none-theless.

On the street below, the dusky hue of dawn painted the trees along the sidewalk in shades of gray. A bird chirped, answered by another. The rumble of a car engine roared to life.

Seth didn't have much time. If he didn't return to his post soon, he'd be locked out for the entire day. Now that would really piss off Drake.

Seth removed his jacket and placed the worn leather coat next to his Stetson. He quickly unbuttoned his shirt. With a flip of his hand, he tossed the material on top of his coat.

Still crouched on one knee, he lowered his head in prayer. His skin rippled as his feather-coated bones elongated and sliced through his skin, the soft pop and crackle escaping into the night air.

He stretched his wings, white as snow with silver-tipped ends, extending them to their full seven-foot span. He released a long sigh. After a full night cramped tight against his back, his wings ached.

A soft breeze swept across his twin appendages, caressing the feathers like a lover and sending sensual delight along the sensitive nerve endings. Self-hatred coiled in his stomach.

When Rhiannon placed a questionable soul into a gargoyle, she provided each one with a unique talent. His goddess had blessed him with wings. White, pure as an angel, damn wings. More of a curse than a blessing as far as he was concerned.

While some other gargoyles had leathery wings that could turn as stone-hard as the rest of their flesh, Seth's white wings couldn't do that and were a weakness he loathed. Embarrassed as he was by them, he'd never tried to fly and never would.

Maybe the useless wings were Rhiannon's idea of a joke, and she'd given them to him to match the wings from his stone gargoyle—a griffin, no less. Why the hell he needed them when he could dematerialize was beyond him.

He'd wanted to ask her, but questions like that were frowned upon. Instead of using his wings, he dematerialized himself everywhere he needed to go.

Fortunately, he'd hidden his "gift" from his teammates for over a century. Although Finn may have suspected, he never once asked. His best friend had remained silent and had earned Seth's loyalty. That didn't matter anymore, though, did it?

Seth raised and lowered his wings, letting the cool, impending dawn air filter between the feathers. Up here, hidden from view, he could afford to let them out, but he'd never, ever, show them to anyone. An angel he was not.

"Finn, I'm sorry I couldn't save you." How many times had he said these exact words about his Emily? Countless.

Like the sun after a winter storm, Emily had brightened Seth's life from the moment she'd stepped off the train. Their whirlwind courtship and subsequent marriage had turned him into the happiest man alive.

Until her death had shattered his world.

Emily, so pure at heart, had trusted anyone and everyone. In the end, that had been her undoing.

He'd blamed himself for not being there to save her, and her death had started him on his own path of self-destruction. Too bad he'd taken so many souls down with him. He'd roamed from city to city, snaring people in his net with his easy smile and quick wit.

Straight up he was the best poker player around and had played anyone who'd dared to challenge him, cheating at every opportunity. His unsuspecting opponents had lost their homes, their businesses, and so much more.

Some may have deserved it, others most certainly did not. In either case, he'd harmed others without remorse, and that's what had turned him into a questionable soul.

Poker. An unholy game. God'll punish you, son, for playing that game. Your dirty, filthy hands are forever stained. Ma's words echoed in Seth's mind.

He no longer gambled, but he'd traded one bad habit for another. Now he was the kind of guy who'd screw just about any woman that came along. His motto was wham-bam-thank you-ma'am, and his stomping grounds included seedy bars or clubs.

Although the women changed from blondes to brunettes to red heads in a constant stream, one thing never changed. His shirt remained on, as if glued to his chest, for he refused to risk revealing his wings. They were sensitive, and in the heat of passion, he might unintentionally release them. That would never do.

The breeze slid over his delicate feathers once more, tickling the ends. He shivered and closed his eyes.

An image of Hannah, similar in appearance and mannerism to Emily, flitted through his mind. After rescuing her from the fae, he'd stood closer to her than he had since the fateful day they'd met.

The chemistry between them had overwhelmed his senses, and he'd wanted to run his hands over every bare inch of her skin. His self-loathing returned, tightening in his gut to the point of pain. Hannah was too pure, too innocent for the likes of him.

"Seth. Sun's almost up. You're running out of time. Damn it, where are you?" Drake's irritating voice echoed through the mind link.

Seth gritted his teeth and retracted his wings. *"I'm on my way."*

"Great. Hey, I can't contact Finn through the mind link. Is he with you?"

Seth grabbed his shirt and yanked his arms through the sleeves. *"About Finn. He won't be returning to his post, not ever again. I'll tell you more when I arrive."*

Silence stretched for several long seconds. *"Damn. That's unfortunate. I await your report."*

The mind link vanished.

Drake's lack of emotion punched Seth in the gut harder than his fist ever could. A bitter taste filled the back of Seth's mouth, and his dislike for his boss grew.

The first rays of the morning sun threatened to crest over the clouds. Time to go.

Seth threw on his coat and his Stetson then dematerialized. His molecules disintegrated at the atomic level and flitted through space, returning to the University of Chicago.

He loathed spending another day trapped in his griffin-like stone gargoyle next to Finn's empty shell and with Drake breathing down his neck, but, hey, that was part of the job. He deserved nothing less.

CHAPTER 4

annah tracked the thermometer's flat surface over her forehead. The electronic beeps pinged against the shower tiles. Ninety-seven point five. Well within normal range.

Then, why did she feel so bad?

Despite the knot in her stomach, she hadn't thrown up. Not once.

Hannah glanced in the mirror. Dark circles ringed her eyes, and although she'd swallowed a couple of Advil after she'd woken up, her headache still pounded loud and clear at her temple.

"Hannah, we're leaving." Sadie's voice echoed up the stairs.

Hannah shoved the thermometer into the medicine cabinet and shut the door. "I'm coming!"

She hurried through the hallway and down the stairs. Her stocking feet pounded against the floorboards, sending shock waves all the way to her aching skull.

When she reached the bottom, a wave of dizziness crested over her, and the coat rack next to the front door seemed to spin in a macabre kind of dance. She placed her hand on the wall to steady herself.

Sadie rounded the corner and almost plowed into her. She gripped

Hannah's arm, her eyes wide. "Hey, bug. The plane leaves in less than three hours. We have to hurry, or we'll miss our flight and—"

"Sissy, it's all right. You'll get there."

Sadie exhaled a quick breath. "I know. I'm just nervous."

"You'll have a great time. Trust me."

Beaumont strode toward the front door, a suitcase in either hand and a small carry-on strapped over his shoulder.

He set down the suitcases and raised an eyebrow. "This is our honeymoon, bandit, remember? You'll be lucky if we see anything besides our private cabin."

A sly smile tugged at Sadie's lip then she peered at Hannah. "You sure you don't want to—"

Hannah placed her hands on her hips. "For the last time, no."

Sadie studied Hannah's features, and a concerned furrow creased her brow. "You look a little pale. Do you feel okay?"

No. I feel terrible. Hannah forced a smile. "Just tired from finishing up that project yesterday."

Sadie bit her lip. "I worry about you."

"Don't. I'll be fine. Go on your cruise. If I need anything, I can contact Wynne." The witch had become a close friend since the night Hannah had reunited with Sadie and discovered the gorgeous and mysterious Seth.

Beaumont ran his hand through his hair. "Speaking of Wynne, if you see her before we return, tell her it's been a while since she's updated the wards on the house. Have her reinforce them."

In Beaumont's new role as head of the Gargoyle Reintegration Guild, they'd moved into this old Victorian a few months ago. Built in the early 1900s, the house had been the home to the Guild Director and his family for many decades. The witches protected this house and its inhabitants from destruction by the fae.

"Will do. Now go, you two." Hannah gripped Sadie's arm and drew her toward the front door.

Beaumont picked up the luggage and strode through the doorway. The beep of the car alarm echoed from the driveway.

Sadie trailed her fingers down Hannah's arm. "I'm going to miss you."

Love for her sister tongue-tied Hannah. She swallowed and forced herself to breathe. "Beaumont will have you so distracted, you won't even have time to think twice about me. Go. Have fun. You deserve it."

Sadie smiled, and her eyes widened. "Oh, I left George's fish flakes next to his bowl. Snookums' cat food is under the sink. Don't forget to clean the litter box every other—"

Hannah steered Sadie over the threshold. "Go, go, go!"

Sadie wrapped her arms around Hannah's shoulder and squeezed tight. "I love you, bug."

"I love you, too, Sissy." Hannah returned the affectionate hug then drew away. "Better hurry. Don't miss your flight."

Sadie nodded and ran to the Toyota Highlander. The slam of the car door echoed off the Victorian's exterior panels.

Hannah stared down the street long after the SUV had driven away.

A wave of nausea churned in her stomach. No, not again. She exhaled a long breath. With only a week off for spring break, she refused to become sick.

She had a picture to sketch for Sadie and Beaumont, and she'd be damned if she'd let a little bug slow her down. Maybe a piece of toast would ease some of the queasiness.

She closed the door behind her and strode into the kitchen. After rounding up a loaf of bread and the jelly jar, she popped a slice into the toaster. She waited for the bread to brown and wiped the back of her hand across her forehead. If she didn't have a fever, why did her skin seem so hot?

An image of the fae's yellow eyes flitted through her mind, sending a ripple of unease along her shoulders. Was it a fluke the fae had pursued her from the library or was she his intended target? If so, why? She was a nineteen-year-old college student with—

"Meow." Snookums rubbed against Hannah's leg, dragging her from her dark thoughts.

The tension in her shoulders eased. She shouldn't let her imagination get the better of her.

"Hello, Snookums." She bent down and stroked her fingers over his ears and along the white patch under his chin.

He rewarded her with the slow rumble of a purr.

The pop of the toaster echoed around the empty kitchen. Hannah gripped the warm bread between her fingers, placed it on a plate, and spread her favorite blackberry jam over the surface.

She snagged the plate, strode to the kitchen table, and set down the dish. As she drew back one of the chairs, the legs scraped against the hardwood floor. She plopped down onto the seat and stared at the toast.

An odd reflective sheen appeared to coat the jam, as if someone had drooled on it.

Her gloomy thoughts returned, flashing back to that night nine months ago when that dark fae, Marco, had forced a single drop of his saliva down her throat. Right after the horrible deed, he'd whispered something in her ear, and she'd fainted shortly after.

Many times she'd tried to remember what he'd said, but the words always seemed to elude her. Good thing Wynne had given her an antidote or who knows what would've happened to her.

As if the toast had sprouted hairy legs and three eyes, Hannah pushed the plate away and rose to her feet. "I can't eat that. Just—no."

She snatched the plate, hurried to the sink, and tossed the bread into the garbage. *Good riddance.*

Sometimes the best medicine was to lose herself in her sketches. Besides, she needed to start that project if she intended to finish the wedding gift by the time Sadie and Beaumont returned.

She strode down the hallway to a spare room Sadie let her use for her art. Her easel, covered in drawing paper, stood in the corner next to the table holding her charcoal. The idea of beginning a new sketch lifted her spirits, bringing a smile to her lips and chasing away some of her worries.

She hurried to the antique rolltop desk, opened the bottom drawer, and withdrew the wedding photo of Beaumont and Sadie.

Beaumont cupped Sadie's chin. The two stared at each other, love evident in their gazes. Hannah couldn't remember ever seeing Sadie look so happy.

Her breath caught. This spark of happiness, right here, was what Hannah vowed to capture.

After everything Sadie had gone through, she deserved a bit of happiness. Love, trust, and companionship were special, were worth fighting for, and were something to cherish forever.

Did you make a wish?

Sadie's question rang in Hannah's mind.

She wanted to love someone with her whole heart and be loved in return. Unconditionally and with devotion. Like Beaumont loved her sister.

She'd read enough romances over the years to believe in happily ever afters and had seen a few happy couples among her friends' parents. Many times she'd relive a fantasy that someday she'd run across an old-fashioned guy. One who called and asked for a date, picked her up in a car that wasn't his brother's or his friend's. He'd take her someplace fun and exciting, or beautiful and romantic, or maybe even both. She dreamed about a wholesome evening that started with good conversation, entailed lots of flirting, and ended with long, slow kisses.

Unfortunately, her dream contained the word "fantasy" and that's what it was. Her father's neglect and her uncle's abuse had left their mark, infusing her with doubt, which she fought against with all her might.

Her thoughts drifted to Seth. Despite not knowing much about him other than he was a gargoyle and Beaumont's friend, she felt an attraction to him she couldn't explain, one that made her toes curl in all the right ways. He kept his distance, yet the look in his eyes contained a heavy longing, as if he wanted to devour her like he hadn't had a decent meal in forever.

Warmth spread over her chest, up her throat, and into her cheeks. She shouldn't want Seth the way she did, nothing would come of it, but she couldn't get rid of her illusion of him. He was her knight in shining armor, her warrior, and her guardian angel all wrapped up in one fine package and totally out of her league.

Not wanting to dwell on what could never be, she shoved her thoughts of Seth aside and concentrated on her task. A stack of charcoal pencils rested in a cup near the easel. She sat on the stool, grasped her favorite one, and stroked the graphite against the paper.

The faint scratching noises and the familiar movement lulled her into her special place, her creative mindset where she lost herself in her art, and the outside world fell away, leaving her at peace. Still, something was missing in her life. If only her dreams of Seth could be real.

CHAPTER 5

"Marco Valentelli, can I trust you?"

Gwawl's voice slid down Marco's spine, but he remained in position, bent on one knee on the cold floor of the large chamber, head lowered. He didn't fear much, but only a fool didn't fear a god. "Of course, my lord."

Mere inches from him on his throne, Gwawl tapped his sandaled foot in short, agitated bursts. The annoying sound beat against Marco's skull.

Lit torches cast strange shadows on the cobbled stone floor that were eerily similar to the dark souls not yet united with their reincarnated bodies.

Of all the places in the Otherworld the god could reside, he'd picked this dark, dank prison-like chamber. Flamboyant he was not.

Gwawl stopped his incessant tapping, and the ensuing silence raised goose bumps along Marco's nape.

"Stand before me, minion."

Marco rose on unsteady feet. He dared a glance at the God of fire and pain.

Gwawl sat on his elaborate throne made of bone from countless ages of human suffering and melded together with the cries of pity long forgotten. The bones swirled and ebbed in a bizarre dance.

The imposing god wore a blood-red robe tied at the waist with a golden chain, and the muscles in his chest and shoulders bulged beneath the material. Dark hair peppered with strands of gray curled in ringlets around his shoulders.

Tight, thin lips and a sharp jaw accentuated his large, bulbous nose. His dark orbs, black as ink, focused on Marco. "A recent acquisition claims you deigned to create a human army. Tell me that isn't so."

Did the god think he planned to overthrow him with a human army? Is that why he questioned his loyalty?

Marco's pulse rose. He'd indeed intended to build a human army, but not to challenge the god, only to earn his favor and possibly a promotion to senior lieutenant over all of Chicago. The humans would've become his ears and eyes during the day while he remained trapped in the Otherworld by the sun.

He'd had just one recruit—Gabriel Rhodes—and that hadn't gone well. Seemed the young man's life had ended a bit early, and, evil to the core, he'd become a fae. Such a pity. Guess now wasn't the best time to pursue the whole "human army" endeavor.

Marco swallowed his fear, lifted his chin, and met his God's gaze. "It wouldn't be wise for me to go against your command, my lord. I'm hurt you think I'm capable of such blasphemy."

"Cernunnos, the Lord of the Otherworld, is the one who ordered we keep humans blissfully ignorant about our little escapades while we war with Rhiannon and her gargoyles. The less humans know, the better. We understand a stray human here or there may obtain information about the fae, but they are to remain few and far between. As such, I wouldn't appreciate a human army."

Marco nodded. "Of course, my lord."

"So, you're saying the new recruit lied?" Gwawl shifted in his seat, placed his elbow on the chair's large, flat armrest, and rubbed his chin. His gaze never wavered. "Hmm. Seems it's a 'he said, she said' situation. Such a mystery."

Marco held his breath. Ever since he'd received the summons that

Gwawl wanted to see him in the God's personal chamber, his eyelid had twitched with worry. The skin fluttered once again.

Gwawl straightened his shoulders and tapped his finger on the armrest. As if alive, the bones slid and rotated under the pressure. "Well, I've made a decision. First, as I have dominion over all the dark souls, I will assign the rookie to New York. Something might happen to our newest recruit if he remains in Chicago."

Good decision. Otherwise, Marco would've hunted Gabriel down, cut off his head, and sent his dark soul into the ether himself.

Marco inclined his chin to his God in deference.

Gwawl smiled, and the tips of his canines glinted in the light. "Second, although you are technically an overlord in my army and command some of the younger, inexperienced fae, I'm giving you a couple of 'more seasoned' teammates, shall we say, until I can assess your loyalty and allegiance."

Teammates? You mean babysitters. A ball hardened deep in Marco's gut. "All I want is to serve you, earn your favor, and become a senior lieutenant in your army."

"Do you now? Well, we'll see about that." A deep chuckle eased from Gwawl. "You're a bit pale. Don't fret, my minion. Your two new teammates will follow your lead."

"Who are these new...teammates?" Marco's voice rose an octave on the last word. He hated the thought that every move he made would be under a microscope.

"You're anxious to meet your new friends. How charmingly sweet. Let's get on with it then." Gwawl clapped his hands together.

At the far end of the long chamber, a door creaked open. Two fae walked in. One had dark braided hair, olive skin, and wore a black leather jacket. A diamond stud pierced each ear lobe along with one in his nose. His emotions remained hidden behind his expressionless features.

Marco's gaze slid to the other fae. The muscles in his shoulders tensed. With his dark hair and green eyes, this guy looked familiar. He wracked his brain, but the elusive connection remained out of reach.

"Come forward, gentlemen." Gwawl rose from his seat. At over seven feet tall, his presence dwarfed everyone in the room.

The two men stepped forward.

Gwawl nodded toward the fae with the diamonds. "This is Zain Roldan. Recently reassigned from Detroit to Chicago. I'm sure you'll get along smashingly."

Zain nodded. A smile curled his lip, revealing a chipped front tooth.

Marco doubted "smashingly" described their relationship, but if the god wanted to mince words, so be it.

Gwawl strode to the other fae and placed his hand on the guy's shoulder. "This here is a rare soul. I'm so very pleased he decided to switch teams. Do you recognize him?"

Switch teams... Marco blinked. Recognition sparked in the back of his mind. "Ah, yes. A gargoyle. I saw him a few times when I fought against Beaumont—"

"Former gargoyle." The guy held out his palm. "Name's Finn. Finn Mahoney."

Finn's sea-green eyes seemed bottomless, his expression tight, his lips thinned.

An odd sense of foreboding crested over Marco's shoulders. In the many decades since Marco became a fae, few gargoyles had failed their test and turned evil, and to go from enemy to best buddies in less than a week stretched the realm of possibility thin.

Was he truly wicked now? Did he really lose his need for redemption? Was he a spy for Rhiannon? Surely, Gwawl would sense if that were true. In either case, Marco was stuck with the guy, at least for now.

Marco accepted the firm handshake. Finn relented first, and Marco had to stifle the urge to wipe his palm on his pants.

Gwawl returned to his throne. As he sat, the bones creaked and swirled, readjusting to his posture. "Now that you're acquainted, I have an assignment for you."

An opportunity. A jolt of hope made Marco's hand twitch. "What can I do for you, my lord?"

The god rubbed his chin. "You mentioned you wanted to serve me, earn my favor, and move up in my army. That's good. Very good, indeed. Because I require tribute as proof of your unwavering loyalty. Something that will please me and make me forget all about your desire to create a human army. Don't make me wait long."

Irony bit Marco in the balls, for he'd once requested a similar tribute from his human minion, and, as if he'd literally been bitten, his scrotum constricted closer to his body for protection. He swallowed then inclined his head. "As you command, my lord."

"A word of advice while you're working on your tribute, don't let your kill record suffer." An uncanny smile curled Gwawl's lip. "Now, we have nothing further to discuss. Dusk approaches, and I have the urge to visit my caged gargoyle pets."

Rumors abounded over the exact number of captured and trapped gargoyle's Gwawl actually kept in a room hidden from most fae, but Marco had no doubt he tortured them mercilessly. With a sweep of the god's large hand, the double doors at the far end of the room opened.

Marco glanced from Zain to Finn. Irritation flared at his temple. One or both might rat him out to Gwawl if he so much as stepped an inch out of line. As soon as they hit the pavement, he'd have a little talk with his new "teammates."

Marco raised his chin and strode toward the exit, his long overcoat billowing around his knees with each step.

Marco materialized in his favorite hiding spot in the human realm, one located in an abandoned old church not far from the University of Chicago. He had turned it into his private quarters with everything he needed to be comfortable. A few bits of dust swirled in the eddy he'd created, but they slowed and came to rest beside one of the well-stocked bar's carved wooden feet. What better place to hide among the humans than in an abandoned place of worship?

Several months ago he'd followed part of Chicago's underground tunnel, and with the help of a few fae minions, stocked the room alongside the bell tower with everything he'd needed to create his own elaborate private quarters.

Tapping into a source of electricity had required more ingenuity, but like the old saying, "where there's a will, there's a way." Besides, he enjoyed having a place of his own in the human realm where he could retreat for some regeneration time after a good battle with the enemy.

A small dust storm rose on his left, another on his right. Moments later, his two companions joined him.

Zain glanced from the liquor bottles on the ornate bar, to the large couch, and then to the giant flat-screen TV. A cartoon flitted over the screen, the volume off. His lips tightened. "You don't seem like the cartoon type. You bring children in here? Hunt them?"

"That wouldn't surprise me." Finn sat on one of the bar stools, snagged a bottle of Irish whiskey off the bar, and took a swig.

Marco clamped his jaw so hard his teeth clacked together. He paced to Finn's side, snatched the bottle, and placed it back on the shelf. "Children hold a special place in my heart. I would never harm a child."

Indeed, he'd learned firsthand what it was like when an adult injured a kid. He rubbed his hand along his nape, and his fingers slid over the tip of one of many scars.

To this day, he refused to wear a belt with a metal buckle. Yet despite or maybe because of his father's abuse, he'd sought the man's approval, never receiving any until the day Marco had left the house for good.

Finn wiped his mouth with the back of his hand. "I'm glad ta hear that."

"Ditto," Zain replied.

A jolt of irritation brought Marco to the couch where he grabbed the remote and turned off the TV. Time to find out about his new Irish friend. "So, Finn, what did you do to fall so far from grace? Try to seduce your goddess?"

"Not on yer life. She would'a strung me up to dry if I'd a tried that." Finn rose from the stool and joined him by the couch. "I did break a rule, though, one grave enough ta turn me into a fae. I killed a human. Can't say I didn't enjoy wringin' the life out of yer old chum, Gabriel."

Marco riveted his attention on Finn. "You killed Gabriel?"

"Aye. I did."

Finn hadn't just killed any human. He'd killed Gabriel. How ironic was that?

Marco's bullshit radar rose a notch. Still, the guy committed a sin to bring his sorry ass down from his exalted perch. Even a righteous gargoyle could fall. Once a gargoyle made his fatal mistake, though, the malevolent side of him came out in full force.

The handle of Marco's cane rested in the crook of his elbow. He brushed his fingers over the smooth surface and studied his new partner. "Seems a bit convenient, doesn't it?"

Finn smiled, and a dimple formed in his chin. "Aye, doesn't it?"

Zain cleared his throat. "Don't want to interrupt your private party, but we have work to do. So, boss, what's our first assignment?"

Boss. The word traveled through Marco like lightning, leaving a jolt of satisfaction in its wake. He'd had other fae who'd worked with him before, but they'd been of the human-just-turned-rookie type. These two were something else entirely. If he used them right, maybe he'd bring his tribute to Gwawl and flush out the spy as well.

Marco smiled. "Well, your timing is perfect, shall we say. I found a special young woman several months ago, a jewel among the rabbits who walk around as humans.

"Pure, innocent, and so very powerful. When I discovered her, she was eighteen, and since the age of majority in the Otherworld is nineteen, still a minor. As I've said, I won't hurt a child, but I did give her some of my saliva so I can track her."

Finn's brow furrowed. "Why do ya want her? When a fae kills a human with a good soul, all ya get is a brief shot of energy before the soul travels ta the Otherworld. Other than that, she'll be no good ta the fae army."

Marco held up his index finger. "Well, now. That's where you're wrong."

Zain blinked. "How so?"

Excitement propelled Marco to the bar. He grasped a decanter of brandy and poured two fingers of the alcohol into a glass. As he swirled the liquid in the snifter, he smiled. "This young woman turned nineteen yesterday, so she's fair game so to speak. The power is in her purity and innocence, which is a rare treat and will make a perfect tribute to Gwawl."

Finn sat on the couch and propped his booted feet on the coffee table. "Pray tell, how will ya accomplish that?"

Marco downed the brandy, and liquid fire burned all the way to his gut. He set the glass on the counter. "She's connected to me. I've already started to pull the wholesome energy from her and placed the essence in a bottle. It's not potent enough yet, but once I have it all, the pure force it contains will be enough to give even a god a nice energy boost. Gwawl will be impressed."

Zain sat on the couch opposite from Finn. He rubbed the stubble on his chin. "Why don't you just kill her and take her essence all in one shot?"

Marco stared hard at the fae. "Have you lived under a rock? I'd like nothing more than to do exactly that, but the taking of a soul is delicate work."

He shrugged off his overcoat and hung it on the wooden coat rack. With a gentle caress, he brushed his fingers over the smooth handle of his cane.

"The urge to suck her dry can be overwhelming. If I'm not careful, I'll kill her before I've completed my task. All that power would go," Marco spread his fingers into the air, "poof. That would be a tragedy of epic proportions."

A puzzled furrow formed on Zain's brow. "If her soul is so powerful, why don't you keep the power for yourself?"

Marco pointed at Zain. "Now that's a valid question. Originally, that was my intent, but based on current circumstances, I'd rather appease a god than challenge one."

Finn set his feet on the floor and nodded. "Ya have a good point."

An idea ignited in Marco's mind. A sense of giddiness rose so fast he wanted to yell at the top of his lungs. He glanced at Finn. "You, my dear friend, will bring her to me."

Finn's eyes widened as he leaned forward. "Ya want me ta capture a young lass and bring her to ya?"

Marco raised an eyebrow. "Not up for the task? Seems pretty simple to me."

Finn smiled. "'Twould be my pleasure. Now tell me, who is this lass?"

"Hannah McAllister."

Finn's smile faded ever so slightly. A twitch curled his lip, but then his smile returned. "Now that'll be as easy as takin' candy from a babe. I know where she lives."

"Perfect. Bring her here." Marco loosened his tie and undid the first button of his shirt.

"Ya don't happen ta have a mind link, do ya?"

Marco pursed his lips. "I'll know when you arrive with her, and in case you forgot, you're no longer a gargoyle."

Finn winked. "How could I ever forget?"

"You want me to go with him?" Zain nodded toward Finn, and his braid slid over his shoulder.

"You'll remain with me. We need to work on increasing our kill record for Gwawl, and I've never had a bodyguard," *or babysitter,* "before. Might be a nice change of pace."

Besides, some ancient leader had said *"Keep your friends close, but your enemies closer."* He'd do exactly that.

Finn tested.

Zain close by his side.

What better way to start a friendship?

"I better get a move on." Finn stepped away from the couch.

Marco raised his hand. "One last thing. The transition from childhood to adulthood is a magical time. Hannah's energy will be at its strongest for the next three nights. Then, it will fade, and I won't be able to claim it. A word of warning. If you don't succeed, fae or not, friend or not, I will kill you. Are we clear?"

Finn inclined his head but didn't lower his gaze. "As the reflection on the water of a still loch."

A whirlwind of dirt swirled in a small eddy, and Finn disappeared.

Marco crooked his finger at Zain. "Let's prepare for our guest, shall we?"

CHAPTER 6

*S*eth materialized on South Street Beach. A strong breeze whipped over his shoulders and threatened to launch his Stetson into Lake Michigan. Even with the strap under his chin he didn't want to take the chance, so he ripped his favorite hat from his head and held it alongside his jeans.

In a brilliant display of reds, greens, and golds, Drake's molecules reformed, and his boss stood next to him. He peered at the shore then lifted his gaze past the sand, the grass, and to the single-story brick building.

Lines in his cheeks drew taut. "Show me where Finn killed Gabriel."

During the day while trapped at their posts, Seth had shared the details of Finn's death. Drake's reaction had been all business, and Seth's dislike for him had grown by the hour. He tightened his grip on his hat. Good thing he had something in his hand, otherwise he'd pound his fist into Drake's face out of spite.

"Over here." Seth marched toward the restrooms. The sand under his boots shifted with each step, slowing him down. For a moment, he considered dematerializing there, but he needed to let out some of his frustration, and the short walk provided some relief.

The full moon, partially covered by a cloud, cast the beach in a soft glow. Visible in the distance, a few pedestrians, a jogger, and a man walking his dog shared this bit of Chicago. Seth and Drake must keep that in mind for what they were about to do.

As they approached the small building, a man emerged from the men's restroom. He wore a pair of dirty jeans and a ripped shirt. Hair loose around his shoulders, he sported several days' growth of facial hair.

His gaze zipped from Seth to Drake and back again. Eyes wide, he wiped the back of his hand over his shirt. "D...don't hurt me. I don't have any money."

Drake stared at the human. "We're not here for you. Be on your way."

A spark of annoyance flitted along Seth's nerves. He placed his hat on his head and retrieved his billfold from his pocket. At night as the gargoyles descended from their posts, Rhiannon provided each one with fresh clothes and a wallet with enough cash for emergencies or any small purchases. You never knew when you'd need a quick buck.

Seth withdrew a one-hundred-dollar bill and held the money toward the man. "Get yourself a shave and a decent meal."

The man studied Seth. Wariness glimmered in his eyes as he stepped forward and snatched the bill from Seth's grasp. "Thanks, man."

He bolted around the building.

Seth couldn't help everyone down on their luck, but when opportunity smacked him alongside the head, he did what he could.

"You're too soft. If you're not careful, that'll come back to bite you." Drake pointed to the women's restroom. "See if that one's clear. I'll check the men's."

Seething inside, Seth strode toward the door with the stick figure in a diamond-shaped dress. He rapped on the metal.

Silence.

He pushed open the door and peered inside. Among the dirt and grime, piles of trash littered the floor, and a single bulb lit up the mirrors over three sinks.

The distinct scent of human feces invaded his nostrils. Seth wrinkled his nose and peered under the stalls. No legs in sight.

Thank you, blessed Rhiannon.

He withdrew from the fetid place in a rush.

Drake emerged from the men's room at the same time. "All clear."

"Same here." Seth nodded. He trailed his fingers along the cord at his wrist, circling the figure eight.

Drake's attention followed a dark stain along the pavement that pooled next to the wall. "Finn killed Gabriel here. I sense the taint."

Memories of Finn ripped through Seth's mind—the anger in his features, his hands wrapped around Gabriel's throat, the snap of bone. Seth tightened his jaw. "Looks like the human authorities took care of the body."

The edge of Drake's lip curled. "Good thing. I'm not in the mood to deal with humans."

"Really? Could'a fooled me, Ace." Seth let the barb hang in the air.

Drake raised a dark eyebrow. "Look, cowboy. We're here to get a job done. If you don't like my attitude, tough shit."

Seth trailed his fingers over the handle of his whip. He was as much on edge as his boss. After losing his best friend, Seth needed to let off a little steam.

A row with Drake might accomplish that task but removing the remnants of Finn's tainted aura took precedence. As it was, he sensed the evil expanding toward him, as if eager to claim another victim.

Seth wouldn't forgive himself if another gargoyle became infected because they'd delayed too long and the "taint" spread like an unseen fog. He gripped the brim of his hat and nodded. "Let's get 'er done, then."

Drake's lip twitched. "You have the potion you picked up from Wynne?"

"Right here." Seth dug into the front pocket of his 501's and withdrew a small vial. Through the glass, the silver and blue liquid swirled.

Seth's boss held out his hand. "The sooner I use the witch's potion to cleanse Finn's tainted aura from this place, the happier I'll be. Can't risk one of the other gargoyles running into this if it spread. That might start an infection among the ranks I don't even want to think about."

Seth tightened his grip on the small bottle and held the special potion close. "I'll do it. Finn was my best friend. He would've wanted it that way."

"That's not protocol." Drake scowled at him. "You're asking me to break the rules?"

"I'm asking you to bend them. A bit of compassion might do you wonders."

A flinch, ever so slight Seth almost didn't catch it, darted across Drake's features. "I can't do that. Protocol must be—"

"Damn protocol."

Drake pressed his mouth into a tight, grim line. "You've been itching for some time at your post, haven't you? Hand over the potion or you'll get exactly that."

Oh hell, no. Seth didn't want to spend any more time at his post than absolutely necessary. He'd hated dark, confined spaces since age five after he'd fallen into an abandoned mine and spent the night there before his father had found him. Besides, he had plans to visit a young woman, a very sweet, innocent one he couldn't seem to get off his mind.

He clenched his jaw and tossed the vial to his stick-up-the-ass boss. "Whatever suits your fancy."

Drake caught the small container. As he uncorked the bottle, he smiled. "Thank the goddess Wynne had some on hand. I don't know what we'd do without her sometimes."

Made from a mixture of herbs, strange liquids, and who knew what else, blue smoke etched with silver striations floated from the opening. Like a brilliant cloud, the potion encircled the area. Within the mist, sparks fizzled and sputtered.

Drake's grip on the vial tightened to the point his fingernails turned white. He closed his eyes. In the old language of the Other-world, Drake spoke the ancient words. *"Toyo non formidia. Lapido sans karoatoc. Asi de, asi do."*

Darkness engulfed some of the cloud as if the malicious stain, left over from Finn's transition, fought for its very life. The swirling eddy grew larger, expanding in the space between Drake and Seth. If Drake didn't move, the darkness would pin him against the wall.

"*Toyo non formidia. Lapido sans karoatoc. Asi de, asi do.*"

The cold fingers of dread skittered up Seth's back. "Watch out!"

Seth lunged at Drake, caught the guy around the shoulders, and tackled him to the ground. The bottle slipped from Drake's fingers.

Glass shattered across the pavement.

A flame burst from the spilled potion, lighting up the area in a brilliant flash. The roar launched Seth into the air.

He landed on the grass several yards away. The muscles in his shoulders and buttocks ached from the impact, and his hat dangled from the cord around his neck.

Not far away, Drake groaned. "Did the potion work?"

Seth glanced at the small building. The twin lights lit up the entrance to each restroom. Bits of blue potion, evaporating quickly, covered the doors, the brick wall, and most of the sidewalk. The dark aura, however, was gone.

"Yeah. All's clear." Seth rose to his feet, settled his hat on his head, and hurried to his boss. "You okay?"

Drake stood and wiped the grass from his pants. "Yeah. Piece of cake."

Seth studied his boss, searching for any signs the "taint" from Finn's aura had reached him.

Drake pursed his lips. "What? Do I have potion on me or something?"

The tension in Seth's shoulders eased. Drake seemed as crotchety as usual. "That was a close one."

"Well, it's done now. Meet up with Damian and Grayson. The three of you can cover the west side tonight." Drake picked up the bottle's cork and shoved it into his pocket.

"Before I join the others, I'll stop at Beaumont's and leave a note for him. He'll want to know about Finn as soon as he returns from his vacation." At least that was the excuse he'd given himself. Although he wanted to leave a message about their friend, what he really needed was to see Hannah.

While on his post today in his stone form, he'd had plenty of time to think about her. He couldn't let her birthday slip by without giving her a gift. His mama had instilled in him from a young age that it was important to honor someone's birthday, and he'd do right by her memory.

Many a day, he'd seen Hannah sit on one of the benches in the quad, pull out her sketch pad, and track the charcoal over the paper. Even now, the image of her swift, sure strokes and her sweet smile filled his mind. She'd love a new set of charcoal pencils.

Drake flitted his discerning gaze over Lake Michigan then up to the almost full moon. "Tonight'll be a busy one for the fae. Make it quick."

"As a jack rabbit in heat." Seth smiled and traced the brim of his hat with his finger. Not waiting for a reply, he dematerialized straight for the campus bookstore with an eagerness he didn't want to contemplate.

CHAPTER 7

*H*annah rolled her shoulders, loosened her grip on the pencil, and brushed the charcoal over the paper. The familiar scratch of the graphite settled over her, warming her on the inside. She enjoyed these brief moments where she escaped into her private world and forgot about nasty things like abusive uncles and dark, dangerous fae.

She traced a few lines around Sadie's ear, filling in some of the details along her jawline then studied the portrait. Beaumont cupped Sadie's chin in his palm, but the texture of Sadie's hair and her appreciative grin needed work. Hannah had spent far too much time on the roses that bordered the edges, wanting every last detail to be perfect.

Pain flared at Hannah's temple, building to a loud, penetrating crescendo.

The charcoal pencil slipped from her fingers and bounced against the floor. Shards scattered over the polished hardwood.

She closed her eyes and pressed her fingers along the bridge of her nose where the pain pounded in tune with her heart.

Her stomach roiled. "No, no. Not again."

She ran from her art room, sprinted down the hall, and rushed into the bathroom. A bitter taste coated the back of her throat while she gripped the edge of the sink, her knuckles aching from strain.

The toilet taunted her. *Ready to get down on your knees and pray to me?*

A part of her wished she'd throw up and get it over with. Instead, a bead of sweat trickled over her brow, and the skin on her arms prickled.

Oh great. The chills...

Apparently, she wasn't over whatever bug had hit her last night. During the day, she'd started to feel better and managed to eat some soup and a handful of saltine crackers. She'd even laid down on the couch for a few hours, catching up on some much-needed sleep. That didn't seem to do much good.

Hannah turned her head and peered through the bathroom window. Darkness crept over the lawn. One of the lone oak tree's branches tapped against the pane. *Tick, tick, tick.*

"I wish Sadie were here." Loneliness weighed heavily on her shoulders and tears stung her eyes.

God, how she missed her sister, but Sadie and Beaumont deserved to enjoy their honeymoon. They didn't need to worry about her.

All her life, whether it was her mother, Sadie, or Aunt Sally, she'd relied on others to help her. Sooner or later, she'd have to take care of herself. Maybe now was a good time to start.

With shaky fingers, Hannah grabbed the cup next to the sink, poured a glass of water, and brought it to her lips. As the liquid slid down her throat, the urge to vomit passed. *Thank you, God.*

After a long breath, she pushed away from the sink. Maybe if she laid down for a while the headache and chills would disappear, but the idea of returning to bed didn't sit well with her. Instead, she headed for the living room and the comfy couch.

"Time to binge on a few episodes of *Riverdale*." Her voice echoed down the empty corridor.

As she entered the living room, she reached for the light switch.

A faint tink pinged off the front window.

The muscles in her shoulders tensed.

On a gentle flutter, the curtains swayed in the draft coming in through the slight opening in the window. Beyond the windowpane, the streetlight lit up the sidewalk in a soft glow. Parked cars lined the pavement, silent and still. The old oak tree's branches swayed in the breeze.

Nerves. It's just nerves.

Still, the sense of unease straightened her spine. In the darkened room, the couch seemed to sprout shadows.

The hair on her nape rose.

She flicked the switch. Light bathed the room in stark white.

The couch, the TV, and the coffee table rested in the same places they always had.

She released a slow breath, and the tension in her shoulders eased.

Tink. Tink. Tink.

She shot her gaze to the window.

With the light on, she couldn't see outside. Yet, if she turned it off, she feared what she'd see.

Tink.

Hannah drew on her inner strength and raised her chin. She turned off the light once again.

Through the window, she spotted a man standing on the sidewalk. Dressed in dark pants and a matching jacket, he had broad shoulders and short jet-black hair. The streetlight behind him bathed his features in shadows. He raised his hand and waved.

Did she know him?

She crept closer to the window to get a better look.

"Hannah, lass, it's Finn." He took a step forward but stopped at the edge of the driveway.

Hannah placed her palm to her chest. A shaky laugh slipped from her lips. "Finn? Just a moment. Let me get the door."

He was one of Beaumont's friends, and she'd seen him around a few times and had liked his soft laugh and easy manner. She hurried to the large front door, unhooked the deadbolt, and tugged on the handle. The door opened on a soft whoosh.

Finn paced on the sidewalk, his strides quick and purposeful. At this angle, the streetlight lit up his features. Tension lines formed around his pursed mouth. He met her gaze, and a smile chased away the strain.

"Hello, lass. It's good ta see ya again."

"What are you doing here?" She stepped onto the front porch and glanced down the street, first one way then the other. "Is Seth with you?"

Her heart skipped a beat. How she longed to see him. Besides working on the same gargoyle squad, she'd heard stories from Beaumont about Finn and Seth's close friendship. Where one went, the other wasn't far behind.

Finn held out his palms and shook his head. "I'm afraid not tonight, lass. That's disappointin' ta ya, I can tell."

She paced to the first step and wrapped her fingers around the rail. Confusion fogged her mind, competing with the headache that threatened to return. "Oh well, if you're looking for Beaumont, he's not here."

Finn inched toward the grass. "He's not, is he? Well, fancy that. I'm really here ta see ya, though, lass. There's somethin' we need ta chat about. Mind if I come in?"

"I guess." She took a step toward him. "What is this about..."

A yellow radiance encircled Finn's eyes, and when he smiled, a set of long, pointed fangs glinted in the streetlight's eerie glow.

A scream lodged behind Hannah's lips.

Finn tore across the lawn.

She sprinted to the safety of the house.

Seth dematerialized across the street from Beaumont's home. He placed his hand over the pencils in his coat pocket. Did he get the right kind? Would Hannah like them? He'd stopped at the campus bookstore and bought the nicest set available. How could she not like—

On an inhale, the metallic scent of fae assailed his senses.

He tensed, his gaze riveting to the old Victorian.

Finn darted across the lawn toward the house.

Hannah bolted for the front door.

Dread spiked in Seth's veins. *No, no, no!*

He dashed across the street.

As Finn scrambled up the stairs, Seth launched himself at the fae. His hat flipped through the air and tumbled into the grass.

He tackled Finn around the thighs, and they landed on the porch.

Seth's elbow slammed into the concrete post. Pain ricocheted up his arm, and he grimaced but didn't break his hold on the fae.

Finn struggled beneath him, and they tumbled down the stairs.

An odd mixture of anger, sadness, and confusion swirled in Seth's mind. To see his best friend as a fae so soon after his transformation, and to have him attack Hannah, brought out a side in Seth he'd thought long dead. Not since his wife passed had such emotion roiled in his veins.

He punched Finn over and over, taking out his frustration on this friend turned foe.

Finn hissed and returned the blows. One struck Seth in the jaw.

Cartilage cracked from the impact. Pain swept up the side of his face. He hardened his skin, turning the flesh as firm as stone.

Finn's fist slammed into Seth's temple. The crunch of fingers breaking echoed into the night.

Seth drew his dagger from its sheath. He held the blade over Finn's left eye.

Finn stopped his struggles. "Do it!"

Seth's fingers shook from strain. As much as he wanted to rid the world of another fae, he couldn't bring himself to bury the tip in Finn's eye. Instead, he rose to his feet and headed for the lawn, dragging Finn with him.

A flash of regret flitted across Finn's features. "Later, ya'll wish ya would'a finished the job."

Grass and dirt whipped around Finn's feet in a swirl, and amid the force of the mini-tornado, Seth lost his grip on his old friend.

"No, damn it!" Seth tugged his whip from his belt and snapped it in the air.

The ends swept into the swirling eddy, but only contacted air.

Finn had disappeared.

The soft click of the front door echoed into the night, and Hannah stepped onto the porch.

Seth glanced at her, checking to make sure Finn hadn't injured her. He scanned from her golden hair to her emerald green eyes, over full, luscious lips, past her tight-fitting pink sweater, down her slim waist, and over form-fitting jeans that hugged her well-rounded hips.

Thankfully, she seemed physically unharmed, but he worried about her mental state. No human should have to witness such evil.

He exhaled the breath he hadn't realized he'd held. "Are you okay?"

She licked her lips and nodded. "Just a little shaken up."

The sudden urge to pull her against him and hold her close whipped through him. His fingers jerked in response, but he resisted the impulse. He didn't deserve to touch a woman as fine as Hannah.

He curled his hand into a fist and glanced over the lawn. No sign of fae, at least not now.

He picked his hat off the ground and wiped away a few bits of grass that clung to the brim. "We should get you inside."

Hannah rubbed her arms and met his gaze. "What happened to Finn? Why isn't he like you anymore, and why did he attack me?"

All kinds of similar questions swirled in Seth's mind, but he needed Hannah in the house, safe and sound. "Good questions. What I do know is when faced with his test, Finn failed. He's now a fae. We can discuss this more inside."

She crossed the threshold, and he followed her, closing and locking the door behind him. He mentally thanked Wynne, once again, for warding this house.

Hannah hurried into the living room and turned on the lights. Soft illumination filled the space. She paced past the couch and stood in front of the side table. George, the Betta fish, swam in his bowl, his red tail trailing behind him.

Hannah turned to face him, her cheeks flushed. Confusion etched her brows. "Finn's a fae? What did he do?"

The urge to withhold the information bubbled in Seth's mind. He wanted to protect Hannah, do whatever it took to keep her safe. The less she knew, the better. When he didn't answer, she crossed her arms.

"Tell me. I want to know."

He strode to the couch, placed his hat on the coffee table, and met her gaze. "He killed Gabriel."

Hannah's eyes widened. "He did?"

"Yeah. Went against our number one rule to protect the humans." Seth ran his hand over his face. "He's a fae. I still can't believe it."

A somber ache tightened his chest. He gritted his teeth, and sharp pain from Finn's blow to his jaw radiated up the side of his face. The lingering discomfort was another reminder that his best friend was now the enemy.

Hannah wrapped her arms around his neck. "You saved me. Again. Thank you."

Her cool, crisp, linen scent eased into his senses, burrowing deep. Smooth and silky, her hair caressed his neck, and the warmth of her skin sent tingles of excitement everywhere she touched.

He wanted to give in to the urge to wrap his arms around her and hold her tight. Instead, he placed his hands on her arms and drew her away. She rested her palms on his chest, and sexual energy flared between them.

He longed for more of her soft caresses over every inch of his skin. Except for his back and his damnable white wings. He never wanted anyone to touch him there.

Hannah studied him, her green eyes shining like perfect emeralds then her brow furrowed, and a frown tugged at her luscious lips. "You're injured."

She stroked her fingers across his cheek and over the tender spot on his jaw. Warmth seeped into his chest at the contact. Oh, gods, he liked her touch far too much.

"Does it hurt?" she asked.

"No." He forced the word past the lump lodged in his throat. "The damage will heal within the hour."

"Oh." She traced the spot once again. "Are there ways to make it heal faster?"

He brushed his thumb over the smooth skin on her arm. "Yes. Water over my skin, nearness to domesticated animals, and sex."

An adorable flush of pink tinged her cheeks. "If you kissed me, would it help?"

A flinch tightened his grasp on her arms. "Oh, darlin', you don't want to become tainted by the likes of me. Besides, I'd need far more than a kiss. I'd need you naked beneath me, my tongue licking your bare flesh with a little chocolate and some whipped cream spread over every delectable inch."

"Oh..." Her beautiful emerald eyes widened, and she tugged her bottom lip between her teeth.

He'd been around enough women to recognize a seductress when he saw one. Hannah wasn't one of them.

The surprise in her eyes portrayed an innocence he'd rarely seen. He'd bet his bottom dollar she was a virgin. He needed to scare her away, show her how dangerous he could be to her.

Seth brushed away a stray hair caught in Hannah's eyelashes. He trailed his fingertips along the smooth skin of her cheek before resting them along her jawline. "I'm not someone you should get involved with. I kill for a living."

She pursed those full, luscious lips. "If you're trying to scare me, it's not working. You're not dangerous to me, I know it."

"So beautiful." The words escaped his mouth before he'd realized he'd said them aloud.

Hannah inhaled, and a small smile brightened her features. "You think so?"

He blinked. Certainly, she didn't doubt her attractiveness. "You're a rare beauty, like sunset reflecting on a lake, snowflakes on a red rose, and the kiss of dew on..."

Before he could stop himself, he wrapped his fingers around her nape and drew her to him. With the softest of touches, he brought his mouth to hers. The brush of their lips burned like blissful fire.

She dug her fingers into his T-shirt, bunching the material in her fists. Her breasts pressed against his chest. Even through the T-shirt's material, he felt the tightening of her nipples. Overwhelming need roared within him.

He deepened the kiss, claiming her with a passion he hadn't experienced since his human days. Deliberately, he licked at the seam along her lips.

She gasped at the contact, opening to him. He slid his tongue along hers, brushing with long, languid strokes. She trembled in his arms, accepting him with trust and naivety.

With his gargoyle speed, he pinned her against the nearest wall, trapping her in his embrace. He continued his onslaught, kissing her with a ravaging passion that burned from the desperate depths of his soul.

Despite not wanting to give in to her request, he'd wanted her from the moment they'd met, and he'd enjoy every moment of this kiss.

She mewled, a desperate sound that burrowed deep inside. He pressed his erection against her abdomen, showing her how much she tempted him. Perhaps that might scare her away.

She buried her fingers into his scalp and held him close.

Not the reaction he'd expected. Although a part of him wanted to pick her up and drag her to the nearest bed, he broke the kiss, released her, and stepped aside.

Their panting breaths echoed in the room.

Hannah sighed. "Wow, just wow. Why did you stop?"

"Don't tempt me, Hannah. You have no idea what I've done."

She blinked, and her brow furrowed. "Then tell me."

He'd never tell her about the crimes he'd committed and the lives he'd destroyed. She'd hate him, and that he couldn't handle.

Instead, he settled for something in between. "I'm a gargoyle, Hannah. There's a reason I have a questionable soul. I've done things

I'm not proud of. You deserve some nice young man. Not to be sullied by the likes of me."

Her beautiful features tightened, but then a smile tugged at her lips. "You're not as bad as you think you are. You know, if you keep rescuing me, I may have to start calling you my 'guardian angel'."

Oh, hell, no. He stepped away and strode to the window. The last thing he wanted to be compared to was a damn angel. He stared into the night, searching for any sign of fae. The street remained blessedly deserted.

Hannah placed her hand on his shoulder. "Did I say something wrong?"

He turned to face her. She reminded him so much of Emily. Dear, sweet Emily who had seen the good in others and had believed people could change given the chance. How wrong she'd been. If only he'd saved her.

He sighed. "We need to talk about Finn. Tell me what happened before I arrived."

Hannah sighed and sat on the couch. Her blonde hair cascaded around her shoulders, the tips resting along the collar of her blouse. With each breath she took, her chest rose and fell, accentuating her full breasts.

The need to tug her into his arms and finish the job flushed through his veins. Blood headed south. That damn kiss had affected him more than he'd realized.

He strode to the side table to adjust his pants and studied George. The fish hid among the plastic fronds. At least George knew a monster when he saw one.

Hannah sighed. "Finn said he wanted to talk to me. When I asked him to come in, he bared his fangs and rushed toward me. That's when you tackled him."

"The wards protected you. He couldn't step onto the property until you invited him in." Seth turned to face her. "Finn targeted you. We have to figure out why."

Hannah wiped her brow with the back of her hand. "I'm a nineteen-year-old college student studying business. Why does he want me?"

Like a snake slithering through the grass, a sense of unease trickled up Seth's spine. "I wonder if this has anything to do with Marco and your kidnapping last summer."

"That was nine months ago. Why now?" Hannah grabbed a *People* magazine off the coffee table and fanned her flushed cheeks.

"That's what we need to figure out." Seth wracked his brain. If Finn worked with Marco, why would the fae wait until now? Was it more than a coincidence that Marco had been in the park last night? Maybe Hannah wasn't just a random target, but what did Hannah have that interested Marco?

A bead of sweat rolled down the side of Hannah's face, followed by another. She wiped them away and leaned her head against the couch's back. "I don't feel so good."

Seth raced to Hannah's side and placed the back of his hand against her cheek. Her hot skin burned with fever. Unease spiked in his veins. "I don't like the looks of this. Did this just come on?"

Hannah shook her head then moaned, as if the movement hurt. "No. I've felt sick off and on since yesterday, but I haven't thrown up or anything. Just a headache, chills, and some nausea."

How had he not noticed Hannah's illness? He'd been caught up in his own world, that's how. Damn, he'd even kissed her, taking advantage of her weakened state.

He clenched his jaw. Selfish bastard. "With Finn showing up here, this is too much of a coincidence. Let me take you to Wynne, have the witch check you out. Would that be all right?"

Hannah sat up and stared at him. "This is probably just the flu—"

Seth gripped her hand and squeezed. "Please, darlin'. I'll be fit to be tied if you don't let me take you there."

Hannah's eyes flitted back and forth as she studied him.

He held his breath. Somewhere deep inside, her answer meant more to him than he cared to admit.

After a long moment, she nodded. "Okay."

Seth exhaled, and the tension in his shoulders eased. "Thank you."

He rose to his feet and grabbed his hat off the coffee table. Before Hannah had a chance to change her mind, he dematerialized, taking her right along with him. Something about her sudden illness nagged at him, and he wouldn't rest until Wynne checked her out. The thought of losing Hannah seized him like a hangman's noose around his neck.

CHAPTER 8

*H*annah's molecules reformed into her physical body, leaving her breathless. She swayed and almost fell against Wynne's door.

"I got 'cha." Seth wrapped his arms around her waist.

She leaned into him, soaking up his strength.

Good God, his powerful kiss had turned her into a wet noodle. She'd forgotten all about the aches and pains and even her headache, but now, the pounding behind her eyes returned full force. Her skin burned so hot, she must have the flu. What else could it be?

Seth knocked on Wynne's door. "Hurry, Wynne."

A car drove by, its engine rumbling into the night.

Hannah closed her eyes and rested her cheek against Seth's chest. His musky, masculine scent, and the steady beat of his heart, calmed her racing mind.

She wanted him to be the right one, someone she could love and be loved by in return, but he seemed determined to convince her otherwise. Yet, the way he'd kissed her made her doubt whether he really wanted to push her away. Her mind spun from both dizziness and confusion.

The door opened on a soft whoosh.

"Seth? Hannah?" Worry etched Wynne's voice.

"Hannah's sick. I don't think it's the flu. We ran into Marco last night. He may have something to do with this. Can we come in?" Seth's words rumbled in his chest.

The vibration tingled Hannah's cheek. She wanted to burrow further into his embrace, but he urged her forward, so she opened her eyes and stepped over the threshold.

Patchouli incense filtered into Hannah's senses. Her stomach churned, and a frustrated moan eased past her lips. "I feel ill."

"You need the bathroom?" Wynne pointed down the hallway.

Hannah shook her head. "I'm nauseated, but I haven't thrown up."

"That worries me," Seth muttered.

Wynne's brow furrowed. "Let me evaluate her in the living room. Come."

Hannah followed her friend, and Seth was right on her heels. He hovered so close, his warm, spicy scent seemed to envelop her in its embrace. She longed for him to touch her again, but he kept a small bit of space between them.

Wynne strode through a doorway into the largest room in the house. When Hannah had visited Wynne, they'd spent most of their time in this room playing games, watching Netflix, and eating. Her stomach lurched and complained. No food would pass Hannah's lips today, though.

Wynne gripped Hannah's elbow and helped her settle into the couch. The soft cushions brushed against the bare skin on her arms, making them burn. "I'm not that sick. You don't need to do this. I'll be fine."

"I don't share your confidence." A tic flared in Seth's tight jaw.

Wynne placed her palm against Hannah's forehead. Hannah had always envied Wynne's blonde hair and beautiful porcelain skin.

The witch removed her hand and frowned. "You're hot. Way too hot for a normal human temperature. I'd guess around one hundred and six or so."

"How is that possible?" Hannah's heartbeat raced, pumping so hard spots formed in her vision. "Am…am I dying?"

Seth knelt next to her. He reached toward her face, but a flash of something she couldn't quite identify, regret maybe, flickered over his features, and he withdrew and placed his hand on the couch cushions.

"You're not dying, not on my watch. Wynne will help you. In my book, she's the best witch in all of Chicago. You couldn't be in better hands."

An encouraging smile broke across his handsome features, chasing away some of her anxiety. God, at that moment, he looked like an angel, a scorching, sexy one. She did what he wouldn't and stroked her fingertips down his cheek.

"Let me in, cowboy, so I can have a look at her." Wynne placed a tray with an assortment of bottles and a white cloth onto the coffee table.

Seth grasped Hannah's hand and tugged her fingers away. "I'll be right here, darlin'."

He rose to his feet and stepped aside, but lingered nearby, clutching his hat.

"Tell me your symptoms." Wynne settled onto the couch.

Hannah sighed. "You two don't need to do—"

"Hannah." Wynne's stern voice echoed around the room. "Just tell me."

Hannah's stomach churned, and she swallowed several times. "All right. I've had chills, nausea, and headaches off and on since yesterday."

The beautiful witch picked up a small green vial and uncorked the lid. She tipped the bottle, and a small drop of yellow liquid landed onto the white cloth in her palm. "I'm going to wipe this on your skin. If you've been cursed, it will change color."

"You think Marco cursed me?" Hannah glanced from Wynne to Seth and back again.

Wynne nodded. "You have the classic symptoms."

Seth glanced at Hannah. "I don't think it was a coincidence Marco was in the quad last night when that fae attacked you."

Hannah's heartbeat picked up speed once again. "You think he's after me."

"That's what we're here to find out." Seth tightened his mouth.

"This will feel cool." Wynne wiped the cloth over the back of Hannah's hand.

A cold blast raised the hairs all the way up her arm.

Wynne withdrew the material and peered at the linen. The yellow spot remained unchanged.

Hannah slumped against the couch cushions. "See, it's just some weird strain of the flu."

"I want to try something else." Wynne grasped a tiny round container and unscrewed the cap. She held the glass to her lips and blew.

Green crystals burst into the air, surrounding Hannah in a light mist. Her skin tingled, and a prickle rippled down her spine.

Wynne focused on the back of Hannah's neck at her hairline. She brushed the hair away from Hannah's ear. A soft gasp escaped her lips. "Seth, look at this."

Hannah sat forward and raked her finger behind her ear. The smooth skin seemed normal. "What do you see?"

Seth placed his hat on the coffee table and settled onto the couch. The cushions sunk under his massive weight.

His gaze riveted on Hannah's neck then flitted to her eyes. "A small mark behind your ear, the swirls twirling around in a circle. The brand of a fae."

"I need to see it." She tried to stand, but Seth eased her back into the cushions.

"Here, Hannah." Wynne snagged her purse from the floor next to the sideboard table, rummaged through it, and withdrew a compact. She handed the round object to Hannah.

Hannah opened the small container and caught her reflection in the mirror. With dark circles under her eyes and a strained look around her mouth, she appeared to have aged five years in the past two days.

She adjusted the mirror to see behind her ear. A dark swirl, like a tattoo, was visible at her hairline.

"It's Marco's brand, isn't it?" Hannah covered her mouth to hold back her scream.

Wynne took the compact, closed it, and touched her arm. "That would be my guess. You mentioned you saw Marco last night. Was that the first time since the event?"

The event...when Gabriel had kidnapped her to lure in Sadie. Hannah nodded. "Yeah. I hadn't seen Gabriel or Marco since then."

Seth rose to his feet and paced to the fireplace. He trailed his fingertips over the braided cord at his wrist then raked his fingers through his hair. "What triggered him?"

"I wish I knew." Wynne's gaze narrowed. "The night you met Marco, after he forced you to take a drop of his saliva, did anything else happen?"

She closed her eyes and pinched the bridge of her nose. A memory surfaced, along with a tightening in her stomach. She removed her hand and glanced between Seth and Wynne. "He whispered something in my ear, but I don't remember what it was."

Seth peered at her over his shoulder. Intensity radiated from his gaze, and the muscles in his back and arms strained against his brown leather coat, pulling the material taut. He looked absolutely formidable. Thank God, he was on her side.

Wynne selected a pair of long, pointed needles from the tray and held them up to the light. Her brow furrowed as she studied the ends.

"Um, those look pretty sharp. You're not going to poke me with those, are you?" Hannah's voice squeaked on the last word.

The witch smiled and placed the needles in her palm. "This won't hurt. I promise. I want to hear what Marco said to you. Is that okay?"

Hannah bit her lip. "I'm not sure I want to know, but okay."

Moyo con tika. Soto a tien. Wynne's soft voice filled the room.

The twin needles rose from Wynne's palm and floated through the air, right toward Hannah. She gasped. The pointed tips hovered near her ears.

Moyo con tika. Soto a tien. The witch repeated the chant.

"You're doing great, darlin'." Seth's encouraging words calmed Hannah's restless nerves.

"Moyo con tika. Soto a tien."

A brilliant flash of light emanated from the needles. As if pulled from behind a curtain, a memory resurfaced. *Hannah strapped to a chair. Marco leaning over her, forcing her mouth open. His long tongue. The drop of saliva that dripped from the tip then slid down her throat.*

"Your pure, innocent soul will be mine. I can hardly wait." Said in a voice much too deep to be her own, Marco's whispered words burst from her lips.

Wynne inhaled, and her features blanched.

"Damn." Seth cursed under his breath as he paced in front of the fireplace. His heavy footsteps vibrated through the floorboards.

Chills rippled down Hannah's arms. "What do those words mean?"

Wynne plucked the needles from the air and placed them on the tray. She intertwined her fingers with Hannah's. "Marco targeted you. Under the right circumstances, pristine, unblemished souls can enhance the power of the fae who ingests it."

Hannah withdrew her hand, her skin suddenly hypersensitive to touch. "What circumstances? Why me?"

Seth stopped his pacing and coiled his fingers around the handle of his whip. A green hue surrounded his eyes, contrasting with his baby blues. "He must've sensed the goodness and innocence in your soul. If I can sense it, so can he."

"What does that have to do with my illness?"

"Everything." Wynne stood and strode to the window. She gripped the edge of the curtain and peered outside. The corner of her mouth turned into a frown, and she let the curtain fall back in place. "He's siphoning the goodness from you, drop by drop. That's why he gave you his saliva, to track you. I didn't understand it when Seth brought you to me last summer, but I do now. We celebrated your birthday last weekend, but you actually turned nineteen yesterday, right?"

Hannah nodded.

"That's the age of majority in the Otherworld. The transition from youth to adult is when your energy is the strongest. Marco placed his tracking mark on you and bided his time until now. Good thing you didn't give in to him willingly or he'd own your soul already."

Unable to sit a moment longer, Hannah rose to her feet. Her headache returned, pounding at her temple. She pinched the bridge of her nose.

"How is he sucking the energy from me? How do I stop him? What happens to me if I can't?" A sob ripped from her.

Seth was by her side in an instant. "Darlin', you don't need to—"

Meoooow.

Wynne's familiar, Neira, strode into the room. She swished her tail, padded to Wynne, and rubbed her whiskers against the witch's leggings.

From what Hannah had learned from Wynne, Neira served Rhiannon as much as the gargoyles. All gargoyles were male, and the goddess placed questionable female souls into familiars. Neira had been in the Becknell family for generations.

Wynne stroked her fingers along Neira's back. The cat purred in response then changed into her human form. Wearing a pair of billowy red slacks with a matching top, she plopped onto the couch.

"I can't stand listening to you all beat around the bush. Hannah, my dear," Neira stared at her over dark eyebrows, "unless you can best Marco, he will suck all your pure, sweet innocence from you, leaving either a dry, hollowed-out husk or turn you into one of them, an evil fae. I wouldn't want to be in your shoes."

"Always blunt, aren't you, cat?" Seth seethed the words.

Neira shrugged. "At least she knows what to expect."

Hannah's mind spun. "What do I do?"

Seth reached out as if to touch her, but then curled his hand and placed it at his side. "I won't let anything happen to you."

"Y...you promise?"

His jaw tightened, but he nodded. "I vow it."

"Such drama." Neira placed the back of her hand over her eyes. "I can't watch."

Wynne exhaled. "Neira, that's enough. Why don't you make yourself that catnip tea you so crave?"

Neira hopped off the couch and strode toward the hallway. A sly smile crept over her lips. "I can take a hint. Nice chatting with you, Hannah. Good luck, you're going to need it."

As she disappeared around the corner, her giggle echoed in her wake.

"Hannah, there is a bit of good news." Wynne marched to the coffee table and grabbed a small green bottle. "Marco has a short window of time to complete his task, four nights to be exact. After that, your soul will no longer be vulnerable to him."

"My birthday was yesterday. One night down, three more to go." Hannah stifled a nervous laugh. "Is there anything I can do to fight this? Any place safe I can go?"

Wynne glanced at the floor before meeting Hannah's gaze. "Unfortunately, once a fae targets a human, it's nearly impossible to stop him. The safest place is at your home protected by the wards. Whatever you do, don't invite him in."

Hannah bunched her brows together. "I'm supposed to just sit and wait this out?"

A pained expression crossed Wynne's features. "I'd come stay with you if I could, but I can't, not tonight. It's just not possible."

Wynne wrapped her arms around Hannah's shoulders and tugged her in for a big hug. "I wish there was more I could do."

Hannah's face warmed at the heartfelt words. She returned the embrace, thankful for her friend.

The witch drew away and placed the green vial in Hannah's hand. "Drink two sips of this every four hours. It will block part of Marco's hold on you and should relieve your symptoms. I'll stop by tomorrow as soon as I can. Okay?"

"Thank you." Hannah took two swallows then shoved the small bottle in her jeans front pocket. The headache receded along with the burning fever. A quiver of relief swept down her arms.

Hannah's life had gone from normal to crazy in two days. Her sister and Beaumont were out of the country on a cruise ship. Even if she did reach them, this would be over one way or another by the time they made it home.

A tingle of unease rippled over her shoulders. Hannah wasn't sure she could do this on her own.

Seth placed his hat on his head and motioned toward the hallway. "Let me take you home."

"Oh." Hannah peered at Wynne. "You mentioned the wards, and I forgot to tell you. Beaumont said they need reinforcement."

"I'll take care of that tomorrow when I see you." Wynne smiled.

"Thanks." A wave of exhaustion settled over Hannah's shoulders, and she shuffled to the front door. As she stepped outside, the cool night air caressed her skin like a lover.

On the doorstep, Seth turned to face Wynne. "Thank you for all you've done. I can never repay—"

Wynne held up her hand. "My service to Rhiannon and her soldiers is my greatest reward."

Seth nodded once, peered at Hannah, and held out his hand. "You ready to go home?"

Hannah wasn't sure what lay ahead, but she nodded and put her palm and her faith in Seth's hand.

CHAPTER 9

Seth materialized on the old Victorian's steps. As the aged wood accepted his weight, it creaked beneath his boots. Next to him, Hannah's molecules reformed into the young beauty he worried about more than he should. She gripped the railing, her knuckles white with strain.

"I don't think I'll ever get used to materializing out of thin air like that." She shook her head, and her luscious blonde hair cascaded over her shoulders.

The urge to brush away the few strands that clung to her eyelashes flicked along his nerves. Fortunately, she did the job for him, wiping at her cheek.

"Oh no. I don't have my key." Her brow furrowed over her pretty green eyes.

"Allow me." Seth placed his finger on the antiquated knob and sent a tiny jolt of energy to the mechanism.

A loud click echoed in the space between them.

He gripped the handle, twisted the knob, and opened the door. "There you go."

She smiled, her eyes widening. "What else can you do?"

Warmth at her amazement settled deep inside. Seth hadn't seen that look in a woman's eyes since Emily.

He returned her smile. "Lots of things, darlin', but let's get you inside."

She nodded and stepped over the threshold. His guardian instincts kicking in, he scanned across the yard and along the street for any signs of danger.

Two teenagers sat in the front seat of an old Buick, the boy's arm around the girl's shoulder. The tender exchange tugged at the empty place in Seth's heart. He rubbed the spot and followed Hannah inside.

She wandered ahead of him into the living room. Her jeans hugged her well-rounded behind, tempting him in more ways than one.

He shouldn't want to place his dirty hands on her bottom and caress her sweet ass, but Christ, he did. Seth ground his teeth and adjusted his stance, his jeans suddenly tight and painful.

Hannah dug the bottle from her pants pocket and placed it on the coffee table. Lips pursed and brow furrowed, she focused on the small container. "Do you think Marco will…"

Dammit. Seth rushed to Hannah's side and fought the urge to comfort her with a touch. Instead, he lowered his head until he met her eye level. "Darlin', Marco won't get anywhere near you."

She studied him for a moment then nodded. "With you here, I feel safe."

He'd promised Hannah he'd protect her when he could never guarantee such an outcome. Why had he done that? He added foolish to unworthy, undeserving, and disgraceful to describe himself, and he could come up with a whole list of other appropriate adjectives.

Besides, his track record didn't instill confidence. Emily and Finn had relied on him, too, and that hadn't worked out well—one dead, the other a fae.

Self-loathing bit him in the ass harder than an angry rattler. He removed his Stetson, tossed it on the couch, and ran his hand through his short hair.

"You're always around when I need you. But how did you happen to be here when Finn ran across the lawn toward me?" Hannah touched his cheek.

Oh, how he relished the light, sensitive stroke of her fingers along his jaw. He wanted to pull her to him, kiss her like he had before, and remind them both of his dangerous side. Instead, he grasped her fingers and drew them away. "I came to see you. Brought you a birthday present."

In all the commotion, he'd forgotten about the gift. Did he still have the pencils? Had they fallen out during his fight with Finn?

He patted his coat pocket. The package's slight bulge conformed to his palm. A relieved exhale escaped him.

With great care, he retrieved the packet of charcoal pencils from his inside pocket. Through the package, a few of the broken bits shifted in his hands. "I didn't get a chance to wrap them, and it looks like some of them broke during..."

Hannah placed her hands over her mouth. Her wide-eyed gaze swept from the pencils to his eyes and back again. "You brought me a birthday gift?"

Warmth he had no business feeling crept around inside and latched on to his heart. He handed the packet to her. "Happy belated birthday, Hannah."

She accepted his offering, and as her fingertips trailed over his, tingles of sensual energy flared along their connection.

"Thank you." She blinked then a big smile bloomed on her face. "These are General's charcoal pencils. I love this brand. Thank you, thank you, thank you."

She wrapped her arms around his neck, hugging him tight. As he inhaled, her fresh scent swept into his lungs. He stood there, stiff for a moment, his Adam's apple stuck in his throat.

At long last, he slid his hands down her back, stopping just short of her bottom. All her luscious curves fit against him as if she belonged there. He wanted this moment to last a lifetime.

After a long few seconds, Hannah drew away. She brushed her fingers over his coat sleeve and onto his wrist. She focused on the twined cord then circled the infinity symbol with her fingertip.

"I've seen you touch this a few times. Did someone give this to you?" Her soft voice tickled his ear.

"I made it." A sense of pride swelled his lungs.

"It's beautiful. The cord is braided together so intricately into the infinity symbol." Hannah tilted her head, and the tips of her blonde hair brushed over her shoulder. "Why do you wear it?"

"It's a reminder of my infinite commitment to my goddess, Rhiannon. You know about the war she's in with Gwawl, right?"

Hannah tapped her finger against her luscious bottom lip. "From what Sadie told me, Rhiannon was supposed to marry him but fell in love with a human and vowed to never wed the horrible god. As retribution, Gwawl killed her lover and built the fae army to kill humans. In return, she created the gargoyles to protect them."

"You have the basics down. I'm thankful Rhiannon took a chance on me. I've done things I'm not proud of, and if she hadn't plucked my questionable soul as I entered the Otherworld, I'd report to Gwawl. The god is heartless. He likes things his way. As Rhiannon found out, don't ever cross him for his revenge is legendary." Seth met Hannah's gaze.

Her eyes darted back and forth as she studied him. Damn, he could get lost in those beautiful emerald greens.

"Seth, do you think…"

"Seth! Where are you? There's a glut of fae around Crown Fountain. We need your help." Damian's voice blared over the mind link.

The muscles in Seth's entire body tensed.

Hannah narrowed her gaze at him. "What's wrong?"

"Seth. Answer me!"

Indecision ripped a hole in Seth's stomach, shredding him from the inside. He paced to the window and stared into the night. When it came down to it, there really wasn't an option. He couldn't leave Hannah. *"Damian. I'm tied up with something. You and Grayson will have to handle it."*

"What? You don't show, Drake'll be pissed."

Seth mentally turned off his internal tracker. He didn't want his boss to locate him.

"Cover for me, would you?" Seth hated to ask this of his new friend, but given the circumstances, he had little choice.

"Damn, Seth, you better have a good excuse. Grayson and I'll do what we can."

"Thanks, Dame."

"Seth?" Hannah placed her hand on Seth's jacket. "Did I do something wrong?"

He gripped her fingers and squeezed before he drew her hand away. "Absolutely not, darlin'. It was Damian on the mind link. Business."

"Oh." She blinked. "Do you have to leave?"

"It's my hard-ass boss, Drake, excuse my language." He ran his hand through his hair. "If you don't follow strict orders, he'll ground you in your stone gargoyle for a few nights or longer. I've avoided that for over a century, but that's irrelevant. I won't leave you."

Her eyes widened. "I don't want you in trouble because of me."

He didn't want to scare her, but he refused to lie to her. "You're safe in the house because of the wards, but I don't trust Marco or Finn. I can watch for fae and handle anything that comes up from outside the house. Don't worry. I won't be far away. Keep the curtains shut and stay clear of the windows. Okay?"

She nodded and tugged her bottom lip between her teeth. Seth swallowed hard at her unintentional sexiness. So tempting, so very tempting.

He picked his hat off the couch and strode to the door before he did something he'd regret later, like kiss her until she begged for more. His palm on the handle, he turned to face her. "You still have Wynne's potion?"

She nodded. "Yeah. I'll take more and get some sleep."

"Good plan. If you need me, just holler. I'll hear you." He opened the door then dematerialized.

A moment later, he landed on the Victorian's gabled rooftop. From this vantage point, he had an excellent view of the surrounding neighborhood. No fae would bother Hannah tonight.

A cool breeze toyed with Seth's hat, catching one edge. He gripped the brim and tugged the material tight against his head. His clothing and skin rippled, taking on the gray and black hue of the rooftop, camouflaging him.

On the ground below, a cat bolted from under a parked car across the street, and then up a tree. The feline's nails clicked over the bark in quick succession. If Lady Luck shined on him, the cat would be Seth's only companion tonight.

Footsteps from inside the house caught Seth's attention. Under his gable, light flared through the window, sending a soft glow into the night. He must be over Hannah's room.

The rustling of clothes slipped through the cracks in the window frame. Images of Hannah's shirt falling from her shoulders flashed through Seth's mind. He groaned. After a few long, agonizing seconds, the rustling stopped.

"Get some sleep, darlin'," he whispered.

Beneath his coat, an ache built along his wings. They often cramped after a long night. That's why he so often visited the church before returning to his post. Not tonight. He'd stay here until the first rays of the sun chased him away, and the fae returned to the Otherworld.

The ache along his back intensified, stealing his breath. He whipped off his coat, and it landed on the rooftop and slid toward the gutter. *Damn.*

He caught the sleeve and hung the coat over the gable at his feet, took off his shirt, and unfurled his wings. The soft sound of his feathers brushing the air echoed in the stillness.

A shiver of relief spread from his shoulder blades, over the bones in his wings, and to the tip of each feather. He released a long sigh.

"Dear God. Listen up. Today was not one of my better days. Seems there's a fae out to steal my soul." Hannah's soft voice filtered out the window cracks and tickled his sensitive ears. "I know you won't let that happen, though. You sent Seth to watch over me, and I'm forever grateful. Would you look out for him, too? Thank you, Lord, in Jesus's name, amen."

Seth's chest tightened so hard, he couldn't breathe.

Hannah didn't pray for herself, she prayed for him. No one had done something like that since his sweet Emily. Raw wonder competed with his self-loathing. After the things he'd done to others following his wife's death, he didn't deserve Hannah's prayers.

The light in Hannah's room clicked off, erasing the glow from her window.

Desire to protect Hannah flared deep inside. He touched the cord at his wrist, his index finger tracing the infinity symbol.

Whatever the consequences, he'd do everything in his power to keep her safe. No way would that sweet, innocent woman lose her soul, not while he was around.

He'd sacrifice himself first. If that's what it took, so be it.

CHAPTER 10

*M*arco materialized in his room in the Otherworld, his cells coalescing into his physical form. His unmade bed remained nestled against the far wall between his dresser and the tall standalone mirror. He glanced at his reflection. Bits of flesh, bone, and a bucket load of blood coated his long cloak.

A flutter of pure delight rippled up his back. Tonight had been a night to remember. Little rivulets of power had seeped into him, courtesy of Hannah, but then it had dwindled to a trickle. Maybe proximity had something to do with it, but he'd also snagged a few hits off some good human souls he'd killed.

He'd used the extra energy with a passion he hadn't experienced in decades, besting his one-night human kill record by five. Good thing, too, because with Finn on special assignment, he and Zain needed to make up the difference.

They had a god to appease, and like it or not, Marco's need for praise from a father figure still had him by the balls. Gwawl would receive his tribute. Hannah's pure innocence was a special delicacy worthy of a God.

The skeleton of his first kill, one he'd accomplished while still human, stood along the opposite wall. After he'd turned into a fae, he'd dug up the bones and reassembled his trophy here, where he could admire his work daily. The unlucky human was a constant reminder of his duty to Gwawl and his required tribute.

"You going to welcome me home, Ralph?" Marco smirked, resting his cane on the skeleton's outstretched arm. "Not tonight, I see. Well, keep trying, my friend, keep trying."

Marco removed his coat and tossed the damaged, stained material into the large stone fireplace. With a snap of his finger, flames roared to life as if eager to consume their next meal. Tonight, he'd conjure up a new coat, just as he did every night.

He knelt next to the fireplace and pressed his thumb against the loose stone at its base. A hidden drawer slid from its track on a soft squeak.

On an intake of breath, he withdrew the silver flask. Made from the melted daggers of the few gargoyles he'd killed over the decades, the container was as precious to him as its contents.

Marco stroked his fingers over the engraved surface and unscrewed the top. He placed his mouth against the opening, then parted his lips.

A small tendril of a white gaseous substance, almost like smoke, slipped from him and into the flask. The extra bit of strength he'd enjoyed ebbed from him in an instant, leaving a hard, empty pit in his gut.

He couldn't fail in his task to appease Gwawl or all might be for naught. After replacing his precious merchandise, he closed the drawer and rose to his feet.

The hands on his Rolex indicated dawn approached in the human realm. Zain and Finn were to meet him here.

"Where are my two babysitters?" he muttered to himself.

They better not be late.

Static electricity prickled the hair on Marco's arm, and a low buzz filled the air.

Two small whirlwinds burst to life, one near the fireplace, the other next to his dresser. The swirls churned faster, growing by the second, then quit as quickly as they'd started. In their place, stood Zain and Finn.

Zain brushed his fingers through his dark hair, now uncurled from his braid, and smiled. His chipped tooth seemed so out of place with his flawless features. "You should've stayed a few minutes longer. The sunrise was a killer this morning."

The idiot must be a masochist. What fae stayed out to watch the sunrise?

Marco narrowed his gaze. "I'm sure it was."

Finn leaned against the dresser, his palms pressed against the wood. He was empty-handed, no Hannah in sight.

Marco's pulse rose. "Where is my prize?"

Finn drew his brows together. "I don't think yer goin' ta like what I have ta tell ya."

Marco studied Finn. "You failed to complete your assignment. Are you inept or did you blunder on purpose?"

Finn pushed away from the dresser so hard, the wood surface cracked. Bits of dust rained onto the stone floor.

Good thing there wasn't a window in this place or Marco would've tossed the guy through it. Instead, he gripped Finn by the shoulder and shoved him into the wall. The rock shuddered from the impact. "If you don't answer me, I'll throttle your measly neck until I pinch your worthless head from your spine."

Zain placed his palm on Marco's shoulder. "Don't. Do you want to piss off Gwawl?"

Marco fisted his hand but stepped aside.

Finn glared at him. "Ya wouldn't have fared any better. Hannah's protected. By a gargoyle."

Unease scurried through Marco's bloodstream. "By whom?"

Finn laughed. "My old friend, Seth. Fitting, don't ya think?"

Marco stormed to the fireplace. As he passed Ralph, he swore the skeleton smiled in amusement.

He placed his palms on the mantle and stared into the fire. A complication like this didn't factor into his plans. "Give me details."

Finn strode up behind Marco. His loud exhale echoed around the room. "I went ta Beaumont's house. Dear, sweet Hannah was alone. She invited me in. As I raced across the lawn, Seth tackled me. We fought. I ne'er would've given in ta him, but I couldn't risk my life. Better ta wait him out."

"We only have two nights left." Marco turned around and stared at him. "You should've tried again."

"Ya think I didn't?" Finn scoffed. "I waited patiently, but I sensed Seth nearby clear until the wee hours of dawn. I'm sure Drake wanted him on patrol instead of watchin' over a lass, but he remained, alert and waitin'. If I know Drake, he'll have his hide for that."

Zain shrugged. "Do you want me to capture her?"

Based on the first night, Marco'd lay odds Finn was the one most likely to betray him, but he'd be a fool to base his judgment on one night. Besides, this might be an even better test for Finn if his old best buddy, Seth, guarded Hannah.

Marco shook his head. "No, I want you with me. We have more souls to bag for Gwawl. I have complete confidence Finn will come through next time."

Finn inclined his head but didn't lower his gaze. "Aye, I will. One thing I noticed. The witches ward the place, but the spell is weak. I can promise ya this. I'll find a way in."

"You do that and bring Hannah to me. Tonight, I want her full power." Marco tugged at his shirt collar. The tight material chafed his neck, and he longed for a hot shower, a nice meal, and a relaxing day with one of his lady friends. "If I have to do this myself, you'll be dead. Now, that's a promise."

Finn nodded. "Have no worries about my ability ta complete my task. I'll get the lass."

Marco waved his hand in the air, dismissing his two new "team-mates." "Go. Go. Both of you. Do whatever it is you do during your spare time. Leave me to mine."

A small whirlwind swirled around Finn. He vanished a moment later.

Zain crossed his arms, and his muscles bulged beneath his jacket. His dark gaze pierced through Marco. "I don't trust him. He was a gargoyle on Rhiannon's team for over a century. I wouldn't be surprised if he's still fighting the transition to fae. You sure you don't want me to handle this?"

Marco clapped his palm on Zain's shoulder. "Not yet, my new friend. If he fails again, you'll get your chance. At sunset, we gather more souls. Don't want to disappoint our boss, now, do we?"

A hard glint flared in Zain's hazel eyes. "I can hardly wait."

The impudent fae vanished in a mini dust storm.

"Trust is such a fragile thing." Marco turned to Ralph and stared at the skeleton's dark, empty eye sockets. "We'll see which one of them breaks it first. In either case, I will see pretty little Hannah again and suck all of the precious goodness from her soul. Then Gwawl will have his tribute, and I will obtain the promotion I so richly deserve."

The morning sun crested over the top of Stuart Hall, bathing the quad below in dawn's soft glow. A bird's quiet chirp echoed in the morning air, followed by another and then a third. The lawn and the walkways within the quad remained eerily silent and peaceful.

No humans roamed the grounds quite yet. Not that Seth expected much activity today. Most students had fled like wild horses to get away for spring break. But not all.

Seth had remained atop the old Victorian until the sun's first rays nearly crested over the horizon then beat a hasty retreat to his perch. His only solace—Hannah would be safe from the fae during the day. The tension flooding Seth's spirit eased, and an image of Hannah flashed through his mind.

She stood before him, brow furrowed. With a profound touch of kindness, she'd brushed her fingertips along his jaw. His chest tightened at the memory, and a longing for affection he'd craved for more than a century threatened to surface.

He fought the emotion, shoving away the warmth that wanted to burrow deep into his soul. The likes of him didn't deserve sweet kindness from someone as gentle and caring as Hannah.

"Seth. Heads up. Grayson and I did our best to cover for you, but Drake joined us at the end of the last battle. He knows you turned off your tracker and went AWOL. Sorry, man." Damian's voice echoed through the mind link.

"Watch out, my friend, he's madder than a hornet," Grayson chimed in.

Seth seethed, but he didn't regret his choice to watch over Hannah. "Thanks, y'all. 'Preciate the effort."

Frustration traveled through him like an electrical current. He stirred within his stone gargoyle but was unable to stretch his arms, legs, and even wings.

Damn, how he hated the confinement, but at least there was enough light for him to see. If he'd ever been trapped in his gargoyle without his vision, madness might've claimed him long ago.

"Seth." Drake's deep voice pinged over the mind link. "Tell me what's so damned more important than sending fae into the ether."

The urge to spin a tale and lie to his boss lingered on the tip of Seth's tongue. Tension tightened around his soul. Since he'd become a gargoyle, he'd left deceit behind along with the cards. He steeled himself and let the words fly. "Protecting a human woman. Marco's targeted her and—"

"You know the rules. We're night guardians, protectors of all humankind. We can't afford to spend time guarding a single human." Drake expelled a long breath. "You're lucky Damian and Grayson handled the fae tonight. If they hadn't, I'd blame you for any human deaths."

"It didn't come to that."

"Good thing. If it had, I'd ground your ass to your post for a week. As it is, I should hold you here for at least a night, but I need you out in the field." His boss exhaled loud and slow. "You're a good warrior, Seth. Don't disappoint me again."

A bitter thickness coated the back of Seth's throat. His job meant everything to him or so he'd thought. Now, doubt plagued him along with his guilt. "I'll do what I can."

Drake clicked off the mind link without a reply.

Although Seth hadn't lied to his squad leader, he hadn't shared the entire truth either. He had every intention of checking in with Hannah at dusk.

Finn or some other fae would try again, and Seth vowed to protect her no matter the consequences. For her, he'd risk a thousand nights trapped in his gargoyle and endure every moment of the torment.

CHAPTER 11

*S*oft fur tickled Hannah's cheek, rousing her from a deep
sleep. The tail end of a dream, one of a tall, dark, sexy man
who looked a lot like Seth, slipped from her memory. She brushed the
fine hairs that were tickling her away and opened her eyes.

A thin shaft of sunlight streamed between the crack in her
curtains, tracked over the floor and onto her bed, the brightness
piercing into her brain. She blinked and focused on her surroundings.

Snookums sat on the corner of her comforter. He licked his front
paw, his long tongue tugging at the fur with each stroke.

She slid back on the pillow with a soft groan. "Why did you wake
me up so early, Snookums? You hungry?"

As if he understood, he rubbed against her shoulder. The rumble
of a soft purr reverberated in his chest. A moment later, he jumped off
the comforter. His nails clicked against the hardwood floor as he
headed into the hallway.

Hannah placed her arm over her face, blocking the sunlight.
Memories of last night resurfaced with a vengeance—Finn's attack,
Seth's rescue, Wynne's potion. How had she ended up in such a situa-
tion? It was all too much to comprehend.

She pushed aside the bedsheets and rolled to a sitting position. The joints in her shoulders, hips, and knees ached, flaring the headache behind her eyes.

"I need medicine." Her words, raspy from her dry throat, echoed in the quiet room. Although she'd snagged the bottle from the coffee table and swallowed some of the medicine before bed, she was well past the four-hour limit. No wonder her head hurt.

Hannah grabbed the small green bottle from her nightstand, uncorked the top, and brought the glass to her lips. The smooth, cool liquid eased down her throat. She exhaled a long breath and set the vial on the table.

The pounding at her temple ebbed to a dull throb. She massaged the spot then glanced at the digital clock nestled on the nightstand— 1:12p.m.

Her heart skipped a beat. Had she really slept through the entire morning?

Wynne would arrive soon. Besides, Hannah needed to work on that sketch for Sadie and Beaumont. She'd finish that drawing even if it was the last one she ever made.

Hannah rose to her feet. White spots formed in her vision and dizziness threatened to take her down. She wrapped shaky fingers around her bedpost and placed her forehead against the cool grain.

A shiver rippled from her shoulders and down her arms to her fingertips. She exhaled a long breath. A moment later, her vision cleared.

With slow, measured steps, she headed for the bathroom. A nice, warm shower should do her wonders.

Thirty minutes later and feeling a little better, Hannah stood in front of her mirror and admired her clothes. She rubbed her hands over the soft material of her rose-colored sweater. Paired with her favorite jeans, she'd picked this particular outfit because the bright, vibrant tone reminded her to stay positive. Things would work out in the end. They always did, didn't they?

She focused on her features reflected in the mirror. Dark circles rimmed her eyes despite the concealer she'd applied. Doubt's cold fingers threatened to creep up her spine. What if she didn't survive? Worse yet, what if she turned into a fae?

"No. That won't happen." Drawing on her inner strength and her faith, she peered at the ceramic angel resting over her headboard. The beautiful white wings, spread wide, flared at the tips.

Her guardian angel watched over her, and his name was Seth.

Thank God, he'd come to her rescue. She'd be dead without him, her soul sucked dry by that vicious fae, Marco.

The hair at her nape rose, and she trailed her finger over the mark behind her ear. How she hated having his brand on her skin. If there was a way to cut it off, she'd do it regardless of any permanent scar.

Bolstered by her belief in her savior and her resolve to survive, she snatched the medicine from her dresser, turned on the ball of her foot, and headed for the kitchen.

After feeding both Snookums and George, Hannah poured herself a bowl of Rice Krispies and settled into one of the chairs at the kitchen table. The little round chunks bobbed in the milk, and the trademark pop, crackle, and snap made them appear alive.

Hannah's stomach soured. "Nope. Not happening."

She shoved the bowl away. A tidal wave of milk crested dangerously close to the brim, and a few pieces of the cereal threatened to escape.

The familiar ding of the doorbell's chime rang through the house.

Hannah rose from her chair, the hard, wooden feet scraping against the linoleum and echoing through her brain. She winced, even as she hurried down the hall. When she reached the front door, she leaned on her tiptoes and peered through the peephole.

Wynne and her sister, Sasha, stood on the front porch. A pretty floral scarf hung around Wynne's neck, the yellow and blue flowers accentuating her blonde hair and blue eyes. Sasha, an older version of Wynne, stared directly at the peephole. A smile broke across her features, and she waved.

"Thank God." Hannah yanked open the door. "I'm so happy to see you both."

Wynne strode through the doorway and wrapped her arms around Hannah. "So glad to see you, too."

Sasha joined in the group hug, and a hint of cinnamon and nutmeg infiltrated Hannah's senses. Tension drained from her shoulders. How she loved her friends.

A moment later, Hannah drew away to close the door.

"How do you feel?" Wynne's intense gaze focused on her, concern etched in the fine lines around her eyes.

Fatigue tugged on Hannah's mind, and her legs seemed to weigh a thousand pounds. "Tired. Sore. A little scared."

Sasha placed her hand on Hannah's arm. "I can imagine. You've had a rough time."

"Let's get you into the light so I can get a better look at you." Wynne grasped Hannah's hand and led her into the kitchen, Sasha following not far behind.

Wynne set her blue Coach purse on the table. She rested her gaze on the cereal bowl, and she furrowed her brow. "What have you eaten today?"

Hannah shrugged. "I just woke up a little while ago."

"Food will give you energy. Eat something. Okay?"

Hannah shook her head. "It churns my stomach."

"The nausea is only a sensation caused by Marco's hold on you. Part of the soul-stealing weakens the victim by making their appetite seem non-existent which makes it easier to prey on them. If you can, ignore the nausea and eat some food. It will help you feel better and give you strength to fight."

Hannah sighed. As much as she wanted to eat, food didn't appeal to her. "Okay, I'll try later. I promise."

Wynne wrapped her arms around Hannah's shoulders and tugged her close once again. "I'm so sorry. This can't be easy for you."

Sasha embraced them both. "No damn dark fae is going to steal your soul, not if we have anything to say about it."

Warmth spread through Hannah, lightening her spirit. She held the two witches near a moment longer then drew away. "I want to thank both of you. Your friendship means the world to me."

Wynne smiled, but her anxious gaze traveled over Hannah's features. "Why don't you sit down and let me have a look at you."

The witches' compassion and fatigue weakened her knees, and Hannah slipped into the nearest kitchen chair before she fell.

Sasha sat next to her and held her hand while Wynne poked, prodded, and studied her with every "say ah," "breathe deep," and "cough."

After she'd completed her examination, Wynne leaned against the table and crossed her arms. "The medicine I gave you seemed to help, but I don't like that you still have a slight temperature and appear fatigued."

She dug through her purse and withdrew a small leather pouch. "I had a feeling this might happen, so I made you a cream. This one has fast healing ability. Should you notice any muscle pain or bleeding, apply this lotion directly onto the spot. Be careful though, too much can irritate the skin."

The hair along Hannah's scalp tingled. "What kind of bleeding? Will random sores pop out on my skin like chickenpox or something?"

"No, nothing like that, but the longer Marco's hold on you persists, you might experience a nosebleed, bleeding cracked lips, or blood seeping from your fingernails."

"My fingernails?" Hannah glanced at her fingers, and visions of blood gushing from the tips raised goose bumps along her arms.

"Hannah. Don't worry. I don't sense that will occur, but I want to be on the safe side." Wynne offered the pouch. "Continue to take the other medication every few hours, as we discussed."

With a bitterness coating the back of her throat, Hannah accepted the gift. She tugged open the string, studied the green paste within the leather, then shoved the small bag in her jeans pocket.

Would she be able to escape Marco? A chilling prickle tracked up her spine. There was only so much the witches could do to help her. "Thank you for looking out for me. I don't know what I'd do without you both or Seth."

Her cheeks heated at the sound of his name coming from her lips. The thought of him calmed her fears, but for so long, she'd kept her interest in him a secret even from her two closest new friends. Now, though, questions about him burned in her mind, and she blurted the words before she lost her nerve.

"What can you tell me about him?"

"Seth?" Wynne raised her eyebrows. "Our cowboy?"

Hannah nodded. "Yeah."

Sasha giggled. "Oh, Hannah, you have a crush on him, don't you? That's so sweet."

Hannah's cheeks flamed hotter. "Well, I'm just curious. That's all."

"Uh-huh. I know how it is. He's one fine looking male specimen, if you ask me." Sasha winked.

Wynne pulled out another chair and joined them at the table. "Sasha. He's one of my charges. I wish you wouldn't talk about him that way."

"Why not?" Sasha narrowed her gaze at her sister. "You used to be all googly-eyed over Beaumont."

Wynne pursed her mouth. "That was a while ago. Not anymore. Now, I've sworn off men."

"Yeah, until the next hottie comes along." Sasha turned her attention to Hannah. "What do you know about Seth?"

"He's honorable and has been a gargoyle for a while. Finn was his best friend. I think there was someone special in his life, maybe a long time ago, but I'm not sure about now."

The lines around Wynne's eyes softened. "You're right about all of those things. He had a wife before he became a gargoyle. He never talks about her, but I've seen a sorrowful look in his eyes sometimes. Makes me wonder what happened."

Sasha straightened in the chair, and a white crystal on the end of a chain around her neck peeked from underneath her blouse. She shook her head. "Honey, you're a sweet, innocent young thing. From what I know of Seth, he'd never hurt you, but he's a gargoyle. On the rare night that he has off, I've heard rumors he frequents some of the dance clubs and bars. Likes the ladies, if you know what I mean."

Hannah fidgeted in her seat. She had no chance with Seth, but after their kiss, she'd let a small part of herself begin to hope for something special with him.

Wynne clasped Hannah's hand. "I can tell you from firsthand experience, don't get involved with a gargoyle. It won't end well. I don't want to see you with a broken heart."

Might be too late for that already. Hannah drew her hand away and raised her chin. "I appreciate your concern..."

"But?" Sasha toyed with the crystal at her throat.

Hannah shrugged and shook her head.

"Unfortunately, I have a long list of things to do today." Wynne pushed away from the table and rose from her chair.

"I'll be outside for a few minutes reinforcing the wards. You," she pointed at Hannah and then the cereal bowl, "finish that."

As if on command, the bowl slid across the tablecloth until it rested in front of Hannah. The spoon clanked against the inside, once, twice, three times, as if in irritation.

"All right." Hannah gripped the utensil, snagged a few soggy pieces and shoved them into her mouth. The nasty mush slid down her throat, but her stomach rumbled in thanks.

After the front door rang down the hallway, a smile spread across Sasha's face, and she leaned forward. "What you really want to know about Seth is—how good is he in bed—isn't it?"

Hannah held the spoonful of uneaten cereal midair. She tightened her fingers around the handle, and the milk jiggled in the spoon. "W...what?"

Sasha glanced at the door before focusing on Hannah. "Wynne doesn't know this, but a few years ago I slept with him once."

"You what?" A pang of jealousy lanced through Hannah.

The spoon slipped from her fingers and landed in the bowl, sending a small wave over the lip. Milk spilled onto the table along with a few Rice Krispies. The cereal pieces floated on the milk river toward the edge but didn't make it before succumbing to their soggy fate.

"Don't tell me you've never dreamed of what it might be like to be with Seth. I can see it in your eyes. You're crazy about him." Sasha leaned back in her chair and fanned her fingers over her ample breast.

"Seth is so very fine. You told me once you were a virgin. You picked a great choice for your first lover, and you won't have to worry about catching anything nasty or getting pregnant from a gargoyle. Trust me, you won't regret it."

Heaviness settled onto Hannah's shoulders. "I've always dreamed my first time would be with someone special, someone that cares about me or even loves me. But I'm not sure I'll live past the next two nights."

Sasha waved her hand in the air. "Maybe Seth is the one for you. It doesn't have to be about love to be special, you know. Besides, you and I both know you're not going to die. You have your faith, and I've seen your fate in the stars."

Hannah's pulse raced. "You have?"

Sasha's smile faded. Apprehension etched lines around her mouth. "Belief in yourself and others can accomplish great things, more than you may even realize. No matter how bleak life seems, never let doubt cloud your mind. Remember that, Hannah, okay?"

Hannah's throat constricted. Sasha's words had left her unable to speak. She blinked away the hot, gummy tears that threatened to fall and nodded.

The front door creaked open. A moment later, Wynne wandered into the kitchen. She untied the scarf around her neck and exhaled. "My, Hannah, that cat of yours can be such a pest, wanting to be stroked all the time. Distracting as the Otherworld. If he wasn't so dang cute, I'd have zapped him with a spell."

Wynne wiped her forehead with the back of her hand. "Well, I fortified the perimeter. The wards should be good for another three months. Would you tell Beaumont when he and Sadie return from their trip?"

"Absolutely." Hannah rose from her seat and wrapped Wynne in a giant hug. "Thank you for watching out for me."

"Of course. My pleasure. Besides," Wynne pulled back enough to stare into Hannah's eyes, "in the few months that we've known each other, you've become one of my closest friends. I want to make sure you're safe so we can have more movies and popcorn nights."

A sensation of weightlessness removed some of the burden on Hannah's shoulders. "With you, Sasha, and Seth on my side, Marco doesn't stand a chance."

Wynne smiled. "That's right. Not a chance this side of the Otherworld." Her gaze slid to the window, and her smile faded. "Time to go, sis. We have a few more stops to make before nightfall."

Sasha rose and strode toward Hannah, her arms extended wide. "You stay safe, okay?"

Hannah hugged Sasha. "Yep. It's all good."

Wynne tied her scarf around her wrist. "If you need anything, reach out to Sasha or me. One of us should be able to help you."

"Thank you. Let me walk you to the—"

Wynne held up her hand. "We can let ourselves out. I'd rather you finish that cereal and take the potion I gave you earlier. Don't forget. Every four hours or so."

Even as Hannah sighed, the headache started at her temple once again. "I will."

As Sasha followed Wynne into the hallway, she peered at Hannah, winked, and whispered, "Remember what I said. Faith in yourself and others can work wonders."

Hannah believed in the virtue of the human spirit, but with an evil fae intent on stealing every ounce of goodness in her soul, would there be enough left to matter?

She didn't want to dwell on that or she'd end up wrapped in a ball of insecurity. Besides, the sketch of Beaumont and Sadie wouldn't finish itself.

With determination radiating from the inside, she finished the bowl of cereal and headed for her art room. The distraction might do her some good.

She picked up her charcoal pencil and tried to focus on Sasha's sage advice, but she couldn't stop the apprehension creeping into her thoughts.

CHAPTER 12

*H*annah brushed the charcoal over the page with long, firm strokes. Bits of the dark carbon filled in the lines in Seth's hair and along the brim of his Stetson. While working on the portrait for Sadie and Beaumont, she'd thought about Seth. Before she knew it, she'd set aside the sketch for her sister, thank God it was almost done, and started on her new project using the charcoal Seth had given her.

She stepped away from the easel and stared at the portrait. Seth, with his piercing eyes, sexy smile, and a dusting of stubble on his chin, peered at her with longing in his gaze. Oh, how she wished that look was directed at her.

Over the past few months when he'd visited Beaumont, she'd seen him stare off into the distance with a similar yearning in his eyes. That look of reverence must've been for his deceased wife.

Hannah shook her head and touched up a spot along one of Seth's wings. Hannah had permitted her muse to take over, and her strokes had become fast and furious, the wings forming beneath her swift-moving pencil. She hadn't intended to add them and didn't know if he had wings, but she'd long ago learned to go with the flow when she entered her creative zone and allowed herself to draw whatever her muse whispered in her ear.

A dull throb started at the base of her scalp, but she didn't want to stop drawing, not now. While in the groove, nothing else mattered. She did her best work that way. A few more strokes along Seth's nose and along the edge of his mouth should complete the portrait.

Warmth filtered from deep inside, expanding in her chest. She'd captured his image the way she'd intended. Seth would like the picture, Hannah just knew it.

A loud thump echoed down the hallway.

Hannah stiffened and held her breath. Maybe Snookums knocked something off the coffee table or—

She stepped to the window and peered through the glass. Dusk painted the surrounding trees in shades of gray. A streetlight winked on and cast a dull glow onto the sidewalk. Somehow, she'd lost track of time.

Her heart pounded, and the dull throb grew more intense.

Silence stretched on for several long moments. Even as her mind raced, she hung a thin sheet over the rods protruding from the easel's frame, hiding the sketch but not touching the material and wiping away the charcoal from the picture.

"Oh no. I forgot to take my medicine." Hannah bolted from the art room and into the hallway. The muscles in Hannah's legs ached from the effort to run, and unusual tiredness stalled the breath in her lungs.

She rounded the corner of the living room, flicked on the light, and glanced at the side table holding George's fishbowl. The green medicine bottle rested alongside the Beta's food containers. Just as she'd thought, she'd left it there after feeding him that morning.

Hannah wiped her mouth on a quick exhale. "Thank God, I found you."

"Why, thank ya, lass. Ya shouldn't worry about me, but I appreciate yer concern nonetheless." Finn stood next to the fireplace. Soot stained his red shirt at the shoulder and along one pant leg of his blue jeans.

He wiped a black smudge from his cheek and smiled. "Good ta see ya again, Hannah."

She gripped the back of the couch. Her fingernails bit into the soft material.

Stalling for time, she blurted out the first thing that came to her mind. "The house is warded. How did you get in here?"

He gazed around the room before focusing on her. The menacing smile that crested over his lips was one she'd never seen before coming from him, and the darkness in his eyes prickled the hairs at her nape.

She tightened her grip on the couch, thankful for the small barrier between her and this fae.

"Ah, well." Finn inched toward her, hands flexing into fists at his side. "Seems Wynne forgot ta reinforce the ward on the chimney. Perhaps the lassie was distracted. In either case, ya did invite me in. So, I materialized down yer chimney. Seems I got a bit dirty along the way."

Hannah's pulse ratcheted up another level. She slid toward the end of the couch, keeping distance between them. Her attention tracked to the fireplace poker, and her stomach clenched. No way could she reach it before him.

A stack of mail rested on the sideboard. Nothing worthy to use as a weapon nearby.

"Now, lass, don't make me do this the hard way." He edged toward her, held out his palm, and waggled his fingers in encouragement. "Come with me. Marco wants ta see ya again."

His eyes glowed an uncanny vibrant yellow.

Energy, fast as lightning, propelled her toward the hallway.

Her sneakers skidded on the parquet floor. She gripped the doorframe, but her momentum carried her into the wall.

Pain ricocheted from her shoulder all the way to her fingertips.

Finn tackled her, and her hipbone slammed against the hardwood floor along with her shoulder. Agony flared at the joints as his heavy weight pinned her to the ground. Her face plastered against the flat surface, she struggled beneath him, but he grasped her wrists and held her tight.

"Calm yerself, lass. Fightin' will only make it worse." Finn's heated breath blasted across her ear.

"Let me go!" She strained under his weight, her heels beating against his thighs.

The front door slammed against the wall, and a loud crack resounded.

One sizable wood splinter landed just inches from Hannah's nose and bounced on the floor.

A moment later, a strong breeze ruffled Hannah's hair, and Finn's weight lifted.

Glass shattered, and something heavy landed with a thud, shaking the ground.

Hannah's breath rushed from her. She pushed herself to her hands and knees, wrenched her head around, and peered into the living room.

Like a blur, two males fought. They moved so fast, she couldn't identify either, but she knew one had to be Finn.

The couch crashed against the wall. One of its legs protruded from the cushion as if impaled. Shards of glass from the broken coffee tabletop lay scattered over the rug.

Between the blurs, Hannah caught glimpses of the fighters. Red shirt. Dark hair. *Finn.*

Brown leather jacket—

A cowboy hat flew through the air and landed on the impaled couch leg. The hat's cord swayed back and forth from the impact.

Hannah's heart skipped a beat.

Seth.

The crack of a whip echoed against the walls, and hope fluttered in Hannah's stomach.

She searched for a weapon, and her gaze landed on the fireplace poker, which mysteriously still rested against the brick amid all the fighting. If she could sneak past both men and snatch it, she might be able to help Seth.

Steeling herself, she inhaled a quick breath then stepped into the room.

~

Seth cracked his whip. The barbed tips ripped across Finn's chest, shredding the material and scoring the flesh. Blood spurted from the wound. An odorous, metallic scent filled the air.

Finn bared his fangs and withdrew his dagger from its sheath. "Ya're too far away. Come closer and find out what it's like ta be bested by an Irishman."

"You're the one that'll die tonight." As soon as the sun had set, Seth had materialized on Hannah's lawn. He'd heard Finn's threat through the cracks along the windowsill. Not wasting a moment, he'd burst through the doorway.

Seeing Hannah pinned to the ground by Finn had sent a rush of energy through him so fast, white spots of anger had blurred his vision. Now, he faced his best-friend-turned-enemy. With a quick snap of his wrist, he sent the length of his whip toward Finn once again.

The ends wrapped around Finn's wrist. Seth tugged, and the dagger dislodged from the fae's grip. The blade slipped from his palm and clattered to the floor.

Finn gripped the whip with his free hand and yanked.

Seth tightened the muscles in his legs, holding steady against the rebounding force that threatened to wrench him off balance. He hardened his jaw, and pain radiated up his face.

Finn leapt over the couch's destroyed remains. His gaze focused on something behind Seth, and a devious smile tugged at his lips.

The scrape of metal against brick echoed from behind him.

Icicles formed from dread skittered down Seth's spine. He turned toward the fireplace.

With fingers white from strain, Hannah gripped the fireplace poker. She raised the pointed tip over her head like a baseball bat. Determination etched lines around her pursed lips.

Finn crouched, preparing for his attack on Hannah.

"No, Hannah!" Seth launched himself toward her.

Finn leapt into the air.

Seth wrapped his arms around her as Hannah's terrified scream echoed around the room. He shimmered and hardened his skin to stone, preparing for Finn's certain assault.

Finn's claws scraped along Seth's jacket, ripping into the material. With his hardened skin, Finn's nails didn't penetrate Seth's flesh, but Seth couldn't fight Finn while he protected Hannah. Helplessness seized him, a feeling he detested.

"Let me help." Hannah's soft words penetrated Seth's brain.

"No, darlin'—"

Finn cleared his throat, the phlegmy sound loud in the enclosed space.

Seth's heart skipped a beat. Finn was preparing to use his poisonous acid. Fae produced a limited supply in a sac at the back of their throat. The corroding substance penetrated even the hardest stone.

Still protecting Hannah with his body, Seth braced himself and tugged his dagger from his waistband.

Finn's wet and sticky spittle landed on Seth's back.

Pain flared along the skin at Seth's shoulder blades and into his wings, stealing the breath from his lungs.

Finn chuckled. Spit glistened on his bottom lip. "Ya can't protect her much longer. Once the acid burns through ya, there'll be no one ta stand in my way. Ya'll be coming with me then, lass."

"Not if I can help it." Seth released Hannah, and with a quick twist, thrust the weapon at his old friend.

Finn ducked, but the blade sliced across his cheek. A high-pitched howl burst from his lips. He bolted to his weapon and retrieved his dagger from the floor. The blade glinted in the subdued light.

In the seconds it took Finn to snag his weapon, Seth embraced Hannah and drew her next to the overturned, destroyed couch.

As he plastered her against the wall, face to face, and covered her with his body, he shimmered. His clothing and skin blended in with the white wall and the couch's brown material.

Hannah's panting breaths tickled his ear. Thank the goddess, she kept quiet. As long as she didn't move, she'd remain hidden behind him.

Finn growled. "Feck. Yer hidin' from me now, are ya? That's a jolt. Ya never were a coward. Guess ya're smartin' more than yer lettin' on. Good. Very good."

The pain along Seth's wings brought white spots before his vision. He breathed deep, forcing his attention to remain on his enemy even as Hannah's sweet scent raced into his lungs.

Methodical and with purpose, Finn tracked along the fireplace and the far wall, his dagger held out in front of him.

Seth turned his own dagger over in his palm until his fingers gripped the sharp blade. Slowly, he raised his hand, aimed, and flicked.

The blade sailed through the air.

With a soft thunk, like a watermelon split open by a machete, the tip embedded in Finn's chest.

The muscles in the fae's shoulders tensed, and his mouth opened on a silent scream.

"Feck. I don't believe it. Ya actually hit me, didn't ya?" Eyes wide, he grabbed the hilt and withdrew the bloody blade several inches before the tip emerged. The weapon bounced on the rug then clattered on the parquet floor. Blood spread over his shirt, darkening the material.

Before Seth could finish the job, Finn disappeared in a swirl of broken glass, shredded couch fabric, and bits of stuffing.

An eerie stillness settled over the room.

Hannah's soft breaths teased the skin on his neck. She trailed her fingernails over his cheek and along his jaw, drawing his attention to her. "You saved me, again. How many more times are you going to do that?"

"As many as it takes."

Her eyes darted back and forth as she studied him. "You would, wouldn't you? You really are my guardian angel. If not for you, I'd be..."

"Hannah, darlin—" Pain lanced along his back. He inhaled through gritted teeth.

"Are you all right?" She bit her lip.

The acid burned over his wings, singeing feathers and flesh in equal measure. Agony surged along his oversensitive skin, lighting up his nerves like a bonfire. A shiver rippled over his entire body. His mind fogged.

As if she were his rock grounding him to reality, he tightened his grip on Hannah's arms.

She grasped his face in her palms. "Look at me."

He did as she commanded.

Her bottom lip trembled, the plump flesh quivering ever so slightly. The urge to kiss away her fear competed with the need to ensure her safety.

In the end, his duty won out. "Don't you worry, darlin'. I won't let Finn take you."

She furrowed her brow. "You're injured. Let me look at—"

He pushed away from her. "I'm fine."

Hannah craned her neck to see over his shoulder.

He kept her at arm's length, his aching back out of her view.

"Stop, Seth. I smell burnt flesh. You need help."

A zip of unease coursed through his veins. There was no way he'd let her or anyone else see his wings. "I'll be fine, really. Just need to sit for a bit."

His vision wavered, and he placed his palm against the wall for support.

Hannah huffed. "I'm calling Wynne."

She bolted into the hallway. A moment later, she emerged with her phone in her hand. The ringing on the other end of the line sounded like a death knell.

"Hello?"

Hannah touched the base of her throat. "Sasha?"

"Hannah?" Sasha gasped. "What's going on? You sound upset."

Seth's breath heaved from his lungs. The pain worsened with every heartbeat as the acid bore through his feathers, his flesh, his bones. He didn't know how long he could stay on his feet. What if he passed out? Not going to happen.

He ground his teeth, and through sheer force of will, locked his knees in place.

Hannah glanced at him, the unease in her eyes morphing to all-out panic. "It's Seth. Finn and Seth fought. Finn spit something onto Seth's back and—"

"Oh no, that's acid!"

"—he's injured and in a lot of pain. Can Wynne come over?"

A long silence echoed over the line. With his extrasensory hearing, Seth heard Sasha's gulp.

"That's not possible."

Hannah blinked, her fine lashes caressing her cheek. "What do you mean, 'not possible?'"

"There's a full moon tonight. Every night of the full moon, Wynne pays penance to Rhiannon for putting Beaumont at risk. She's locked in stone, just like the gargoyles during the day. I also received notification that one of the gargoyles died in a fight tonight and another is coming in for severe lacerations. Per Rhiannon's rules, I must stay here. But I have—"

Sasha's words faded as Hannah met Seth's gaze.

He forced a smile. "It's okay. I'll be fine."

His leg buckled.

His knee crashed against the floor.

Breath stalled in his lungs.

The phone slid from Hannah's hand. It skittered across the floor and under the remnants of the couch.

She rushed to his side. "Seth. Tell me what to do—"

"Need a shower..." Seth forced the words from his lips. Even on his knees, he had the presence of mind to keep his shoulders back so Hannah didn't see his wings. He didn't want to admit how bad the injury hurt, but if he didn't repair the damage and soon, the wound might never heal.

"Hannah! Hannah! Talk to me. I have an idea how to help him."

Even without his extrasensory hearing, he would've heard Sasha's loud words. Apparently, so did Hannah. She glanced at the couch, pushed off the floor, and raced to retrieve her phone.

Hannah reached between a crack in the frame and withdrew the device, her fingers gripped tight around the case. "Tell me."

"Wynne gave you a cream. It's similar to the salve we give the gargoyles. Rub some on the injury. The balm should relieve the pain and speed the healing process."

Hannah's shoulders visibly relaxed, but the hand holding the phone shook. "Thank you, Sasha."

"Good luck. Call me if you need anything else."

Hannah shoved the phone in her pocket and raced to Seth's side. A caring Seth hadn't seen in well over a hundred years reflected in the depths of those emerald green eyes. His chest tightened, but not from pain.

"Seth," she placed her arm under his shoulder then glanced around. Her brows furrowed, putting a sadness in her features he didn't like. "Come with me. There's a chair in the next room. Besides, it's cleaner in there. After all this destruction, I don't trust you won't get an infection."

Struggling with consciousness, he didn't have the strength to argue with her. Between the two of them, his arm draped over her shoulders, they trudged down the hallway and into the adjacent room.

Various landscapes and portraits, mostly sketches, lined the walls. The illustrations calmed him in a way he didn't fully understand.

Hannah helped him into a chair next to an easel.

Hot, fevered pain rippled down his spine. White spots in his vision turned to blizzard-like conditions, eating away at his consciousness. He placed his head between his knees and breathed deep.

Hannah's inhale echoed loud in the room. "Oh my god. You have feathers. Are those...wings?"

Darkness threatened to take him down, and he almost wished it would. After over a hundred years of hiding his wings, Hannah had discovered his secret.

CHAPTER 13

*H*annah gaped at Seth. He sat hunched over in the chair in her art room, white feathers protruding through the large gashes in his leather jacket.

She held her breath. "I didn't know you had wings."

He straightened his back, placed his elbows on his thighs, and peered at her. Tightness formed lines around his eyes, and vulnerability and pain embedded within his blue depths. "No one knows, except you, now."

No one else knew? Hannah's heart picked up speed, and determination to help him pushed her into action. "Let's get this jacket off so I can look at your injuries."

She tugged at Seth's collar and eased the soft leather over his shoulders and down his arms. A grimace pursed his lips, but he didn't cry out. Respect for him swelled inside. He was her warrior, her guardian angel, and he'd risked his life for her.

Visible through several long slashes in his ripped T-shirt, the soft down of his feathers protruded from his damaged skin. She guided the shredded top over his head.

White as fresh snow, bits of his feathers jutted from beneath his skin, the tips shimmering as if they'd been dipped in shiny, silver metallic nail polish. Their beauty stole her breath away. The T-shirt slipped from her fingers and landed next to the jacket with a soft plop.

A strained moan eased from Seth's lips. The muscles in his back clenched, and his skin rippled as if bones adjusted and moved beneath the surface. She never would've known the hidden wings existed if he hadn't received his injury.

Like a tide receding from the shore, his skin drew away and two beautiful white wings unfurled. They grew with each beat of her heart until they extended almost to the ceiling.

Blood oozed from a nasty gash between his wings at the center of his shoulder blades. Even as she examined the injury the wound grew, heading to his lower back and eating more of his flesh with every breath. Along his wings, visible holes among the feathers showed more damage from the fae's horrific acid.

Anger like she'd never experienced swelled deep in Hannah's soul. He'd received his injuries protecting her.

She placed her hand on his arm. "I'll get the salve. Be right back."

A bead of sweat rolled over his brow and dripped onto the floor. He gave her a quick nod.

Fear for his well-being chased after her as she bolted to retrieve Wynne's lotion. She took the stairs two at a time and burst into the bathroom. The small pouch rested on the counter. She grasped the sack in her palm and fled back down the stairs.

A wave of exhaustion nearly took her down, but she pushed through the sluggishness. Seth needed her.

She reached him and tried to untie the cord, but her shaky fingers fumbled over the knot. Adrenaline, fueled by her frustration, zipped along her nerves.

Seth placed his palm over her hand and gripped the pouch in their combined grasp.

Hannah peered at him.

He smiled, and the look of reverence in his eyes just about brought her to her knees. "It's all right, Hannah. I'll do it."

She swallowed and shook her head. "I want to do this for you. Please, let me." Would he trust her? She held her breath and waited.

Seth met her gaze, nodded, and then squeezed her hand before he let her go. "Thank you, darlin', just don't touch the feathers."

His familiar term of endearment rumbled in the space between them and settled over her with an easy warmth. Unexpected tears blurred her vision. She blinked them away before one escaped and slipped over her lashes.

With a new determination urging her on, she exhaled a quick breath, focused on the knot, and untied the strands.

A soft hiss of magic eased from the pouch. Hannah set the string on the table next to her easel. Wisps of blue smoke unfurled from the bag and drifted toward Seth's back.

Her breath stalled. "How do I..."

"Place some on your fingertips and spread the solution over the wound. Don't worry, the acid won't burn your skin through the salve."

She wiped the back of her hand across her damp forehead then dipped two fingers into the cream. With tentative, gentle care, she reached between Seth's outstretched wings and rubbed the salve onto the wound.

He hissed, and the muscles in his back tensed.

Hannah inhaled. "Did I hurt you?"

"Nope. You're doing great, darlin'." Seth's encouraging words slipped through her, giving her the strength to continue.

As she rubbed the salve over the wound, the smoke the cream created changed to green then yellow before turning to an off shade of white. Between Seth's shoulder blades, the skin on his back knit together, the wound closing with each brush of her fingertips.

The tension in Seth's muscles eased, his shoulders relaxing under her tender strokes. When the last of the wound disappeared, Hannah's attention turned to the holes in several of Seth's feathers. Despite the injuries, the soft, beautiful down of his wings mesmerized her. Unable to resist, she stroked her fingers along the velvety plumes and—

Seth rose from his seat and grasped her arms, his wings folding slightly. With a speed she couldn't track, he pinned her against the wall. The pictures rattled from the impact. His pupils dilated, and he raked his gaze over her with feral, lustful intensity.

"I told you not to touch the feathers." His husky voice rumbled from his chest into hers.

She blinked, and tried to piece together what had just happened. "I don't understand. Why not?"

He trailed his fingers along her jaw until he cradled her head in his palm. With his other hand, he gripped her hip and tugged her close against him. "You have no idea what your touch does to me."

"But, your wings. They're injured, too." She licked her lips.

He glanced over his shoulder at them and then returned his attention to her. "My feathers are very sensitive. In an arousing sort of way."

Hannah inhaled. As her lungs expanded, her breasts pressed into Seth's chest. He was a wall of pure, masculine strength, and her body reacted on its own, her nipples peaking beneath her bra.

She bit her lip. "How aroused would you become if I touched them some more?"

A low, feral growl eased from him, and a greenish hue ringed his eyes. "You play with fire, Hannah."

Seth brought his lips to hers in a bruising kiss. Passion ignited within her, sending a rush of endorphins through her blood at lightning speed. He slid his hand along her hip, over her bottom, and squeezed.

Gasping, she opened to him, and he deepened the kiss, exploring her with his tongue. She slid her fingers through his hair and poured the rush of emotions swirling through her into her kiss.

He trailed his fingers up her hip and along her ribs, dangerously close to her breast. She ached for him to touch her there, too, but instead, he drew away and placed his forehead against hers. Their panting breaths echoed in the space between them.

He pushed away from the wall and scowled at his hands. Torment and regret crossed his features. "Dammit, Hannah. A man like me has no business putting his hands on you."

As he whipped around to turn his back on her, the tip of one wing caught the cloth over the easel. The material slid to the ground and pooled at Seth's feet. His gaze tracked to the sheet then rose to the sketch.

He glanced at her, and a darkness she hadn't seen before from him flared in his blue eyes. "What is this?"

~

Seth focused on Hannah, his mind reeling. How had she known about his wings? He'd never shared his special gift with anyone. There's no way she could've known. Yet, the truth was so boldly laid out on that picture.

Hannah shifted her gaze between him and the sketch. Her mouth opened, closed, opened again. "I drew a picture of you."

A strange urge to laugh bubbled up from deep inside, but he kept it in check. Hannah should fear him, this gargoyle with a questionable soul, the one who murdered for a living.

Instead, the trust and innocence he'd sensed from the first moment they'd met remained on full display in her response.

He traced his finger over the cord at his wrist and tried to ignore the stinging pain along his wings. "Yes, it's a picture of me. A fine one at that. You have great talen…"

He peered at his image on the canvas. In the depths of his eyes, he noted something he hadn't seen since his human days—happiness. A groundswell of emotions roared through him. Confusion, desire, want, and need, swirled to such intensity, he crashed to one knee.

Hannah placed her hand on his shoulder and knelt next to him. "What can I do?"

Her concern for his well-being poked at the tough lining around his heart. He shouldn't let her in, shouldn't care for her, but he couldn't battle an enemy he didn't know how to fight.

"Talk to me. Just, talk to me. I need to hear your voice." He sucked in a deep breath, and Hannah's fresh scent burrowed into his senses.

She trailed her fingers down his arm until her hand rested on top of his. "Sometimes I draw and don't know why. My mind wanders and half the time I don't even know what the picture will become. I drew you. The wings, they just happened."

Her voice and her calming touch soothed into his soul, easing away the tension. Pain still pulsed along his wings. Although the salve had healed his back, he wasn't sure he could handle Hannah's sweet touch caressing his sensitive feathers.

He inhaled, gripped her hand, and rose to his feet. "Tell me why you draw."

"I…" She studied his features, the slightest hint of tension forming lines around her eyes. "When Mom left and Dad decided he liked spending more time with his beer than with us, Sadie would play games with me, cook for me, basically take care of me. I worshipped her and wanted to repay her any way possible."

Hannah pulled away from him and strode to the easel. She picked up one of her pencils and studied the dark charcoal. "Sadie always liked my sketches, so I worked hard on them, did my best, gave her way too many."

A soft laugh escaped her lips. Her face brightened, and her beauty slammed into Seth, the force of it rocking him on his feet. *Dearest Rhiannon, you mean to torture me.*

"Sadie praised and kept every single picture I ever made for her." Hannah's eyes shimmered with unshed tears. One crested over her lashes and slid down her cheek. "I didn't know what I would do without her."

Seth closed the distance between them and cradled her head in his palm. He brushed the back of his finger over her soft cheek, wiping away the moisture. "That must've been hard for you, the time you were apart."

Hannah nodded and leaned into his caress. "My uncle beat my aunt. She protected me from him, but one time I came home early from cheerleading practice. She wasn't there."

"But he was. He hit you, didn't he?" The urge to beat the man to a pulp surged through him, and he tightened his jaw so hard his teeth ached.

Hannah nodded. "After that first time, I never let myself be alone with him again. Not long after, I learned how much he feared God, and I figured out how to use that against him. I can't believe how many times mentioning the wrath of God kept him at bay, but it worked for both me and Aunt Sally. I think my guardian angel had something to do with that too, though."

"You really think an angel protected you?" He leaned closer and stared into her eyes.

She blinked, studying him with an intensity that bore deep inside. "Yeah, I do."

Her belief radiated from her in waves, the brightness in her soul almost too much for him to handle. Goodness, light, trust, faith. She was all of those things and so much more. His heart ached, swelling with respect for all that she represented.

"I think you did what you needed to survive, and it seems you helped protect your aunt as much as she protected you."

She stroked her fingers along his brow and over his ear, tangling her fingertips in his hair. "Well, I believe in guardian angels. I'm looking at one right now."

His breath lodged behind a lump in his throat. After a long moment, he swallowed. "I'm no one's guardian angel, darlin'. I'm a creature of the night."

An innocent smile curled her lip. "Maybe you're my night angel instead."

He shook his head. "Hannah..."

Hannah focused her attention on the spark stone embedded in his chest right over his heart. She ran her fingers along the hard surface.

The sensual touch lit up his nerves, and in response, his stone changed from its normal opaque color to a vibrant shade of red.

"So, this contains a piece of your soul?" Her soft voice held a hint of wonder.

"It does. Rhiannon hangs on to the rest of my foul spirit. She seems to think I'll redeem myself someday." He laughed darkly. It'd take eons serving in her army to make up for all the lives he'd destroyed during his human life, but dammit, he still clung to hope.

"What did you do..." She fixated on something over his shoulder.

Worry knitted her brow. "Seth, your wing... There's a hole, it's growing. Please, the salve. Let me help you."

So focused on their conversation, he'd shoved the pain in the far recesses of his brain. Awareness brought the agony front and center again. Although not as fierce as the pain on his back, the pinpricks along his feathers burned like fire.

He'd hated his white-as-a-dove wings from the day he'd been recruited into Rhiannon's army. He wasn't an angel—guardian, night, or otherwise—and didn't deserve Hannah's devotion and care, but he didn't deny how much he craved her touch.

Maybe he'd secretly wanted to reveal his wings to her. No. Absolutely not. He kicked that idiotic notion to the ground. Before he had a chance to think about having her tend to his injured wing any further, he nodded and sat in the chair once again.

Hannah retrieved the sack containing the salve from the floor. How had the small bundle survived the chaos? Witch magic. Had to be.

She stood, determination etched in the fine lines around her lips. Those beautiful, perfect lips. A stirring of another kind rippled through him, pumping blood south. He adjusted himself in the chair and spread his wings as wide as possible. Even within the enclosed space, the tips of his wings almost spanned wall to wall.

Hannah's soft intake of breath echoed through the room. "They're magnificent."

His chest expanded, and he berated himself for enjoying her compliment. He was despicable and didn't deserve the likes of someone as sweet and innocent as Hannah. If only his wings were good for something.

The first brush of her fingers along his feathers lit up his nerves. Part pain, part arousal, all very sensitive. He inhaled. Held his breath.

She stopped for a moment. "Am I pressing too hard?"

Oh, sweetheart, not nearly hard enough. The words were on the tip of his tongue. Instead, he shook his head and peered at her over his shoulder. "You're doing fine, darlin'. Just fine."

She gave him her special smile that lit up her features and put a spark in her emerald green eyes. "You let me know if I do, okay?"

"You bet." His deep voice came out on a rasp.

Hannah smoothed more of the salve onto his wings. A ripple of delight followed in her wake, and with each stroke, his erection lengthened, tightened, and pressed painfully against his pants.

Exchanging one pain for another hadn't even crossed his mind, but he refused to let Hannah see what she did to him. Rather, he basked in her attention, soaking up each caress of her fingers with a hunger of a man starved for decades.

"Seth. Tell me about your wife."

The muscles in his back locked hard as steel. He peered at her over his shoulder. Part of one wing blocked his view, so he moved it until he saw her eyes. Curiosity, coupled with the slightest bit of hope, reflected in her gaze.

He swallowed. "Why do you ask about Emily? She's long dead."

Hannah flinched, but continued her ministrations, soothing him with each brush of her fingertips. Gods, she'd be the death of him, yet.

"How did she die?" Hannah's soft words slipped under his skin.

He didn't want to face the disappointment that would darken her eyes, so he turned away. "She died of pneumonia in 1884. My Emily had the biggest heart of anyone I've ever known. Kind and generous, she'd help anyone who needed helping, and in the end, that's what killed her."

Hannah stopped for a moment then resumed her long, sensuous strokes on his wings. When she didn't say anything, he spoke to fill the void.

"I'd gone to town on the pretense of needing supplies, but in reality, I wanted to get away. It's a bad habit of mine left over from childhood. A storm came up out of nowhere. My wife, four months along with our first child, sent the help home before the storm hit so they could be with their families." A chagrinned laugh burst from him.

"The last of the help, Jimmy Watson, a new guy I never trusted, stayed behind. I should've followed my instincts. He backhanded Emily, knocked her into the wall, and stole the money we'd saved for a new roof from the canister in the kitchen. He ran. She chased him into the rain."

Raw emotion choked the rest of the words from him.

Hannah continued her care of him, stroking his feathers with her light, sensitive touch. A tremble, part sorrow for his past, part need for a future he could never have, rippled through him.

"Please, tell me the rest." Hannah's voice wavered, as if she experienced his emotional pain right along with him.

Seth released a slow breath. "Jimmy freaking Watson got away. My Emily, she caught pneumonia and died a few weeks later."

"Did you kill Jimmy? Is that how you became a gargoyle?"

A tic in his jaw pulsed to life. He shook his head, refused to look at her. "I never saw the asshole again, forgive my language, but if I had, I would've tortured him until his screams turned hoarse and he died awake and aware of everything I'd done to him. No, I never had my revenge."

"Then, what did you do that would make me believe you're a horrible man, other than love your wife and blame the man responsible for her death?"

This time, he did look at her. Better to see the rejection in her eyes so she'd stay away from him. It was the best way to protect her from him. "After Emily died, I sold the farm, roamed from town to town, city to city, searching for Jimmy and playing poker, stealing from as many others as possible."

Hannah held his gaze. "What else?"

"I ruined countless families' lives, those stupid enough to bet against me. Some didn't believe my luck, said I'd cheated. Sometimes I did. Most of the time, I was just that good." He shrugged.

"I never shared my uncanny skills with anyone. Two years into my spree and after one too many wins, a group of men caught me outside of town and strung me from a tree. Poetic justice, wouldn't you say?"

Hannah blinked, but her usually expressive features remained unreadable. "What did you do with the money?"

His erection had long deflated from their mood-killing conversation. He folded his wings, rose from the chair and strode to the

117

window, eager to put distance between them. The salve must've worked for his wings no longer burned. He drew aside the curtain and stared into the night.

Streetlights lined the empty road like sentries in a storm. Absently, he traced the figure eight on the cord at his wrist. Memories of his past surfaced in his mind, tormenting him.

Hannah padded across the room until she stood right behind him. With a gentle tug on his shoulder, she urged him to face her. Determination lined her pursed lips and her furrowed brow, but there was no judgment in her eyes, only concern. "Seth. Tell me."

Hannah's commanding words opened the floodgate, and he shared with her something he swore he'd never tell another. "A few months before my death, I ran across this rancher. I could tell he had an addiction to cards, so I kept playing him. The guy had the better hand, but I cheated him out of his home and left him penniless."

Seth kept his focus on the empty sidewalk. "A couple weeks later, I saw the guy enter a saloon, leaving his wife and their young daughter to wait on a nearby bench. Tears streaked the little girl's face. That was the last straw for me. I'd realized I'd made some big mistakes. After that, I left town, spent what I needed to keep myself alive, and continued my search for Jimmy. The rest," he shrugged, "I gave to the few hospitals I found and the orphanages."

Tears welled in Hannah's eyes. "Not just for the woman and the girl, but also for Emily and your unborn child."

He nodded once.

"If the rancher was addicted to cards, then he would've lost to someone, eventually. At least you learned from your mistake, and I'm sure you helped many along the way with your donations." Hannah wiped her hand across her brow.

He shrugged. "That's why Rhiannon considered my soul questionable. She took a chance on me."

"I'm so glad she did. In the end, you helped those in need. That makes you an angel to me." Hannah's gaze bore into him, her eyes narrowing. "You mentioned you needed to get away and said it was a bad habit from childhood. What did you mean?"

Seth swallowed, but refused to look away. Hannah deserved to know the full truth. "When I was five, I fell through a hole at the back of our property and into an old, abandoned mine. Sprained my ankle and wasn't able to climb out. I wandered further into the tunnel but ended up spending the night before my father found me. Since then, I don't like dark, confined places and have this incessant need to be free. That's why I left Emily that day and why I'm responsible for her death."

"You can't blame yourself for that. Jimmy's the one responsible." Hannah's cheeks, red and rosy, glowed with a fine sheen of sweat.

A chilliness rippled along Seth's wings. He trailed his fingers along Hannah's brow. Damp, clammy, and too warm to the touch, her skin burned with fever. "Hannah, when was the last time you took some of Wynne's medicine?"

She shook her head, her eyes glazed, unfocused. "I'm not sure. Before sunset, I think."

"Let me get it for you, darlin'. Where is it?" Seth glanced around the room.

"I left it on the table next to the George in the living room." She pointed to the hallway.

Seth bolted from the room, grabbed the bottle, and returned a moment later. Fingers laced around the sloping neck, he held it out to her.

She blinked and accepted the vial. As she drew the cork from the end, the vial slipped from her fingers.

Seth reached for the bottle, but the damned thing careened off his finger and flipped end over end. The smooth glass skittered against the hardwood floor, leaving a trail of liquid in its wake, and ended up alongside the doorstop. Green potion slid along a crack in the wood and disappeared.

"Oh no!" Hannah's whispered words, full of despair, echoed between them.

"I'm sorry. I couldn't stop it." Heart racing, Seth entwined his fingers with Hannah's and squeezed her hand. "I'll contact Wynne. We'll get you more."

Hannah shook her head. "Wynne's in her punishment, remember? Sasha can't come over either."

"Then I'll take you there. The medicine can help stave off Marco's hold over you."

"No, that won't work." She glanced at their linked hands and rubbed her thumb along his.

His heart skipped a beat. "Why not?"

She shook her head.

With his free hand, he placed his fingertip under her chin and encouraged her to look at him. "Please, tell me."

Her tear-filled gaze met his. "I didn't want you to know, but I'm growing weaker. I can feel his pull on me. The medicine isn't strong enough to stop him."

He gave her hand a gentle squeeze. "I won't let anything happen to you, remember?"

"I remember." A small smile bloomed on her face. She studied him for a long moment then her eyes widened. "I just thought of something that might work."

The excitement in her voice eased some of the tension in his shoulders. He tilted his head. "Like what?"

She withdrew her hand from his then laced her fingers around his neck. "When you touch me, the pain goes away. A little, anyway. But I think there's something that might help even more."

A blush turned her cheeks rosy. She glanced away for a moment before meeting his gaze. "It might stop him from wanting me altogether."

Seth didn't like the sly look in her eyes. His gut tightened. "What?"

"Love me, here, now. I won't expect you to stick around, but I want this. I want you. If I'm no longer a virgin, he—"

A virgin? Christ, no. He hadn't slept with a virgin since Emily. He tugged her arms from around his neck then ran his hand through his hair. "Hannah, darlin'. It's not right. I won't take advantage of you."

"Y...you don't want me?" Hannah's shoulders sagged.

He wanted her with a passion he hadn't experienced since his Emily and didn't want to see her in such pain much less be the cause of it. He grasped her hand, brought her fingers to his lips, and placed a tender kiss on her delicate skin.

"I want you more than I can say." With a lump lodged in the back of his throat, his voice came out strained.

The tension in her features disappeared, replaced with a coy smile. "Then, what's stopping you?"

"I've slept with more women than I can count, but that's not the only reason I'm stained and tainted. I've been no good from the beginning."

"Who told you that?"

"My mother. When I learned how to play poker as a kid. She said cards dirtied my soul as well as my hands. She was right."

"She was wrong. There's good in everyone, Seth, including you. Good is stronger than evil. I believe that in my very soul. Make love to me." Hannah pressed her lips against his, chasing away his mother's words with a single kiss.

His jaw tightened as his resolve wavered. Hannah might be right. Taking her sweet, virgin innocence might do the trick.

Damn him.

He'd give in to her demand and his self-interest, but in return, he'd show Hannah what making love to someone was all about. Gods help him if he ended up losing his heart to her in the process. He didn't see any way for them to be together.

CHAPTER 14

*T*he loud squeak of metal hinges grinding together echoed down the deserted back alley. Marco pressed his palm against the grime-encrusted dumpster and peered over the lid.

Two men, arm in arm, emerged from the back door of a seedy night club. The short one staggered into the taller one and laughed. The lanky man gripped his companion's butt covered in a tight pair of leather pants and gave it a squeeze.

A pleased smile tugged at Marco's lips. *Easy pickings these two.*

Zain leaned close and nodded toward the couple. "You want the pleasure, boss, or do you want me to take care of 'em?"

A trickle of energy slipped along Marco's nerves, bolstering his power and heightening his senses. Ever since darkness fell, bits of Hannah's spirit had flowed into him on a constant stream. Anytime now, he'd sense that Finn had completed his task and transported her to the private sanctuary in the old church. In the meantime, though, the wait had turned him into a bundle of charged nerves.

Eager to expel some of his excitement, he focused on Zain and shook his head. "I'm feeling a bit spry at the moment. You can have the next kill."

Zain smirked, revealing his chipped tooth. "Have fun."

Marco straightened his shoulders then rested his palm over his cane's handle nestled in the crook of his arm. With quick, efficient strides, he approached the couple from behind, not bothering to mask his footsteps.

"Excuse me, gentlemen," he called.

The tall man stiffened. He glanced over his shoulder. A glimmer of fear flitted through his dark brown eyes before his gaze narrowed.

His buddy, who had on a pair of large, green iridescent hoop earrings, turned to face Marco. "Can I help you with something?"

The urge to extend his claw and swipe the sharp tip across both their throats in one fell swoop zipped through Marco's mind, but he resisted. Sometimes it was more fun to toy with prey first.

He extended his palm, furrowed his brow, and forced a frown. "Well, yes, actually. I'm in need of some assistance, something only you can provide."

The tall one tugged on his lover's arm. "We should go, Jake."

"Stop it, Lance." Jake yanked his arm away and met Marco's gaze. "What do you mean, something only I can provide?"

The thrill of impending death sizzled through Marco. He put on a smile and inched forward. "I require your soul. Must match the daily kill quota, you know."

"Run, Jake." Lance pulled on Jake's arm, dragging him down the street.

Marco withdrew his blade from its sheath and gave them a two-second head start. His heartbeat raced double time.

The men's footsteps echoed off the surrounding brick buildings along with their panted breaths.

Marco tore after them. He closed the distance, but a familiar sensation that he couldn't ignore nagged at him from the inside.

A summons.

His heart skipped a beat.

Before he could catch his prey, he disappeared in a swirl of dirt and grime. Damn. He'd really looked forward to that kill.

~

Marco reformed in Gwawl's chamber. Flames flickered in the sconces on the wall, and the overwhelming scent of dampness and decay infiltrated his senses. The urge to gag churned in his gut.

"Marco Valentelli." Gwawl's deep voice ricocheted around the cavernous room.

At the far end of the chamber, the god sat in his chair. The bones ebbed and swirled in a macabre dance around him.

Marco sheathed his sword and bent to one knee. His heartbeat hammered loud in his ears. "Yes, my lord."

"Come closer." Gwawl tapped his clawed finger on his armrest. The tink, tink, tink scraped along every one of Marco's nerves.

Marco rose to his feet. Before he stepped forward, his body flew through the air. An instant later, he dangled in front of the god. He couldn't breathe.

Gwawl's eyes narrowed, and a puff of steam burst from his nostrils. "Where is my tribute?"

Marco scratched at the invisible bond choking the life from him. How did the god expect him to answer like this?

With the force of an earthquake, Marco plunged to the floor. Head, shoulders, and hip slammed against the stone. Pain ricocheted all the way to his brain.

He cut off the moan before it escaped his lips.

"Stand, minion, and give me a reason not to dispose of you on the spot." Gwawl's voice boomed across the room.

A few stones dislodged from the ceiling and pinged along the floor.

Marco set the nub of his cane on the flat stone and leaned on his staff. He rose to his feet, but bowed low. "At this very moment, I'm working on my tribute. A human woman with the power of pure, virginal innocence is under my influence. It won't be long before I deliver her essence to you, mighty one."

Gwawl's exhale and the soft cries of the chair's souls were the only sounds in the room. Marco dared a glance at the god. Even beneath his overcoat, goose bumps rose along Marco's arms.

Gwawl rubbed his chin, and a devious smile curled his lip. "A pure, innocent, virginal soul, you say?"

Hope, thin and fragile, sprung to life in Marco.

"Yes, my lord. She turned nineteen a couple of days ago. I've already bottled some of her essence, but I need a bit more time—"

"Virgins, untouched and unblemished, hold a special place in my heart, but without their virginity, they're just another utterly horrible good soul. Bring this virgin's essence to me. I shall enjoy devouring her delicacy like a fine wine. Besides, that would irritate Rhiannon, and I'd love nothing better than to stick it to her by absorbing an innocent girl's soul." The god's smile turned cold. "You have one more night. Please me and you shall be rewarded. Fail me... Do I even need to go there?"

Marco's blood froze. A niggle of doubt threatened at the edge of his mind, but he shoved the thought aside. Instead, he pulled on the determination burning in his gut. More than anything, he wanted to please his God and vowed to do everything in his power to ensure he succeeded.

Marco bowed low but kept his gaze on Gwawl. "I look forward to giving you such a unique prize."

"As you should." Gwawl waved his hand in the air. "Better get back to it, then."

A swirl of dust swarmed around Marco's feet. An instant later, he reformed in the back alley.

The scent of a recent kill swept by on the breeze.

He glanced down the dark passageway.

Movement between two dumpsters caught his attention. A muffled cry escaped into the night.

Marco withdrew his sword from his cane and strode toward the commotion. He raised the weapon above his shoulder.

As he crept past the dumpster, a tall guy with a long, dark braid and a black leather jacket crouched over an unrecognizable mass of human flesh.

Annoyance flared at Marco's temple, and he sheathed his sword. "Zain. Did you take my kill?"

Zain turned to face him. His brow rose, and he wiped his blood-covered dagger over his dark jeans. "You're back. Where'd you go?"

"Took an unexpected trip to see Gwawl." Marco crossed his arms, and his overcoat billowed around his knees. "Seems our God has little patience. He wants his tribute by tomorrow night."

Zain rose to his feet and crossed his arms, his biceps bulging beneath his jacket. "Guess we better check in with Finn."

"Agreed." Marco nodded toward the dead human, the flesh already turning to dust. "Now, I'll ask again. Did you take my kill?"

"Nope. Those two guys got away." Zain curled his lip. "I found this one, though, breaking into a car. A bad soul for sure."

The last of the human's clothing and flesh disintegrated and blew away in the breeze. Just like all the humans the fae killed, no trace remained.

Marco pointed down the alley, a sense of urgency strumming through his veins. "Let's see how many more we can bag on our way to my private sanctuary. I look forward to meeting Finn there. He better have my prize."

CHAPTER 15

*H*annah stood next to Seth in her art room, dug her fingers into his hair, and pressed her lips against his mouth. As she inhaled, his dark, musky scent washed over her, beating back the headache behind her eyes. Her heartbeat accelerated as arousal consumed her.

With deliberate intent, she licked the seam of his lips like he'd first done to her, requesting entrance. When a low, masculine groan rumbled in his throat, and he opened to her, a sensual thrill sped along her nerves. She stroked her tongue against his, enjoying how he responded and toyed with her in return.

He broke the kiss long enough to sweep his arms under her legs, cradle her against him, and head toward the hallway. Along the way, he brushed his lips against her forehead, her ear, and on the top of her head.

"Which way to your bedroom?" he asked.

Hannah pointed to the staircase. "Second floor, third door on the right."

Seth tugged her tighter against him and took the stairs two at a time. She bounced in his arms and gripped his shoulder to steady herself. As he proceeded down the hallway, his heavy boots echoed off the walls.

Once in her room, he knelt on the rug and set her on the messy, unmade bed with a tenderness belied by his strength. For a brief moment, embarrassment at her shoddy housekeeping flashed through her but fled when she looked into his eyes and only saw desire.

His gaze roamed over her features, and then he focused on the wall over her head. He arched his dark eyebrows. "You have an angel over your bed?"

The wonder in his eyes lifted Hannah's spirit. "My guardian angel watches over me every night."

A sly smile bloomed on his lips. "Well, now, guess I had some competition I wasn't aware of."

Her heart leapt at his words, hope teasing her with longing. He cared for her, something she treasured, but she wanted more from him. At least she could pretend. That would have to do.

On a whim, she tugged the angel off the wall and handed it to him. "I want you to have this. As a reminder of what you are to me."

His attention darted from the ceramic angel to her eyes. He shook his head. "Put it back, darlin'. I can't take that from you."

She placed the small bauble in his palm and closed his fingers around her favorite treasure. "I won't take 'no' for an answer. Take this, please."

Seth nodded and placed the angel in his pocket. He visibly swallowed, his Adam's apple bobbing several times. "I'll cherish it, always."

Bolder than she'd ever been before, she stroked her fingertip along his bottom lip, tugging at the soft flesh. "If you want to thank me, you better make love to me good."

He grasped her wrist and placed affectionate kisses along the pad of each finger then one in the middle of her palm. A zing of excitement flared along her skin with each brush of his lips.

His smile lit up his gorgeous features. "Darlin', I'm going to make your fingers and your toes curl before the night's over."

Sweat rolled down the side of her face and landed on her shirt, darkening the material. Blood pounded at her temple, and she rubbed between her eyes to ease the pain.

Seth knelt beside her and trailed his fingers over her brow, tucking a few stray hairs behind her ear. "Darlin', what can I—"

"So hot." Hannah sat up and tugged at her shirt. A whisper of insecurity flitted through her mind. How could she ever compare to all the women Seth had been with, not to mention the love and devotion he'd had for his wife?

She shoved the thought away. All that mattered was being with Seth, right here, right now. The future might never come. She refused to die without ever experiencing the physical act of love.

"Let me help you with that." Seth gripped the hem of her shirt, drew it over her shoulders, and tossed the discarded clothing on the floor. He focused on her lace bra.

Desire glimmered in his eyes as he traced the edge of one cup, then slipped his finger between her breasts, and followed the lace along the other side. Everywhere he touched, her skin tingled from the contact.

A crease formed between his brows. "I'm worried about you. Are you certain you want to go through—"

"Yes, yes, yes. Please, yes." Palms sweaty, heat rolled off her skin in waves.

He nodded once. With a skill he couldn't possibly have learned on the battlefield, he unhooked her bra with a single twist of his fingers. The material slid over her arms, and he tossed the bit of clothing onto the floor.

Seth focused on her breasts. A small twitch stretched the skin around one eye, and reverence reflected in his gaze.

"You are so beautiful." His husky voice rumbled in his chest.

Her heart melted at his words. She wanted this man with her heart, body, and soul. After wrapping her arms around his neck, she leaned against him.

The warmth of his skin and the soft hairs along his breastbone tickled her breasts. Her nipples tightened from the contact, and heat pooled at the juncture between her legs.

Hannah trembled in his arms, nervousness she hadn't expected flitting through her like a strong wind and stealing her breath away. Despite her desire for him, she didn't know what to expect. She'd heard from some of her girlfriends that the first time hurt, and the tiniest bit of fear followed in the wind's aftermath.

The muscles in Seth's shoulders stiffened. He drew away enough to look at her. Concern etched lines around his eyes. "What is it? What's wrong? Are you in pain?"

"I'm scared." She blurted the words before she lost her nerve.

Seth's features softened. "Darlin', I'll go slow. I promise, and if you want me to stop, just say so. I would never, ever, do anything to hurt you."

Hannah's throat tightened so hard, breathing became difficult. Tears swelled in her eyes, blurring her vision. She swore a halo formed around Seth's head.

After blinking several times, she inhaled a long breath and slowly let it out. "Okay."

He traced his fingers down the side of her face and cupped her chin. With loving care, he trailed kisses from her ear and along her jaw until he reached the edge of her lip.

Her mouth tingled with anticipation.

He brushed the barest hint of a kiss across her parted lips. "May I touch your beautiful breasts?"

She inhaled. "Y…yes."

Seth slid his fingers along her ribs, cupped one of her breasts in his palm, and traced his thumb over her nipple. A shiver of delight raced along her nerves and settled at her core. He lowered his head and drew the hard peak between his lips.

She gasped and writhed at the contact. Never in her entire life had she experienced anything like that.

He chuckled, and the reverberation set off a new spark of excitement that wound into a taut cord inside.

"Seth, that tickles."

"It does a lot more than that, doesn't it, darlin'?" He smiled at her as he went for the other side.

Tenderly, he licked at her other nipple then nipped at the hardened peak. She wriggled from his gentle touch and wondered what other new sensations he'd share with her tonight.

The need to ask burned on her tongue, but the words wouldn't come. "W…what…"

With one sweep of his arms, he drew her legs onto the bed. A flutter tickled her insides.

That sexy smile, the one that made his blue eyes glint, tugged at his lips. The spark stone on his chest darkened to a deep red. "You look fabulous in those jeans, darlin', but it's time for them to go."

Seth straddled her knees. His chest, ripped with hard, taut muscles, bulged beneath his skin, and the edge of his wings poked from behind his shoulders. Her night angel's hands were large enough to cover her hips. He gripped her jeans with deft, nimble fingers, and unbuttoned her pants.

The release of the zipper echoed through the room, and she sucked in a sharp breath.

With a quick yank, he removed her jeans and underwear in one swift move. The garments landed on the nearby chair.

His affectionate gaze roamed over her breasts and along her exposed hips and legs.

Naked before him, she felt exposed, and her insecurities returned full force, tightening like a vice around her heart. She didn't expect him to care for her. This was a means to an end for him. He'd promised to take her virginity to save her from losing her soul, but he wouldn't stick around afterward. He was a gargoyle and had a long track record of sleeping with women. She'd just be another in that long list.

"Hey, hey, we can't have this." A crease formed between his brows. "You're not smilin'. That's not right."

Despite the ache inside, she smiled at his words.

A gleam reflected in his eyes. "Now, that's much better. You're beautiful, darlin', so very, very beautiful."

If only he'd said those words because he loved her and not from her looks. She steeled her heart, afraid he'd break it long before the fae sucked out whatever remained of her soul.

"Remember how I kissed your lovely nipples. I'm going to do the same down here." He slid his hands across her ankles, over her knees, and up her thighs, spreading her legs along the way.

A thrill fluttered in her stomach, part anticipation, part nervousness. She'd never been with a man before and wasn't quite sure what to expect. Although she trusted Seth to be compassionate and kind, uncertainties ran rampant in her mind.

Taking his time, he brushed soft kisses along the inside of her calf and up her thigh.

She clutched the sheets in her fist and squeezed as tingles rippled in his path.

Seth reached the juncture between her legs, and a blissful scream threatened to burst from her lips. Every muscle taut, she quivered beneath his touch.

The rough edge of his stubble tickled her skin as he smiled. "I can't neglect the other one, now can I?"

The sheet bunched in Hannah's grasp. He trailed fresh kisses along her other thigh, and her leg trembled in response.

As Seth nuzzled his mouth between her legs, he gripped her hips, holding her in place. He stared at her, his deep blue eyes swimming with a hint of amusement and something unidentifiable embedded in their depths. Caring? Love?

She pushed the thoughts from her mind, for even if she survived, they couldn't be together. Hannah doubted he could ever love anyone more than Emily. Besides, he was a gargoyle and had a job to do. She wouldn't fit into the picture.

The flick of his tongue along her folds made her buck and bite back a moan. Seth held her in place with steady, strong hands. Another swipe of his warm and wet tongue crested over her clit, and a cry burst from her lips.

Seth relentlessly licked and sucked, twirling his tongue along the most sensitive part of her.

Hannah squirmed under his onslaught. Muscles tight, she jerked and thrashed, the new sensations ripping through her body in a torrent.

A rush of blood like she'd never experienced headed south, stars burst in her vision, and warm wetness coated her inside. The blissful, pulsing release lasted for several long seconds before the wave receded, leaving her limp and happy.

As a warm glow spread through her body, Hannah relaxed into the pillows. "Wow, that was fantastic."

"Was that your first orgasm?" Seth's deep voice rumbled in the space between them.

Hannah's cheeks heated. She nodded.

"Well, I'll be. You never," he held up one finger and flexed it, "did this on your own?"

Hannah bit her lip and gave her head a quick shake. She hated admitting that she'd never given herself an orgasm, but she refused to lie to him.

A flash of pride crested over his features so fast, she almost missed it. "I'm honored you let me be the first."

She sat up then trailed her fingers down the side of his face, enjoying how the stubble tickled her fingers. "I'm glad it was you. I wouldn't want it to be anyone else."

Seth's eyes flicked back and forth as he studied her. Maybe he didn't believe that she'd wanted him to be her first. After a long moment, he lowered his gaze. "How're you feeling, darlin'?"

She'd felt wonderful under his focused attention, but now, a hollowness ached in her chest as if something tried to claw its way out from the inside. Her heart skipped a beat. Would her soul rip apart at any moment?

Hannah didn't want Seth to see her unease, so she put on her best smile and gripped the waistband of his jeans. "Relaxed and ready for more."

Seth curled his fingers along her nape and brought his lips to hers in a passionate kiss that left her breathless. She liked his devoted attention and hated herself for wanting more from him than he would be able to give.

A long moment later, he released her and stepped off the bed. With a hard yank, he unhooked his belt and popped the buttons on his jeans, shoved them down, and tossed them onto the chair with her pants.

His erection stood straight from his body. Veined ridges covered the long, hard length all the way to his round, plump crown. The velvety tip glistened with a bead of moisture.

"Oh. My. God." Hannah clamped her hand over her mouth. Mortified she'd spoken the words, she dared a glance at his face.

"I'll take that as a compliment." A sexy smile drew across Seth's lips.

"I'm sorry, it's just that I've never seen a man's erection before. Not in real life anyway, and you're so big." She leaned forward to touch him.

A gasp escaped him, and he stepped out of reach. "You have wings…"

CHAPTER 16

Seth held his breath. He fixated on the set of wings tattooed over Hannah's left shoulder blade. Outlined in black ink, the white feathers sparkled in the lamp's soft glow. How had he not noticed this before? Caught up in Hannah's safety and well-being, he'd focused on giving her an orgasm she'd never forget. At least he'd succeeded at that.

"You have a wing tattoo? How? When? Why?" The questions tumbled from his lips.

Hannah withdrew her outstretched hand, the one she was about to wrap around his hard, straining erection and rubbed her other arm. She met his gaze. "Aunt Sally took me to get it after Uncle Frank hit me that one time. It's a reminder that my guardian angel watches over me."

He stared at her tattoo in disbelief. His wings, her wings, the similarity was uncanny. Could this get any weirder? No. Well, never say never. He'd seen a lot of strange things over the years. This was just another one you didn't want to examine too closely.

He opened his mouth, but words eluded him. After a long silence, he untied his tongue and cleared his throat. "They're very nice."

Her gaze slid to the spark stone on his chest before heading south and resting at his semi-engorged flesh. A flush spread across her cheeks, darkening into a red rosiness and accentuating her full lips, small pixie nose, and gorgeous eyes.

"But they pale compared to your beauty, Hannah. You're a rare gem among many."

Hannah's eyes widened. She tugged her bottom lip between her teeth, pulling at the plump flesh.

As if it had a mind of its own and wanted to join in the fun, his erection jerked. She placed her fingertip over the sensitive slit on the end of his crown, swiping away the moisture that had beaded there.

Ripples of sensation tracked all the way to his balls, tightening the sac taut against his skin. He closed his eyes and moaned. Gods, she'd be the death of him yet.

"Did I do something wrong?" Her voice held an edge of uncertainty.

He opened his eyes and met her gaze. "No, darlin', you did everything right."

At his encouraging words, her features brightened, and she wrapped her fingers around his hard length, capturing him in her grasp. She drew her fingers from his balls all the way to his tip and back again. His moan turned into a groan, one that rumbled deep in his chest.

"Your skin, it's so soft, yet you're as hard as steel. I had no idea…" A bead of sweat rolled from her forehead and down the side of her face. She was sick, not in the body, but in the soul.

Although he didn't want to sully her with his tainted flesh, he'd made her a promise, one he intended to keep. If taking her virginity would break Marco's hold, then he'd do it and try not to lose his heart in the process.

He clasped his fingers over hers, drew her hand away, and encouraged her to lie back on the bed. With a tenderness he had no business feeling, he crawled onto the sheets with her.

She peered at him, her brow furrowed over those green eyes he'd lost himself in the first night they'd met. "What're doing?"

"Tonight, my darlin', is all about you." He lay on top of her, one leg between her thighs. As he brushed her hair away from her features, he studied her, committing each and every detail to memory.

He wanted to remember her, like this, in the long days to come while trapped at his post, for sure as the sun rose in the sky, he'd earned a long stay in his stone gargoyle. She, however, was worth any amount of time in the darkness.

As he brushed the tip of one wing across her breast, the feather-light caress flared the flames between them. She toyed with the ends, tracing her fingers from the tip of one feather, over the interconnecting bones, and along one wing. Everywhere she touched burned like a deep, sensual fire.

His spark stone flared a brilliant red, casting a glow over her features. The ends of his wings followed suit, blazing in a deep shade of crimson.

Hannah gasped. "Your feathers, the silver tips changed color. How?"

He smiled. "As I mentioned before, they're sensitive—"

She stroked her fingers along the tips once again. Sexual electricity rippled between them, and the silver ends of his wings changed from red to green to yellow before returning to the deep russet.

"Your wings are so beautiful." The admiration in her gaze became quizzical. "How come they didn't change when I put on the salve?"

"The pain kept them in their silver state." His heart pounded as she stroked along the silver tips once again. He remained still.

"The changing colors remind me of rainbows. Rainbows need sunshine and water to exist. The happy and the sad. A balance. As do we all." Hannah's whispered words burrowed deep into his chest, unlatching the lock around his heart.

Seth cupped her head in his palm and brought his lips to hers, devouring her with all the passion he'd kept trapped in his heart. He'd thought his Emily was the only one able to unlock the craving inside. How wrong he'd been.

Hannah moaned and writhed under his passionate onslaught. She thrust her fingers in his hair, her nails digging into his scalp and holding him there. He deepened the kiss and slid his free hand along the soft contours of her ample bosom and over her flat abdomen until he cradled her firm behind in his palm. With a quick tug, he drew her close.

The skin hot and stretched tight, his erection pressed along her thigh. She squirmed underneath him, driving him crazy. He broke the kiss, and he trailed his lips along her jaw with butterfly soft nips until he reached her ear. "I can't get enough of you."

She arched against him, and a soft giggle eased from her. "That tickles."

Her endearing words carved notches into his heart, marking him in ways no one else ever had. She was so young, so innocent, and so beautiful, on the inside as well as the outside, and he cared for her more than he wanted to admit.

Seth drew away enough to look at her. He stroked a finger along the bridge of her nose then over her bottom lip. "You're so much fun to tease."

The smile she gave him sent a tremor of delight over his wings. A spark of sexual energy crackled loud in the air.

Hannah's eyes widened. "Your wings. Light, like lightning bolts, sparked from the tips."

Seth's chest tightened. "Only for you."

"Really?" Hannah bit her lip.

"That's never happened before." He winked at her. "Must be your charm."

He brushed his fingertip along her collarbone and over her shoulder then pressed himself against her, letting her know how much he wanted her. A veritable whirlwind of emotions flashed across her face—uncertainty, fear, acceptance, love. Had he really seen that last one? Was it possible she wanted someone as tainted as him?

"There's good in everyone, Seth, including you." Hannah's earlier words flitted through his mind.

The pink in Hannah's cheeks had spread to her neck and across her chest. A thin sheen of sweat coated her skin. He wanted to believe that was from his devoted attention to her, but he understood the sickness took its toll.

Although he didn't want to rush her, waiting any longer to take her virginity wasn't an option.

He kissed her again, enjoying how their tongues tangled together, stroking each other in just the right way. As he broke the kiss, he eased his hand from her bottom and spread her thighs.

She tensed beneath him.

"It's all right, darlin'. You're doing great." He smiled at her and, with his free hand, stroked his fingers along her collarbone. Sex for the first time might be painful. She was smart enough to know that was a real possibility, but he'd do everything in his power to make sure she experienced as little discomfort as possible.

The tension drained from Hannah's muscles. A smile full of trust and faith curved her lips. "I believe in you, Seth."

His lungs stalled even as his heart swelled. Love, an emotion he hadn't experienced in over a hundred years, filled the empty spot deep in his soul.

I love you, Hannah.

He wanted to say the words, but she couldn't love him in return, not with his jaded past. Instead, he'd show her just how much she meant to him.

Seth showered her with kisses as he inched closer to her opening. With all the tenderness she deserved, he slid his finger between her folds. Wet and warm beyond his dreams, she was ready for him.

As if she read his mind, she arched into his palm and spread her legs, further opening to him. He repositioned himself over her, giving him easier access, all the while caressing her with his attentive kisses.

Stretched tight with need, his erection strained against his inner control. He circled his finger around her clit, and the nub hardened. Faster and faster, he stroked her while ravaging her with kisses. She trembled beneath him on the edge of another orgasm, and he waited to enter her until she broke their kiss.

"Seth, oh God, Seth!"

As she screamed his name, he nudged inside her tight entrance. He drove onward against the pressure. Like a rubber band pushed to the breaking point, the tension released, and he slid all the way inside her.

He held himself still.

Hannah's orgasm pulsed around him, her sweet channel stroking him with each beat. He peered into her eyes.

Love reflected in the depths of those beautiful emerald greens.

Wrapped in a bubble in this precious bit of time with her, he allowed himself the briefest glimpse of what it might be like to love someone again and be loved in return. How he longed to stay here forever.

Worry for her broke through his thoughts. "Are you all right, darlin'? Did I hurt you?"

She smiled and shook her head. "I felt a tightness and a quick pang, but it didn't last. Did you, um, you know…"

He returned her smile. "Did I come? Is that what you're asking?"

She bit her lip, drawing the plump bottom flesh between her teeth in the endearing way that drove him crazy.

"Not yet. I don't want to hurt you if you're sore."

Her eyes sparked, and she circled her hips as if she'd done this many times before.

He groaned. "Gods, Hannah, what you do to me."

She quickened the pace. From the satisfied and happy look on her face, she didn't seem to be in pain. He took that as a good sign and settled into a rhythm. As he stared into her eyes, he crested over the brink and lost himself to the beautiful young woman who now owned his heart.

CHAPTER 17

*M*arco hid from his prey in the doorway of the closed Books and Curios bookstore. The glow from the streetlight across the street didn't penetrate the small stairwell and reveal his location. That was good. Better to catch his prey that way. This time of night, only the brave or the foolish ventured into this part of town.

Soft, feminine laughter echoed down the street, followed by an answering male chuckle. A couple, arm in arm, stumbled over the sidewalk, holding each other upright. Their combined snickers and the way they clung to each other indicated their level of intoxication as well as their lust.

Marco traced his fingers over the handle of his cane. Nestled in the crook of his arm, the handle's smooth, bone surface calmed his racing heart. Soon, very soon, he'd score another kill to add to his record. Although these two didn't seem inherently corrupt, he'd at least obtain a small power boost from their deaths.

He peered at Zain, his partner in crime, who hid behind a dumpster along the adjacent alley kitty-corner from the bookstore. His dark form blended in with his surroundings, but Marco caught the glint from the stud embedded in his nose. Zain bent his head in an almost imperceptible nod. He was ready.

Good, so was Marco.

He tightened his grip on the cane's handle and withdrew the sword's blade.

The couple's footsteps neared.

Marco burst from his hiding spot and raised his sword.

The man, wearing a blue suit and a white button-down shirt, stopped short. His eyes widened.

In a short skirt that showed more leg than it covered, the woman released a loud, nervous laugh.

As if her voice had sprouted knives and scraped over his flesh, the skin on Marco's back tightened. "How irritating. Perhaps you'd sound better without your tongue."

Her companion bolted down the street, leaving her behind.

Coward.

Marco pointed after the man. "Zain, he's yours. I'll take the woman."

Zain slipped past like a shadow.

The woman quivered from head to foot. She conveyed her plea for mercy within her wide eyes, and fear, hot and bitter, radiated from her pores.

Marco inhaled, enjoying how the smell flushed through his lungs and into his bloodstream. A heady sense of excitement traveled along his nerves.

The woman took a step back and held up her hands. "I...I have money. You can have it. Just let me go."

He slid his finger along the edge of his blade.

"I have no need for money, dearest one." He met the woman's gaze and smiled. "But your soul is an entirely different matter."

She turned and bolted, her heels clicking on the pavement. Catching up to her took little effort. He grasped her arm and spun her around.

The sound of her scream rebounded against the building until it skyrocketed into the night air.

Marco's skin crawled as if ants had clamored up his arms and across his nape. He clamped his palm over her mouth, silencing her. "I can't take any more of that screeching. Let's fix that irritating sound from ever happening again, shall we?"

The woman struggled in his grasp but was no match for his preternatural strength. He squeezed his fingers along her jaw, forcing her mouth open.

She inhaled, the whites of her eyes reflecting the streetlamp's glow.

Before she could release her lungful of air and issue another wild wail, he snagged her tongue between two fingers and sliced through the organ with his sharp nail.

Like a piece of uncooked liver, the flesh landed on the pavement with a sickening plop. Blood, along with a slew of unintelligible sounds, dribbled from her mouth.

The high of the impending kill lightened Marco's chest, and a giddy laugh bubbled from his throat.

He placed his palm over the woman's mouth and nose, blocking out the air. She struggled, but then her muscles relaxed.

As the woman's eyes glazed over, a quick zing flickered through Marco's nerves. Her good soul had departed for the Otherworld, but not before he'd received a nice boost.

The body started to disintegrate in his arms, and he released the corpse. It slid to the ground in a pile of dust.

A warm breeze blew across Marco's cheek. The distinct scent of aged stone followed in its wake. *Gargoyles...*

Marco gripped the hilt of his sword. He glanced over his shoulder and down the alley.

Two dark forms sped toward him at inhuman speed.

He focused on the closest adversary—a dark-skinned guy with short-cropped hair and a crooked nose. The glint in his eyes promised Marco pain and a swift death.

He'd seen this particular gargoyle a few times over the past several months and had heard his name was Damian. He'd never fought the guy.

Prepared to take him on, Marco set his stance and raised his sword.

The gargoyle barreled toward him. "I've got this one, Grayson."

"Perfect. I'll track down the other," the second gargoyle echoed from behind. His red scarf reflected in his dark eyes, making them shine.

Marco didn't wait for Damian to take the first punch. He met him half-way and thrust his sword at the oncoming gargoyle.

The tip sliced through Damian's shirt and skittered over his hardened skin.

Damian's fist, solid as stone, grazed Marco's cheek. Pain flared at the impact.

Marco dove to the ground and rolled to his feet a few yards away.

The second gargoyle sped past in a blur.

"Incoming!" Marco screamed, warning Zain.

Damian charged again, his features determined.

Marco swung his sword. The blade caught on Damian's rock-hard arm.

A shudder reverberated through the steel, and Marco strained to maintain his grip.

Damian grasped Marco around the neck and lifted him into the air. Marco struggled to breathe.

His sword slipped from his fingers and clattered against the sidewalk.

He scraped his claws along Damian's arms, but they didn't penetrate his hardened skin.

Victory sparked in Damian's dark eyes.

Anger, along with the will to live, surged through Marco. Gargoyles didn't often turn their entire bodies to stone. It took too much energy. Marco kicked the guy in the gut and prayed he found this gargoyle's weak spot.

Damian inhaled and slipped to one knee, releasing his grip on Marco in the process. Marco fell to the ground.

His knee banged painfully against the pavement. On an intake of breath, cool life-giving air flowed into his lungs.

A menacing growl emerged from Damian's throat.

Filled with renewed battle rage, Marco elongated his knife-like nails. He scraped the sharp tips across Damian's chest. The point of one caught on the edge of the gargoyle's spark stone, scratching the surface.

Damian's penetrating howl echoed off the nearby buildings. He staggered to his feet.

Marco's sword lay in the street, the shiny steel glinting in the light. Eagerness to finish off his enemy ripped through him with a force he hadn't experienced in years. He grasped the handle—

Pain burned in his gut, the agony so fierce white spots formed in his vision. He held his breath. What was happening to him?

Damian wiped his hand across his chest. Blood coated his palm and dripped onto the pavement. He careened into a garbage can. The metal bin tipped over, and the lid rolled into the street and clattered against the gutter.

The pain intensified, burning up Marco's esophagus and into his brain. A moment later, the intense torture ended. The muscles in his legs shook.

Hungry to restore his energy, he drew on his connection to Hannah.

Nothing happened.

Fear slid along his spine, raising the hair at his nape.

He tried again. Nothing.

His connection to Hannah was gone. Panic sent his heart racing.

Was she dead? What if he'd lost her somehow?

A mixture of fear, anger, and confusion rolled in Marco's gut, blending into a deadly concoction. She was his ticket for redemption with Gwawl.

Damian leaned against the brick building then slid to a sitting position. His head lolled to the side.

The need to locate Finn and find out why his link to Hannah had severed wrenched on Marco's damaged soul, but first, he'd finish off his enemy. He raised his sword.

Heavy footsteps echoed down the street, moving at a rapid pace and coming closer.

Marco tensed and glanced in that direction.

Zain bolted toward him. Blood dripped from a cut over his eye and dampened his dark shirt. "Can't kill the gargoyle. Hurry, we have to go."

Over Zain's shoulder, a gargoyle's dark figure dashed toward them. Hatred for the vile creatures burned in Marco's gut.

He sheathed his sword. "I agree. We leave. Now."

Marco grasped Zain by the shoulder, concentrated on Finn's location, and vanished in a swirl of old newspapers and empty plastic bags.

If Hannah was dead, Finn's own death wouldn't be far behind.

CHAPTER 18

A deep-throated bullfrog croaked from beneath Hannah's window, its incessant song rousing her from sleep. Seth spooned her from behind, his taut chest and ribbed abdomen resting against her back. As she inhaled, his warm, masculine scent settled into her lungs.

She glanced at the digital clock on her dresser—5:47a.m. Hannah let out a soft sigh, closed her eyes, and tugged Seth's arm tighter around her waist. After they'd made love last night, she'd headed for the bathroom to clean up. Blood had dried on the inside of her thighs, and a small amount had stained the sheets.

I'm no longer a virgin. She still didn't believe it.

By the time she'd dressed in a thin, rose-colored nightie, Seth had found some sheets in the closet and remade the bed. They'd snuggled beneath the covers, and it hadn't taken long for her to fall asleep.

Hannah's chest tightened, squeezing the breath from her lungs. He'd stayed with her the whole time. God, she loved this man.

Nestling deeper into Seth's arms, she tried to block out the world, but like the impending dawn, thoughts about the future invaded her mind. Did Marco still have a hold on her? Did he even want her now that she'd lost her virginity?

She did an internal assessment—no headache, no stomach pain, no exhaustion. Hope, frail and thin, grew like a tiny sprout in her heart.

"Darlin', I can hear your wheels spinning from here." Seth's deep voice broke through her thoughts.

Hannah peered over her shoulder at him.

He studied her with a reverence in his blue eyes that left her breathless. He trailed a finger along her tattoo. "How's my gal doing?"

Seth's caring words and tender touch flared the love for him in her heart. "I think I'm okay, but I'm not sure."

He sat up on one elbow, his brow furrowed. "What's wrong?"

She shook her head and roused to a sitting position. At the change in angle, blood rushed from her brain. Her vision dimmed.

Seth cupped her chin. "Hey, darlin'. Stay with me."

"I...I'm okay. Just a head rush." Hannah leaned into his embrace. "I don't feel ill or anything, and I don't have a headache."

The tension in his shoulders eased. "That's good to hear."

His gaze tracked to the spot behind her ear.

She held her breath. "Is the mark still there?"

Although relief flitted through his eyes, his brow remained furrowed. "It's faded."

"But still there." Hannah's throat constricted, and she rubbed her fingers over the spot. If only she could wipe the mark away so easily.

"Do you think he still wants me?" Lord, she'd thought sleeping with Seth was the answer. Maybe she'd let her desire for him cloud her judgment into accepting what she'd wanted to believe.

"Hey, hey." He smoothed his thumb over her cheek. "You said you feel better, and the mark has faded. His power over you has diminished. That's progress in my book."

"Seth, I'm scared. What if Marco still comes after me?" She stared into his eyes.

His gorgeous smile tugged at his lips. "Then I'll be here to protect you."

Seth's touch and his comforting words chased away her unease. "Thank you for staying with me all night. You shouldn't have. Your work—"

He placed his finger against her lip. "Is not as important as your safety."

She clasped his fingers and drew his hand away from her mouth. "Would Drake say the same?"

The spark stone embedded in Seth's chest turned a dark shade of red. "Drake's such a stickler for the rules, they're practically shoved up his—"

Seth rose from the bed. The tip of his left crimson-edged wing caressed her skin. He grabbed his jeans off the chair and thrust each foot through the pant legs.

After hooking his whip onto his belt, he strode to the window, moved the curtain out of the way, and glanced through the pane. His handsome features were stark with strain and consternation.

Beaumont had told her once Drake expected his gargoyles to follow strict orders, including returning to their posts at dawn. If they disobeyed, he'd mete out punishment by locking them in their stone forms overnight. Her thoughts drifted to her and Seth's earlier conversation about his time in the abandoned mine. She didn't want him to suffer in his gargoyle statue at night, unable to see.

She joined him at the window. The cars lining the sidewalk, the trees, and the houses were all bathed in a pre-dawn glow. She wrapped her arms around Seth's waist and snuggled against him. "The sun'll be up soon. You should go. I'll be fine here during the day."

Jaw set, he shook his head. "Darlin', I'm not going anywhere. Not today."

That Seth would risk being locked in his stone form for disobeying orders was a testament to how much he cared for her. Her throat tightened so hard, she struggled to breathe.

She stepped from his embrace and strode to the dresser. "I don't want you in trouble with Drake because of me."

Seth's heavy footsteps echoed in the room as he approached her. He wrapped his arm around her waist, tugged her to him back to front, and planted a soft kiss on her shoulder right over her tattoo. The edge of his wings tickled her arms. "Let's not talk about him. How about we spend the entire day in bed—"

149

The chair under her vanity rumbled, the feet bouncing against the hardwood floor. The rat-a-tat-tat echoed like gunfire. A moment later, a man she'd never met materialized in her room.

He had a short military-style haircut, and he wore a pair of camouflage pants and a navy muscle T-shirt. The forbidding scowl on his hardened face could've chewed the rubber off a tire.

Her heart skipped a beat. Was this another fae sent by Marco?

∽

"Drake." Seth couldn't believe his boss had tracked him down. The muscles in his arms quivered with the need to lash out at his boss, and his hands fisted at his sides. "What are you doing here?"

Drake's gaze flicked over Seth's wings. His eyes widened, but then he narrowed his attention to Seth's features.

Like a bug under a microscope, Seth grew uncomfortable, his insides squirming.

"What the hell, Seth? You shut down the mind link all night. I only caught a trace of it as dawn approached. I could ask what you were doing, but from the looks of it, I can guess. Couldn't wait until your next night off?"

Irritation flared along Seth's nerves, and the urge to pummel his boss until he ate those words curled Seth's fingers into fists. "This isn't what you think."

"It isn't, is it?" Drake spread his legs and crossed a pair of beefy arms. His attention focused on Hannah. "So, this is the woman who's clogged your mind and made you forget your responsibilities?"

Seth wrapped his hand around Hannah's waist and drew her close. "Marco's targeted her. She needs protection—"

"We needed you tonight. A fae raked his claws over Damian's spark stone. He..."

A tic ran rampant along Drake's jawline.

Seth's pulse spiked. "Is he all right?"

Drake shook his head. His gaze tracked to the window and the forthcoming dawn. "I left him in Sasha's care at Wynne's house. With Wynne paying her penance during the full moon, Sasha did as much as possible, but she's not Wynne. Come daybreak, my hope is that Wynne can heal him. He'll stay there today."

Self-loathing coated the back of Seth's throat. He hated that one of his teammates suffered a serious injury. One he might've prevented if he'd been there for the fight, but he didn't regret his time with Hannah. She'd needed him more.

"I'm sure Wynne will fix him up good as new." Seth rubbed Hannah's arm, soothed by her nearness.

His boss ran his palm over his features, but then the stern look Seth knew so well returned. "You've earned yourself a week of reflection at your post."

An image of his stone griffin with its lion body, eagle head, and widespread wings formed in Seth's mind. A knot coiled in his gut. "Sorry, boss. Not happening."

Drake blinked, took a step forward, and flexed his hand at his side. "Did you just disobey an order?"

"I'm staying here with Hannah today." Seth straightened his spine and wrapped his wing around her shoulders. The tips sparked at the contact.

Drake's face reddened. "You follow my orders, cowboy. That's how this works. Nice, pretty set of wings, by the way, didn't know you had them. Now, let's go."

Seth folded his hateful appendages onto his back, shrinking them beneath his skin, but he refused to give in. "I won't leave Hannah."

Hannah drew away from his side. She stepped forward and raised her palms as if approaching an injured, wild animal. "Seth's a good, honest soul. I was under a dark fae's spell, and he helped me. He doesn't deserve any punishment."

Drake's laughter rolled through the room. "A good soul? Sorry, sweetheart, he has a questionable soul, just like the rest of us gargoyles and has to face his punishment. It's the rules."

That Hannah would defend him in front of his boss made Seth's chest swell so large, his ribs ached. He would do anything to protect her, and he wasn't sure she was out of the woods when it came to Marco.

"Drake, Marco has—"

Drake raised his hand, and green glowed behind his eyes. "Not another word, Seth. The sun rises. We're done here."

The knot in Seth's stomach tightened into a hard ball. He palmed his whip.

Drake crouched, his muscles bunching beneath his shirt. "Think twice, cowboy."

Seth yanked his belt from its clip. With a flick of his wrist, he snapped the supple leather. The warning crack echoed against the wall. "I won't leave Hannah and be trapped in my gargoyle—"

Drake wrenched his shirt collar down, uncovering his spark stone, and tapped his finger over the gem.

A shaft of blue light burst from the jewel and locked onto Seth's spark stone. He froze, his whip hanging loose in his palm. The muscles in his shoulders, arms, and back tensed as he struggled to break Drake's hold. The light's power drew him forward like a tractor beam.

"Stop! Leave him alone!" Hannah pounded on Drake's arm.

He shoved her aside. She tumbled onto the rug, her knees scraping along the coarse weave. Hannah glanced at Seth, and her beautiful green eyes widened with fear for him.

"Damn you, Drake!" Seth yelled. Unable to break free of Drake's magic hold, he couldn't help Hannah to her feet. Gods, he couldn't even help himself.

Drake shook his head and frowned. "You're coming with me."

As the day's first rays penetrated through the window, Drake dematerialized, taking Seth right along with him. Seth's agonizing scream echoed in their wake.

CHAPTER 19

*M*arco sifted into the fae medical facility, Zain close on his heels. Soft moans, punctuated by an occasional cry, filled the large room. Tables with injured fae lined the walls, some moving, others not. The scent of disinfectant permeated the place but didn't quite cover up the stench of impending death. He curled his lip. How he hated the weak.

Injured fae from all over North America came to this location seeking treatment. Finn was here, somewhere. Marco sensed his essence. The need to find the guy in all this chaos spurred him on.

He rushed past a fae with a large shard of glass protruding from his abdomen. With every heaving breath, blood pumped from the gaping wound. The guy met Marco's gaze, a pleading frenzy lodged in his yellow eyes.

He gripped Marco's arm. "Please, don't let Gwawl take me. Kill me first."

Marco yanked free of the fae's weak grasp. "Perhaps I should alert him of your condition. Move the process along a bit. What do you say to that?"

On Earth's realm, fae died in one of three ways—severing the jugular vein, fire, or a blade embedded in an eye. Here in the Otherworld, they also died at the hands of their God. Gwawl didn't tolerate weakness.

If a fae didn't heal fast enough from his non-lethal injuries or, Gods forbid, dared to beg, Gwawl would torture him in ways only a god could then smite him down faster than a...

"I've got him. No need to call in our master." A medic ran down the aisle, his sneakered feet squeaking on the hard, stone floor.

Marco peered at the injured fae and bared a fang. "Well, seems you're a lucky dog today, aren't you? Perhaps I'll ask Gwawl to put you on my team as a new, expendable shield."

The guy's mouth quivered, but he was smart enough not to respond. Marco smirked at him before dismissing the injured weakling.

The need to find Finn seized him, and Marco glanced across the injured lined up on numerous tables.

Zain followed Marco like a good little puppy. He grabbed a towel from a nearby medic's cart and wiped the congealed blood from the gash at his temple. "You see Finn?"

"Does it look like I've found him?" Irritation flared along Marco's nerves. He'd failed to obtain Hannah's pure, innocent soul for Gwawl. If he wasn't careful, he'd be the one tortured by the testy god.

Zain's eyebrows rose, but then his eyes darkened. "Don't stress. He's here somewhere. We'll find him."

They paced down another aisle and another one after that. The number of wounded fae seemed to go on forever. Where was Finn?

Zain stopped as one of the injured fae took its last breath and disappeared in a tiny dust devil. He pulled the sheet over the remaining trace. "There's a lot of injured in here, but it looks like you took down one of the gargoyles tonight. Damian was his name, right?"

Marco nodded. "It was a good battle, I'll give you that, but I doubt he's dead. Those bastards are incredibly hard to kill."

With a lift of an eyebrow, Zain stroked the stubble on his chin. "Difficult maybe, but the guy rubbed at his spark stone. If you damaged it, he won't live long."

Marco crossed his arms. "Well, we'll see about that, won't we?"

"Feck. Just give it ta me."

A familiar voice echoed over the noisy chaos, drawing Marco's attention.

Two aisles away, Finn sat on the edge of a medical bed. Blood stained his red shirt a darker shade of crimson. He snagged a flask from one of the medics and brought the glass to his lips. As he drank, the dark liquid disappeared from the glass with each swallow.

Where was Hannah? The pulse at Marco's temple beat double time. "Finn!"

Finn met his gaze. His lips thinned.

The female medic attending Finn glanced at Marco, grabbed the empty bottle from Finn, and fled down the aisle, her long, red hair swinging against her back. At least someone here had a healthy respect for authority.

Marco leapt over a cot holding an injured fae. He landed on the stone floor next to Finn, his overcoat billowing around his knees.

The irritating fae slid off the bed. At over six feet, he stood eye to eye with Marco.

Marco grasped Finn's shirt collar, the material bunching in his fist. "Where is my little tribute?"

"Do ya really want ta have this chat, here, in the middle of the infirmary?" Finn raised an eyebrow.

Marco tightened his grip, but Finn only smiled.

Zain placed his hand on Marco's shoulder. "Maybe we should find someplace a bit quieter."

Anger and resentment bubbled over, and Marco shoved Finn, hard. He crashed into the bed. Metal groaned as it bent under Finn's weight, and then the bed frame collapsed into a heap.

Finn shook his head and rose to his feet. A yellow glow rimmed both of Finn's eyes. "I'm not yer enemy, and I didn't appreciate that."

"You're alive because I allow it." Marco gripped his cane. Touching the smooth handle calmed his nerves and prevented him from killing the idiot on the spot. "Transport to my quarters. We'll discuss the details there."

Curling his lip, Finn disappeared in a swirl of dust.

Marco turned to Zain. Although he still didn't trust the bastard, the guy had a keen eye. "Join us. I want your assessment of him."

Zain smirked. "My pleasure."

Marco settled his cane in the crook of his elbow and returned to his quarters.

As he reformed in his room, the smell of burning cloth and dried blood assailed his senses. A fire roared in the fireplace. Flames licked greedily at Finn's shirt.

Finn paced to the tall standalone mirror then returned to the fireplace. He ran his fingers through his dark hair, and the muscles in his bicep flexed tight. As a gargoyle, Finn had been a challenging warrior, but as a fae, he was formidable. Marco would hate to lose such an asset.

A small swirl of dust rose next to Marco's unmade bed. Zain joined them a moment later.

Marco strode to Ralph and rested his cane on the skeleton's outstretched arm. "So, Finn, you failed. That's twice now. Tell me what happened and this better be good."

Zain paced to the fireplace, leaned against the brick, and crossed his arms. His focused attention never wavered from Finn.

"I got past the wards, as I told ya I would. Had the lass in my hands, but then Seth appeared." Finn curled his hand into a fist. "We fought. He threw his dagger at me, pierced my heart, but not before I spit acid on him. Injured as I was, I had ta leave. He'd a finished the job, so I came ta the infirmary."

Marco studied Finn, noting the twitch of every muscle in his features. As much as he wanted to believe Finn lied, he sensed the truth in his words. He tapped his finger along his jaw. "Time is of the essence as you well know. Why didn't you return?"

The annoying fae furrowed his brow and raised his palms. "Did ya not see the number of injured in the infirmary? I laid on that bed, bleeding for hours before they got ta me. There wasn't time."

Marco glanced at Zain, and the fae shrugged and tilted his head.

Finn straightened his shoulders. "I sprayed Seth with acid, got his back real good. He'll die if he's not treated. I'll get Hannah tonight. That's a promise."

"Your weak promises don't hold much weight with me. So, Hannah was alive when you saw her last." Marco tapped his finger against his bottom lip.

"Very much so." Finn placed his hands on his hips. "Why are ya askin'?"

"My connection to Hannah severed while I battled a gargoyle. The break ripped through me with such intensity..." Marco clamped his jaw closed so hard his teeth rattled. "Well, let's just say it's a good thing I injured the guy, or he'd have killed me. What I can't determine, though, is what happened to Hannah."

Finn cleared his throat. "I think I might know."

Marco's gaze riveted on the Irish fae. "Tell me."

The male glanced into the fire. His jaw tightened. "Seth has had a hankering for Hannah since the night he met her. The way that lass looked at him, it's possible she gave her virginity to him, and as well as I know Seth, he was more than happy to accept it. He's the reason I haven't been able ta capture her."

"If that's true..." The muscles in Marco's shoulders tensed. He raced to the fireplace, opened his hiding spot, and drew out the small flask. With trembling fingers, he uncorked the bottle. No essence escaped.

His mouth dried.

He tipped the bottle upside down.

Empty.

"Hannah's essence is gone. That damned gargoyle stole her virginity, and I no longer have a tribute for Gwawl." His hand shaking, Marco set the vial on his dresser with a gentleness that covered his barely concealed rage. He paced to the mirror and back again, the ramifications flitting through his mind at lightning speed.

As he passed Ralph, his anger erupted, and he shoved the skeleton into the stone wall.

Bones splintered and scattered across the floor.

His cane slid underneath the bed, as if it feared his wrath.

"Gwawl has an old-fashioned penchant for virgins and thinks their purity and innocence are tied to their virginity." Disgust tasted bitter on Marco's tongue. He disagreed with the god and believed goodness and virtue were aspects of the soul.

Based on the amount of energy he'd pulled from Hannah, she seemed to have those in spades. Even if Gwawl would no longer desire her, Marco wanted to capture the power of her decency and grace for himself.

In order to do so, though, he'd have to take her energy just like any other human and needed to be close enough to see the whites in her eyes before he killed her.

That, however, didn't change his need for a tribute. Pleasing his god remained his number one priority.

"What do you want to do, boss?" Zain, still leaning against the fire-place as if he didn't have a care in the world, tugged at the diamond stud in his left ear.

Marco chose to keep his change of plans with Hannah a secret. After all, trust was still an issue between these fae, and he wanted Hannah's death for himself.

He raised his chin. "We come up with an alternative, something that will please Gwawl as much or more than that worthless woman."

"Aye, I have an idea." Finn's eyes sparked.

Marco pursed his lips. "Let's hear it."

"From what I've heard, Gwawl likes ta torture gargoyles. It's another way for him ta jab at Rhiannon. How about we give him one?"

Marco tsked. "Are you out of your mind? Gargoyles are hard enough to kill, much less capture. No fae has accomplished that in nearly a decade."

Finn kicked Ralph's femur out of the way and strode to the mirror. Through the glass, he pegged Marco with a stare. "Proves my point. What a valuable prize that would be, now, wouldn't it?"

Marco studied the guy. He was right. To capture a gargoyle would be an accomplishment like no other. Gwawl would be impressed and the reward generous. The risk, however, was great. Marco stewed for a moment, considering his options.

There wasn't another one available to him, not on such short notice. He ripped off his overcoat and flung it onto the bed. "I assume you're referring to your old friend, Seth. How, pray tell, do you intend we capture him?"

"Wait..." Marco raised his hand. "Clever, clever. Since Seth took Hannah's virginity, he might have a sense of duty to protect her more than other women. Besides, as a gargoyle, it's his job to save humans from the likes of us."

Finn placed his index finger on his nose. "Bingo."

Perfect. Absolutely perfect. A zip of excitement rippled along Marco's nerves. Like the old saying "kill two birds with one stone," Marco would do exactly that.

Zain ran his hand along his braid then flipped it over his shoulder. "Seth's one of the strongest gargoyles I've ever seen. How do you plan to capture him, boss?"

Marco tapped his finger against his chin and glanced at Finn. "You knew him well, didn't you?"

"Aye, I knew him better than anyone." Finn smiled, a devilish fae grin that sent a shiver along Marco's arms and reminded him Finn had been a deadly gargoyle, too.

Marco returned the smile, flashing his fangs. "I'm all ears."

"Seth's wife died from an illness she contracted after a man robbed her. Seth blames himself for not savin' her. We capture Hannah, Seth will come runnin'. Knowin' him as I do, he'd sacrifice himself ta set her free."

Marco crossed the room, a sense of giddiness lightening his step, and he sat in his large armchair next to the fireplace. The wood creaked under his weight. As he stared into the flames, his mind raced, and he formed a plan.

"I'll obtain one of the crystal-lined crates Gwawl uses to keep his pet gargoyles. Seems they can't dematerialize through the crystals' powerful magic. The box won't fit in my private chamber in the church, so Zain and I will transport it to the nave. Sunset is at seven, so we'll be ready by eight." He stared at Finn. "Bring the bait to that location, tonight. Do. Not. Fail. Me."

With a solemn nod, Finn straightened his shoulders. "I'll get

Hannah this evening."

"You better, or it'll be the last night for all of us." Marco waved his hand in the air, dismissing his minion.

Finn's mouth thinned before he disappeared in a swirl of dust and debris.

Marco stroked his chin and glanced at Zain. "Impression?"

The fae pushed away from the fireplace. His braid swayed from the movement. "He's either lying or holding something back."

"What makes you so sure?"

Zain shrugged. "Seth was his best friend, and Finn's been a fae only a few nights. How do we know he won't turn on us?"

A large crackle burst from the fire, and Marco returned his attention to the flames. "Perhaps you're right. At nightfall, help me secure the cage then tail him. If he fails in his attempt to capture Hannah, kill him, and bring me the girl. We need her as bait." *...and for me to suck her energy dry.*

A sly smile bloomed on Zain's face. His broken tooth gleamed in the firelight's glow. "My absolute pleasure."

"Now, go. Enjoy the rest of the day doing whatever it is you do." Marco waved him away.

In the midst of a small whirlwind, Zain disappeared.

Marco rose from his seat and strode to the mirror. He glanced at his reflection, noting how the tips of his short blond hair caressed his cheek and accentuated his brown eyes. "I figured you'd say that, Zain. I would, too, if I were a spy."

Deceit was harder to conceal than most people realized. Marco knew that from experience. The problem was who to believe? Zain or Finn? Both? Neither?

Marco grabbed the bottle from his dresser that had contained Hannah's essence and heaved it into the fireplace. The glass shattered. Flames erupted, but quickly died.

He rubbed his palm over his face. Best to assume both fae lied. One of them had to be Gwawl's spy, sent to trip him up. He was sure of it. One way or another, though, he'd obtain a tribute for Gwawl. As for the young woman, well, she'd end up dead and that was a pity.

CHAPTER 20

*H*annah adjusted herself in the chair next to her easel and stroked the charcoal over the page. The rhythmic scratch of graphite on paper echoed around the room, calming her nerves. After Drake had seized Seth and disappeared to their stone gargoyles, the beautiful sunrise had crested over the neighbor's roof and unleashed a gusher of tears from deep inside her. She'd cried until the hitching sobs had stopped, and her tears had left dried streaks down her cheeks.

The tears threatened once again, and she blinked several times to keep them at bay, but guilt sat hard and heavy on her shoulders, and a few slipped over her lashes. Pencil still clasped between her fingers, she wiped away the moisture with the back of her hand.

"You've earned yourself a week of reflection at your post." Drake's harsh words echoed in Hannah's mind.

Seth had received the punishment because he'd been protecting her. She understood just how difficult it would be for him to remain there, unable to see and reminded of the dark, enclosing mine he'd been trapped in as a child.

Damn it. She hung her head and ran her fingers along her nape. She'd paced the house most of the morning, frustration running rampant through her veins. Countless times she'd ended up in the bathroom, holding the mirror in her hand, studying Marco's mark behind her ear. Each time the mark had faded a bit more until the circular outline was no longer visible. Losing her virginity to Seth had done the trick after all.

Her attention drew to the picture of Seth she'd set against the wall. She'd captured the subtle curve of his lips as he started to smile and the affectionate glint in his eyes that appeared every time he looked at her.

How was Seth? Was he all right knowing he'd have to remain in his stone form after dark?

An ache built in her chest, and Hannah rubbed the sore spot. There was no way they could be together. Seth was a gargoyle. She was a human. He fought fae at night and slept in his post during the day. She was a nineteen-year-old college student. Where could this possibly go?

Even if they did see each other on his occasional day off, what would happen when she grew old and he remained young? She didn't want him to stick around to see her wrinkles and gray hair. People would think he was her son or, even worse, her grandson. There was no future for them.

But Sadie and Beaumont are together...

Hope, thin and fragile, clung to her heart, holding on for dear life.

Beaumont had passed his test, though, her rational brain countered. Yeah, and he'd fought in Rhiannon's army for over eight hundred years. Who knew when Seth would face his challenge?

"Stop, stop, stop!" Hannah closed her eyes and exhaled.

She'd beaten herself up many times over the situation with Seth. Her biggest regret was she'd ended up causing him pain.

Hoping the brush of her pencils would bring her peace, she'd sought out the sketch of Beaumont and Sadie, intent on finishing it before they returned from their honeymoon.

Fingers sore and tight from hours of sketching, Hannah flexed her hand and glanced through the window. Visible between the oak's branches, bright, fluffy white clouds filled the sky. Based on the angle of the tree's shadows along the grass, the sun hung well past midday.

Sadie and Beaumont will be home in three days. Time to finish this.

Hannah tapped the pencil's tip against her bottom lip and studied the black and white sketch. Shading within the roses along the border framed the happy couple, and fine, detailed lines brought out the love in Beaumont's smile along with the joy in Sadie's eyes. Yet, something wasn't quite right.

Hannah crinkled her brow. What was missing?

Outside the window, the leaves rustled in the soft breeze. From between the foliage, sunlight played along the windowsill and onto the drawing, accentuating the ends of Sadie's hair.

Hannah's chest swelled on an intake of breath. "Yes, yes, perfect!"

Pink accents on the tips of Sadie's hair would add the finishing touches to the picture. Excitement rushing through her veins, Hannah pawed through her assortment of charcoals and colored pencils. Her fingers grazed over the new pack of General's Seth had given her and heaviness settled inside, but she kept up her search.

"All the colors of the rainbow, except the one I need." Hannah huffed.

She peered through the window once again. Carried in the breeze, the tree's shadows danced over the grass like small fairies out to play. If she hurried, she had time to run to the bookstore, buy more pencils, and return home before dark.

"You shouldn't be out here at night, especially alone." Seth's words from the other night after he'd rescued her outside the library whispered through her mind.

She glanced at his picture. He seemed to watch her.

A knot formed in her stomach.

She placed her hands on her hips, stared at his drawing, and spoke to him as if he stood in front of her. "I don't have a headache. The mark on my neck is gone. I'm fine. Marco's hold over me is broken." ... *along with my heart.*

Heaviness threatened to crush Hannah's shoulders, but she brushed it away and raised her chin. "Sadie and Beaumont deserve the best picture I can sketch, and Sadie must, absolutely, have pink in her hair. Besides, I'll return well before the sun goes down."

Hannah rose from her chair, and the legs squeaked against the polished wood floor. After a final glance at Seth's picture, she raced down the hall, grabbed her light jacket, and bolted out the door.

～

Trapped in his daytime gargoyle post, Seth peered across the library's rooftop. The sun's warm rays radiated across the sky in a brilliant display. Night would come, but not soon enough.

Several times during the day his thoughts had drifted to Hannah, returning to Marco's faded mark on her neck. Did the fae still have a hold over her?

Worry permeated into his psyche like a black cloud, ominous and potent with dread. He struggled against the invisible bonds that chained him, but like countless times before, made no headway. How he hated his confinement.

Hannah had also surprised him by pleading with Drake for his leniency. Not that he'd deserved any. His mother had been right all along. He wasn't worthy of someone as fine as Hannah. Damn his hide, he had no business caring for her, but care for her he did.

"Drake, any word from Damian?" Grayson's deep voice echoed along the mind link.

Drake growled. *"Not yet. If I don't hear by nightfall, Wynne's house'll be my first stop."*

"He's my best friend. I'd like to join you." Grayson replied.

"Count me in," Seth added.

Drake audibly sighed. *"Grayson, you can come along. Seth, you're side-lined for a week. Enjoy your R&R. You earned it."*

Seth wanted to rip out his whip and crack the ends in frustration. Instead, he snarled. *"You need me out there. Let me take out my frustration on our enemy."*

"You know the rules. Break 'em. Pay the price. One week, Seth." Drake exhaled.

Irritation flared bright inside Seth. If he could move, he'd punch Drake in the mouth.

No one spoke for several long minutes.

A few students enjoying spring break tossed a frisbee in the grass in the middle of the quad. One errant throw sent the disc up the library steps. A young woman with shoulder-length blonde hair chased after it. She looked so much like Hannah, fear spiked through Seth.

When she turned, and he got a good look at her features, he relaxed. The woman wasn't Hannah. Safe from fae during the day because of the sun, he hoped she'd stay within the protection of Beaumont's home come nightfall. The wards should keep her safe.

Although the mark had faded from her skin, Seth wasn't convinced she was out of the woods with Marco. The fae might still come after her. Seth hated that he'd remain trapped here after dark, unable to protect her.

Fear trickled along the edges of his soul, leaving him cold.

"Grayson, I need a favor."

"What's up, Seth?"

"Would you check on Hannah for me?"

"Dude, you've got it bad for her, don't you?"

"I think Marco may come for her."

"I thought you, uh, took care of that problem by staying with Hannah and—"

"Just do it. Please." Seth wanted to scream, but he held himself in check.

"All right. I'll stop by after Drake and I are done at Wynne's house."

Seth relaxed a bit, but the fear still gnawed at him. *"Thanks, man."*

The first rays of the setting sun coated the sky a light orange. He wasn't sure how he'd handle being cooped up all night, for a whole week no less, but he'd find a way to endure it. Otherwise, he'd drive himself crazy.

Movement along the sidewalk caught his attention. He glanced over the edge of his perch. A young woman, blonde hair cascading around her shoulders and onto her pink coat, walked by. He recognized the way she swung her hips. She turned her head, and he caught a glimpse of her beautiful features he knew all too well.

"Hannah!"

A sense of claustrophobia whipped through him. He fought against his bonds, straining, stretching, until he ached from the effort.

Why was she walking through the quad so late in the day? She knew better than to tempt fate.

The sun hung lower on the horizon. A few stars twinkled in the twilight sky.

"Drake, you gotta let me go. Hannah's in danger. I have to help her."

Drake tsked. *"Not tonight, cowboy. You stay here. If we sense fae in the area, we'll come."*

"That's not good enough. Release me." Seth demanded.

Drake growled. *"Watch your tongue or it'll be two weeks."*

Drake was a lost cause, and further argument wouldn't help Seth's case. Seth renewed his struggles. As the sun disappeared and night claimed it's due, his teammates dematerialized from their posts, leaving Seth alone, frustrated, and fighting to break free. All he could think about was Hannah's well-being.

CHAPTER 21

*H*annah clutched the packet of colored pencils and hurried down the aisle toward the cashier. The swish of her sneakers on the tiled floor echoed in the nearly empty bookstore. When she'd first arrived, the shelves that usually held a large quantity of drawing supplies were almost empty and there were no colored pencils in sight.

Fortunately, an employee had checked the stockroom and had found a box of drawing supplies with colored pencils as part of the assortment. Unfortunately, that had taken a while.

As Hannah approached the cashier, she glanced out the bookstore's window. Light from the lampposts illuminated the empty bicycle rack and the lines of benches along the sidewalk.

Underneath her light jacket, the fine hairs along her arms rose. Darkness had fallen.

I shouldn't have come.

She toyed with the ends of her hair then tightened her grip on the pencils.

No. Sadie deserves the best, and I need the pink pencil to finish the drawing.

Hannah raised her chin and slid the colored pencils across the counter.

The cashier, a young man in his twenties who wore a Chicago Bulls T-shirt and a Cubs hat, caught the pencils before they slipped off the edge.

"You got a good arm there." He smiled, revealing a gold tooth. "Are you on the softball team?"

Hannah glanced past his shoulder to the darkening night. The chill returned, and she forced herself to meet his gaze.

"Uh, no. I'm just a business student who likes to draw," she replied.

He shrugged and rang up her purchase. "That makes sense, I guess."

Hannah dug her debit card from her back pocket and inserted it into the card reader. After a few seconds, the machine beeped. She withdrew her card and returned it to her pocket.

The cashier handed her a receipt. "You want a bag?"

"No thanks." Hannah snagged the pencils from the counter and shoved them into her jacket pocket.

As she exited through the double doors, a cool breeze caressed her cheek. Streetlamps along the sidewalk stood like lone sentinels, their illumination lighting the path.

Hannah wrapped her fingers around her coat collar and pushed into the wind. The house wasn't too far from campus. She increased her pace, eager to reach home and—

The crack of a branch echoed through the air.

Hannah glanced toward the sound.

A pair of yellow eyes gleamed between the leaves of a nearby tree.

Panic rippled along Hannah's nerves, and she bolted.

The sound of her footsteps competed with the pounding of her heart. In her path, a small swirl of dirt and debris burst to life.

The dust devil disappeared as quickly as it came. Finn, wearing his traditional dark pants and red T-shirt, stood in its place.

Hannah skidded to a stop.

"Ah, lass, so good ta see ya again." Finn smiled and spread his hands. "What's a nice bonnie like ya doin' out here all alone?"

Hannah's pulse beat double time. She glanced over her shoulder. Maybe she could outrun him.

"Hannah, dear lass." He took a step forward. "There's no place for ya ta go. Why don't ya come with me? It'll be easier that way."

Hannah stepped backward, one foot behind the other, putting distance between them. "Why do you want me? I'm no good to you or Marco anymore."

A deep chuckle bubbled from Finn. "Oh my, that's a good one. Did ya think because ya gave yerself ta the gargoyle that Marco wouldn't want ya?"

She kept moving, but a knot formed in her gut. "What do you mean?"

"Just because ya're no longer a virgin doesn't mean ya no longer have value ta us." Finn winked and strode toward her, closing the distance.

A mixture of disbelief and fear rushed through her veins. She bolted the way she'd come.

Hot on her trail, Finn closed in on her, his footsteps echoing along the pavement. She didn't get far before he grabbed her by the arm and yanked her off her feet.

As she collided into his chest, the impact knocked the breath from her lungs.

Finn tightened his grip on her arms.

Pain rippled all the way to her fingertips as she fought to catch her breath.

"I'd hoped ya'd see my logic, but that's okay, lass. We'll do it yer way." He picked her up and slung her over his shoulders.

She kicked her feet and pounded his back. On an intake of breath, she screamed.

He laughed. "No one ta help ya, lass. It's just ya and me."

Seth wasn't coming. Her night angel wouldn't rescue her this time. Fueled by the heartache that Finn was right, she fought harder, kicking and pounding with all her strength.

When they arrived on the street, he threw her into the back seat of a black sedan. The click of the locks reverberated in the enclosed space. She wrenched at the door handle, but the door wouldn't open.

Fear leached along her spine in an all-out panic. She frantically hit the window's smooth, curved button over and over in rapid succession. The dark-tinted glass didn't move an inch. She was invisible through the pane.

Dread enveloped her, crushing her lungs, her heart, and her spirit in its grasp.

Finn slipped into the front seat. The car's engine roared to life.

He peered at her in the rearview mirror. "Id've dematerialized and transported ya ta Marco, but alas, I'm no longer a gargoyle, and fae don't have the ability ta transport another. Enjoy the ride. Ya'll meet up with yer destiny soon enough."

Hannah's fingers shook so hard she shoved them under her armpits. As she rocked back and forth, dismay pushed all thoughts but one from her mind. *Seth was trapped in his stone form, thanks to her. She was on her own.*

Seth struggled against his invisible bonds, stretching his patience thin. He'd kept up the effort since the sun had set and the moon had risen in the sky. Unable to break the chains that bound him to his stone form, at least the silvery orb provided enough light to see.

Damn you, Drake. Even as he cursed his superior, he knew it was his own fault, but he didn't regret rescuing Hannah or the time they'd spent together. Memories of the caring and trusting look in her eyes along with the passionate way she'd kissed him flitted through his mind.

The breeze picked up, rustling the leaves on the trees. Placed every ten feet, the streetlamps lit up the sidewalk around the quad. The empty place reminded him of a tomb.

A feminine scream, one that seemed all too familiar, echoed between the trees.

Fear skittered over his skin, raising the hair along his arms.

Had the wind and his active imagination played tricks on him?

He strained to hear the slightest sounds.

Feet pounding on pavement and breath exhaled in a rush filtered through the rustling leaves.

Tension coiled deep in his soul. *Hannah?*

He renewed his struggles, pouring all his effort into breaking free. The futility of his efforts sank in, and a cry of pure frustration echoed in his mind.

On the far side of the quad, movement caught his attention. Hannah's familiar form lay hunched over Finn's back, her blonde hair dangling toward the sidewalk. With his eagle-like vision, he noted Marco's mark on the back of her ear was gone.

Seth put the pieces together in an instant. Even though Seth had slept with Hannah, taking her virginity, Marco still wanted her either for revenge or for his own vile reasons. There was no other explanation. Otherwise, Finn wouldn't have bothered to capture her. He would've killed her instead.

Seth tracked Finn as he strode between the library and Stuart Hall then disappeared from view. Regret that he hadn't killed Finn when he had the chance slipped down his throat like a bitter pill.

I can't fail her. Seth swallowed his pride and contacted his boss.

"Drake. You have to release me. Finn captured Hannah. I must help her."

Several long seconds that seemed like hours passed.

Dammit. Drake must've turned off his mind link.

The roar of an engine echoed from the street.

Fear knocked at Seth's psyche, but he forced himself to relax. He closed his eyes and his ears, blocking out sight and sound. He stretched his mind as if reaching for the stars.

"Rhiannon."

He floated, no awareness of either time or place.

"Rhiannon," he repeated.

"Ah, Seth. If you weren't one of my favorites, I'd add another three weeks to your punishment. Why are you calling me?" Rhiannon asked.

Relief flitted through his mind. *"Please free me so I can rescue Hannah. She's a good soul and—"*

"I'm well aware of her purity and that she's no longer 'innocent' in the traditional sense thanks to you." Rhiannon chuckled softly.

"I'll willingly do three times my punishment or more if you free me."

Rhiannon sighed. *"I sense how much this means to you. Very well. Once you're done, you'll serve triple your penance."*

A moment later, he materialized on Harper Quad's lawn bent on one knee. The scent of grass, damp with dew, infiltrated his senses. He touched his wristband. "Thank you, my goddess."

He rose to his feet and bolted for the street. The single lit taillight of a black sedan disappeared around the corner.

A roar burst from Seth, and he beat his fist against his thigh. His hand crashed into something hard. He dug into his pocket and withdrew the object—Hannah's angel, her gift to him. His heart shattered even as determination took hold.

Seth stared at the corner where the car had disappeared. He didn't know where Finn took Hannah, so he couldn't dematerialize there to meet them, and tracking wasn't his special skill.

Special skill...

His heart skipped a beat. He looked at the angel's wings.

Yes, yes, yes.

Seth shoved the angel into his pocket, threw his hat on the ground, yanked off his jacket, and ripped his shirt in two. The material slid from his fingers and landed on the pavement.

He unfurled his wings, and a sense of rightness unwound right along with them. As he flexed his appendages and captured the air beneath his feathers, pure instinct drove him onward.

Using the determination boiling in his blood, he rose in the air and flew over the buildings in search of the dark car with the one lit taillight and the woman he loved.

CHAPTER 22

*S*eth soared on the breeze, the rush of air lifting him higher. A zing of adrenaline slipped through him fueled by the excitement of flying for the first time. He flapped his wings, and the gentle sound of the air under his feathers helped calm his beating heart.

Taking flight was more liberating than he'd imagined, and although it had taken him a few seconds to get the hang of flying, he'd taken to it like a bird. Even as his senses took in what the new stimulating experience had to offer, he couldn't dwell on it. He needed to focus on Hannah.

At least he'd had the forethought to camouflage himself and blend with the night sky. If any humans glanced up, all they'd see were a few stars amidst the darkness.

Streets below stretched between tall buildings. Several cars, their red taillights visible, formed long lines, and exhaust fumes filled the air with a foul taste.

The sedan with the missing taillight stood out like a black eye, dark and broken. Once Finn stopped, Seth planned to give him a whole lot more than a black eye. If anything happened to Hannah…

A tic pulsed to life in Seth's jaw, and he let out a slew of curse words.

Where the hell was Finn taking her? To Marco, no doubt, but where was the damn bastard?

The car finally turned left, leaving the city central for the south side. After several blocks the vehicle turned left again. Most of the buildings in the area didn't exceed five stories and appeared run-down, some with bars on the windows, others with broken panes, all neglected.

The car slowed, and Seth's pulse picked up speed.

He dove toward the corner of a nearby building, landing on the tiled roof quiet as a whisper. As he folded his wings against his back, he tracked the car with the attention of a predator after its prey.

The vehicle rolled to a stop next to an abandoned warehouse. A single streetlamp flickered nearby, its irregular pulse eerie and ominous.

Finn cut the engine and opened his door. A soft click echoed against the brick.

The muscles in Seth's legs bunched in preparation. He brushed his finger over his wrist cord. *Thank you, Rhiannon, for releasing me.*

His old friend emerged from the car and glanced down the street, first one way then the other. A slight, smug grin tugged at his lip.

A mixture of hatred and grief festered in Seth's stomach, and his spark stone flared hot and painful along his chest. He wished Finn had never become a fae.

Finn gripped the passenger door's handle and yanked. The door opened, and a familiar, feminine gasp echoed from within.

Hannah...

A war cry burst from Seth's lips, and he leapt from his perch.

Finn's attention focused on him. He hissed and raised his razor-sharp claws.

Seth tackled him, Finn taking the brunt of the impact, and they rolled across the pavement. Bits of rock and broken glass crunched beneath their combined weight.

Finn sliced his nails across Seth's biceps. Pain rippled all the way to his fingers, but he shifted the skin on his arms, turning the flesh hard as stone. The fae's claws slid over the impenetrable surface, ineffective and useless.

"What did you do to Hannah?" Seth tightened his grip on Finn's shoulders. As they struggled on the ground, dirt and debris kicked up in their wake.

Somehow, Finn ended up on top. He cleared his throat, the precursor to an acid spray, and his features distorted, his eyes turning a putrid shade of yellow.

Seth bashed his skull against Finn's forehead.

Finn's eyes glazed, and his muscles relaxed.

The soft rustle of a shoe on gravel caught Seth's attention. He wrenched his head toward the sound.

Hannah emerged from the car. Her beautiful eyes widened.

"Seth! On my God, Seth." She stumbled toward him.

Fear for her safety hardened his stomach. "Run, darlin'. I'll find you."

A few feet behind Hannah, pieces of shredded paper and a plastic baggie whirled into a small dust devil. They had company.

Seth's adrenaline spiked. "Hannah!"

She made it to the front of the sedan before the whirlwind stopped. Zain, a new fae he'd fought a couple of weeks ago, stood in its place.

A growl burst from Finn's throat, and he raked his claws across Seth's chest.

Pain rippled along the scoured flesh. So focused on Hannah, he'd lost track of his enemy. A big mistake. One he'd rectify immediately.

On a burst of adrenaline, Seth bunched his knees beneath Finn and, using the strength endowed in him by his goddess, launched his former friend into the air. Bones crunched as Finn slammed into the brick building.

"Seth, you're injured!" Hannah crossed the car's headlights.

Zain snagged her arm and hauled her to him.

Her scream ricocheted down the alley.

"Hannah!" Dread coiled around Seth's chest, forcing the cry from his lips.

He rose to his feet and yanked his whip from his belt. Blood from his chest wound dripped onto the ground.

Zain dragged Hannah toward an open doorway in the adjacent building. She struggled against his grip, her pursed lips displaying her resolve.

Seth raced toward them. The crack of his whip echoed against the building. He wanted to slice the barbed ends at his enemy but wouldn't risk injuring Hannah.

As Seth closed the distance, a low hiss from behind registered in his brain.

Finn...

Seth turned to defend himself, but his best friend's claws sliced down Seth's back, shredding his wings and nearly ripping one from its socket.

Pain crashed over his shoulders and into his chest, squeezing his lungs and burying the scream inside.

His vision wavered.

He fell to one knee.

Zain jerked Hannah through the open doorway, and her worried gaze landed on Seth.

"Seth! Watch out!" she screamed.

Finn grabbed Seth's injured wing, crushing bone and feathers in his grasp.

Needles of fire licked over Seth's skin. A tormented scream escaped his lips.

The devious fae chuckled. "Nice wings. I guessed ya had a secret but never imaged this. Sure look sensitive."

He stamped his boot across the damaged tissue and ground one of Seth's wings into the pavement like he was crushing a bug.

Seth howled as his bones snapped and excruciating pain seized him. Finally, darkness claimed him and offered him some peace.

~

The terrible crunching of Seth's bones carried on the wind. Hannah's chest ached as if her heart had suffered a similar fate. She jerked from Zain's hold and bolted out the door. "Seth! Seth!"

Zain caught her by the wrist. He yanked hard, drawing her off her feet. Her sneakers skittered on the loose gravel, and she slammed into his chest.

Pain ricocheted down her arms, but anger-fueled adrenaline lashed along her nerves with such raw intensity, she pummeled her free fist against his cheek, his chin, his nose, anywhere she could reach.

Zain chuckled. "Feisty, aren't you?"

He snagged her hand and shoved it behind her back to join the first.

She spat in his face. "I hate you!"

"Aw, how sweet. Too bad I don't care." Zain shoved her in front of him through the doorway, his grip around her wrists tight and painful.

As the door closed, she caught one last glimpse of Seth. Finn stood over his unconscious form, a malicious smile plastered on his face.

She choked back a sob. Seth, her night angel, had come for her after all. Somehow, he'd escaped Drake's long punishment only to be tortured by a fae in order to protect her.

A mixture of pain and regret bubbled to the surface and slid over her lashes in a wave of grief. Finn had damaged Seth's magnificent wings, and she was responsible. She prayed Seth wouldn't lose his life, too.

"Where are you taking me?" Hannah glanced at her captor.

Zain's dark braid trailed over his shoulder, the tips swaying across his black leather jacket with each step. He smiled and gave her a shove. "To see Marco, of course."

Marco.

She inhaled to catch her breath, and the smell of urine and feces burned in her nostrils. Doors spaced every six feet or so lined the building's corridor. Paint peeled from the wooden frames.

Zain hauled her to a stop in front of one painted with a red "X." He twisted the handle and swung the door wide. A loud squeak echoed down the hallway.

Damp, cold air filtered from the room. The hair at her nape rose.

Hannah didn't want to go in there. As if she had a hope of preventing the inevitable, she dug in her heels.

Zain thrust her onward, and she tripped over the threshold.

Hands splayed forward, she crashed into a chair, the only piece of furniture in the room. The edge of her coat caught on the back and ripped.

She toppled to the ground. New bumps and bruises ached from the contact, but the dread grinding at her psyche overshadowed the pain.

"Grace wouldn't be your middle name, now would it?" Zain held out his palm.

She drew on her courage and stuck out her chin.

Yellow flashes of anger pulsed within his eyes. He grabbed her by the hair and yanked her to her feet.

Pain exploded along her scalp. She scratched Zain's arms, but he tightened his grip in retaliation.

The pounding of booted feet echoed in the hallway.

"Seth!" Hope lightened Hannah's spirit.

Zain shook his head. "Oh, honey. That's not your boyfriend."

A moment later, Finn burst through the doorway. He narrowed his gaze on Zain.

"Ya couldn't of waited for me, could ya?"

Zain smirked and shoved Hannah toward Finn. "Here's your prize. You can thank me for the help anytime."

Finn caught her in his arms. She struggled to break free, but he held her tight.

"Ya didn't need ta get involved. I had it under control." He pursed his lips and glared at his partner. "Did Marco ask ya ta follow me?"

Zain shrugged, strode to the apartment's closet, and opened the door. Dim light penetrated through a large hole in the back. "Marco's waiting. We should go. Did you handle the gargoyle?"

Finn guided Hannah toward the closet. "Ya. I did. He's injured, but not out of the game per Marco's orders. He'll be on his way in no time."

Anger spiked through Hannah. She whirled on Finn. "What did you do to him?"

The Irish fae arched one dark eyebrow. "My, my, lass. Ya shouldn't care so much for the likes of him. He's just a gargoyle."

Just a gargoyle...

He was more than that to her, so much more. Anger roiled from deep inside, and before she knew what she'd done, her palm connected with Finn's cheek.

The sound of flesh hitting flesh echoed in the empty room.

Hannah's fingers stung from the impact, but Finn's head didn't even move.

"Now, lass. That wasn't nice." Finn bent down, grabbed her behind the knees, and hauled her over his shoulder.

Not again...

She pounded his back.

"Zain. Go first, I'll follow ya."

"It'll take us a few minutes to get there in the tunnels. If she gets to be too much for you, I can carry her for a while." Zain chuckled.

Hannah swung her fist at Zain's nearby thigh but only connected with air so she continued her assault on Finn's back. "You will both rot in hell for this."

Zain laughed and disappeared through the hole at the rear of the closet.

Finn adjusted her on his shoulder. "Oh, lass. We've been ta some-place far worse already, and after we're done with ya, ya'll be joining us."

Before she could reply, he dragged her through the opening.

CHAPTER 23

*C*onsciousness returned to Seth, bringing a Mack truck driving over him right along with it. Pain rippled over his back, the intensity so fierce it almost pulled him under once again. The gentle tinkle of rain caught his attention, and he held on, using the lulling chime as a life raft amid the agony.

As the cool and refreshing moisture splashed over his damaged flesh, his skin, bones, and feathers knit together from its healing touch. Far from full power, though, he'd need more than a few raindrops to recoup his strength.

Memories of how he ended up here refused to surface, and a frustrated groan eased from his lips. He opened his eyes to see where he was.

Light from a nearby streetlamp flickered over a black car, its rear passenger door ajar. His mind hit the recall button, and the recollections flooded through his brain.

Hannah...

She was in trouble.

He placed his hands on the roughened blacktop, a few broken bits digging into his palm, and pushed himself to his knees. The newly healed flesh on his wings tore at the movement. He sucked in his breath, held it.

Seth gritted his teeth and rose to his feet. He swayed, his brain threatening to go off-line again as his body adjusted to the tilt of his damaged wing that pulled him sideways.

The rain pelted his skin, plastering his hair to his face. He swiped at the wet strands. How long had he laid in the street, unconscious? Long enough for the clouds to come in and bring the healing rain. Thank the goddess they did, or he might've died from his wounds. At least darkness still reigned.

He staggered toward the doorway Zain had dragged Hannah through. The door handle turned without protest, but the hinges squeaked, announcing his approach.

He cursed under his breath and entered the condemned building.

The faes' stench assailed his nostrils. At least he knew which way to go.

He trailed his fingers over the leather handle of his whip and proceeded down the hall. At the open doorway halfway down the corridor, he entered a small apartment. The lone piece of furniture, a broken chair with one of its legs bent at an odd angle, lay in the middle of the room. A shred of bright pink material hung from the ragged end.

Seth's heart skipped a beat. He grabbed the strip and brought the material to his nose. Hannah's cool, refreshing scent wafted into his senses. *Dearest Goddess, help me find her in time.*

After a quick glance around the room, he spotted the open closet. He strode to the doorway. An opening emerged large enough to walk through, and a faint glow permeated from the other side.

Prickles raised the hair over his scalp, but he tamped down his fear of the dark, damp, underground tunnels. He could do this as long as the light remained.

"Drake, Damian, Grayson, I'm heading into the tunnels after fae. Could use some backup."

He counted the few seconds he dared wait for a reply by the beat of his pounding heart. *Dammit.* No response. He was on his own, but nothing else mattered except Hannah. He'd find her, protect her, and give his life for her if that's what it took.

"Hannah, I'm on my way."

Seth took a deep breath and plunged into the gloom.

While Finn carried Hannah on his shoulder, she glanced down the tunnel. Lit torches every few feet lined the long corridor. Water seeped from cracks in the walls, and a small stream raced down the middle of the path.

Finn's boots splashed in the water with each step, sending a constant spray over Hannah's arms and face. The cool wetness blended in with her tears.

How was Seth? Was he alive? Heaviness settled onto her shoulders. *Please God, let him live.*

She renewed her efforts to free herself, kicking her legs and pounding Finn's back.

He tightened his grip around her thighs and ascended a flight of stairs. "Take it easy, lass. We're almost there."

A moment later, they emerged into a large room of what appeared to be an abandoned church with its high ceiling and broken stained glass windows. Concrete shards, dirt, and other debris coated the floor and the steps leading to the nave. Beneath its massive archway stood a large metal crate, big enough for a horse, surrounded by a thick chain and secured by a lock.

Finn tossed her onto the floor as if she were a discarded sack of potatoes.

She scrambled to her feet, and painful tingles of awareness woke her numb feet. Her gaze drew upward to the remarkable domed ceiling. Visible through the glass at its peak, a few stars twinkled between breaks in the clouds.

"Welcome, Hannah. It's been a while, hasn't it?" Marco's deep voice ricocheted off the walls.

The muscles in Hannah's shoulders stiffened. She turned to face him.

He strode toward her, a smile plastered on his deceptively handsome features. His large overcoat billowed around his knees, and his cane rested in the crook of his elbow.

"Now, where are my manners? I'm sure you've had a very difficult past few days. Please, join me." He held out his hand in invitation.

Hannah tried to swallow, but her mouth turned dry. "What do you want from me?"

"You?" Marco sneered and withdrew his proffered hand. "You're my bait."

"Bait?" Her mind clouded as she pieced together his words. *Seth... Oh my God, Seth!*

Her chest tightened, squeezing her heart. She took a step back, then another. If she made it into the tunnel, maybe she'd have a chance—

Zain and Finn strode toward her, flanking her and preventing escape.

Marco tsked. "Come now, we both know you wouldn't make it five feet."

She met his gaze and raised her chin. "You'll never take him down."

"Oh, my dear, that's where you're wrong. He'll fall and rather easily, I might add. Now, come here." He crooked his finger, and a long, pointed claw extended from the tip.

A scream swelled in her lungs, but she refused to give Marco the satisfaction of hearing her terror. Instead, she pursed her lips and took another step back.

"Go on, lass. Can't wait all night." Finn shoved her from behind.

Momentum forced her off balance, and she careened forward, her feet skittering over the floor's dirt-encrusted surface.

Marco slipped his arm around her shoulders. As he tugged her close, the edge of his coat wrapped around her like a blanket.

"It's too bad you gave yourself to that gargoyle. Your pure, innocent essence would've made a nice tribute for Gwawl." He waved his hand in the air. "But that doesn't matter in the grand scheme of things. The gargoyle will do nicely."

Hannah's mind raced as she stalled for time. "Why do you want him?"

Marco swung her toward the large black box. "Gwawl is into torment. He'd love to get his hands on another one of Rhiannon's gargoyles. She'd hate him even more and that would be fine by him. I plan to collect the reward and obtain a promotion to lieutenant of the Chicago fae army."

"If Gwawl doesn't kill ya instead," Finn muttered under his breath.

Marco's gaze riveted on the fae. He grasped the handle of his cane, his fingers white with strain. "What's that supposed to mean?"

Finn shrugged. "Nothin'. Forget I spoke."

Marco drummed his fingers against the cane's handle.

Realization dawned on Hannah. Marco feared Gwawl. She tucked that piece of information into the recesses of her mind.

The dark fae returned his attention to the box.

"As for your gargoyle. Seth, isn't it?" He slid his finger along the metal casing in a gentle caress. "This is his transport crate and future home."

A tingle of unease skittered over Hannah's shoulders and down her spine. "You…you can't. He—"

"That's enough!" Marco raised his hand and stepped away.

Hannah flinched, but then anger rushed through her. "Seth will kill you all."

Marco raised an eyebrow, and a laugh burst from his lips.

"You think too highly of your precious gargoyle. He'll do as he's told and do it willingly. Now, why don't you sit on the stairs, right here?" Marco patted the top step near the large metal crate.

Hannah tightened the muscles in her legs, locked her knees in place, and lifted her chin. "No."

"Sit down!" Marco's commanding voice reverberated off the walls.

A chunk of rock from the ceiling hit the floor and bounced at her feet, followed by another.

Before she could react, Marco tracked to her side and shoved her onto the floor. Her hands splayed on the grungy tile, and her knee cracked against the step, sending a bolt of pain down her shin.

She pushed herself to a sitting position, and her fingertips grazed the box's dark metal. A foul and bitter darkness swirled around her. She jerked her hand away and glared at the fae. "You'll never take Seth down."

He backhanded her, and her head whipped to the side.

Heat seared her cheek. The taste of blood slipped onto her tongue.

Marco laughed darkly. "Watch and see."

She spat at him, her bloody spit landing on the edge of his polished shoe. "Over my dead body."

Marco tsked. "Oh, honey, that's the plan."

"Not on my watch." Seth's deep voice rumbled through the room.

Hannah's lungs expanded with relief even as fear for him coursed through her veins.

Seth stood, shoulders squared, at the cave entrance. His wings rustled behind his back, one drooping at an odd angle, but a strong, determined glint reflected in his eyes. "She's not the one dying tonight."

CHAPTER 24

"Seth, thank God you're all right." Hannah's soft words came out in a rush and filtered into Seth's ears.

His wings quivered from relief.

"He won't be for long." Marco scowled at Finn. "Capture him and bring me his wings as a souvenir."

Seth yanked his whip from his belt and cracked the ends in the air in warning. The movement sent a round of pain over the tender flesh on his damaged wing. "Step away from Hannah."

"Glad ya joined us, boyo, and sorry about yer wing, but I'm goin' ta have ta rip them both off now." As Finn trod down the stairs, his pointed claws extended from his fingertips, and he launched himself into the air.

Seth hurled his whip at his old friend, and the strands wrapped around Finn's waist. Throwing all his anguish, frustration, and heartache into his grip, Seth yanked on his whip.

The ricocheted intensity jerked Finn from his trajectory, and he crashed against the stone wall. As he slid to the ground, a groan eased from his lips.

"It figures I have to finish the job, Finn. You worthless piece of..." Zain circled Seth from behind, a dagger in his palm. A shaft of moonlight pierced through the dome and flickered against the blade.

Seth coiled his rope and turned to face his next opponent. "Come closer. I'm itching for a fight."

Zain's lip curled, revealing a chipped tooth. "If you insist."

The fae scrambled toward Seth, his feet skittering over the dirt-encrusted floor with uncanny speed.

Seth cracked his whip. The ends snaked toward Zain's throat, but the fae dodged the barbed tips. He plowed into Seth's shoulder, his momentum taking them both down.

Seth landed on his back. Pain rippled along his injured wing and jabbed into his brain. As they struggled for dominance, they rolled across the floor.

"Seth, watch out!" Hannah screamed.

The fae swiped his blade at Seth's throat, but Seth jumped to his feet and lunged out of the way.

Instead of severing his jugular, the steel sliced through his jeans and across his thigh. Blood swelled along the cut.

His breath heaved from his lungs, and his limbs, heavy as boulders, shook from his injuries, but he wouldn't let anyone harm Hannah. For as long as he continued to breathe, he'd protect her.

From across the room, Finn moaned and shook his head.

Zain rose to his feet, and a sharp hiss burst from his lips.

Both Zain and Finn rushed Seth.

As they descended upon him, each gripped a wing.

"Yes, yes, rip those horrendous appendages from him," Marco yelled.

Seth hardened his skin but weakened by his injuries, he didn't have the strength to protect himself.

Finn and Zain sliced his back with their daggers and yanked on his wings.

Bones snapped, flesh tore.

Overwhelming pain blinded Seth, and he staggered on his feet.

Blood dripped from the open wound, dragging the strength from him.

Zain tossed Seth's wing to Finn, who caught it with one hand. He held both wings up like war booty, triumph evident in his malevolent grin.

Air wheezed from Seth's lungs in short, uneven breaths. At the sight of his white wings encased in Finn's grasp, a knot weaved from remorse formed in his gut. How was it possible he mourned the loss of his wings when he'd despised them for so long?

"Time to finish the job." A devilish smile curled Zain's lip. He rushed toward Seth, his crimson-stained dagger tight in his grip.

Seth drew on his remaining energy and grasped his rope with both hands. As the large fae attacked, Seth sidestepped him, slid the rough cowhide over Zain's face, and yanked the rope tight against his neck.

Zain clawed at Seth's hands, his sharp nails digging into his skin like knives.

Despite the gnawing pain, Seth refused to let go. As Zain struggled in Seth's grasp, the muscles in Seth's arms shook. With his injuries and his decreased energy, he wasn't sure how much longer he could keep his hold on the fae.

Hannah's sharp cry erupted in the room, and Seth whipped around toward the sound.

Marco hauled Hannah off the floor and into his arms. She fought against his hold, her heels digging for purchase along the rough stone floor.

Seth's heart pounded, fear for Hannah whipping through him faster than lightning.

Marco clamped one hand over her mouth, and with the other, placed the tip of his long steel blade to her throat.

Hannah's skin dimpled from the pressure. Her wide eyes, swimming with a mixture of regret, determination, and love, met his.

His mouth went dry. *Love? Was it possible she really loved him?*

"Release him or I'll kill the girl!" Marco nicked Hannah's skin. Blood pooled along the cut.

Seth stilled.

He loosened the rope from one hand, and the barbed end smacked the ground. With a hard shove, he pushed Zain away. It killed him not to finish the job, but he refused to risk Hannah's safety.

Finn set Seth's wings against the nave's wall. The once-sparkling silver ends seemed dull and lifeless.

Marco stepped in front of a large metal box with a chain around the middle, using Hannah as a shield.

Zain and Finn flanked their leader.

A low growl rumbled in Seth's chest. He tightened his grip on his whip but kept the weapon at his side. He couldn't attack the fae without risking injury to Hannah.

"Release Hannah, now, and I'll make your death quick."

Marco's menacing chuckle reverberated off the ceiling. "You're in no position to make demands. What price are you willing to pay to save this worthless girl?"

With Marco's hand clamped over Hannah's mouth, she couldn't speak, but she shook her head, her eyes pleading with him not to do this.

Seth's stomach hardened into a ball. "What do you want from me?"

The smile that tugged on Marco's lips embodied pure evil. "I offer a trade. You for her."

"How do I know you, or any of your fae, won't kill her?" Seth's back screamed from the pain, but he inched closer. If he stepped within reach, he might be able to snag Hannah from Marco's grasp.

A malicious spark flashed through Marco's eyes, and he dragged Hannah further away. "Other than my word, you don't. Contrary to what you might believe, I do have some standards. The question is, though, can you reach her before I shove my blade into her throat? I think not. Are you willing to take that gamble?"

No, and the damn fae knew it. A knot of pure hatred burned in Seth's gut even as a sense of foreboding crested over his shoulders. It seemed fitting that he'd turn down a gamble after all the times he'd cheated others. The irony wasn't lost on him.

Marco's snide chuckle rolled through the room. "Good choice."

The dark fae withdrew his hand from Hannah's mouth and snapped his fingers. The padlock on the box slipped free, and the chain rattled as the heavy metal hit the floor. The door opened, as if on its own.

Cool, dark dampness radiated from its depths, and the interior had the dull green glow of magical crystals, the kind that prevented a gargoyle from dematerializing.

Cold sweat broke out along Seth's brow. Memories of the cave from his childhood threatened to surface. He ground his teeth and forced the images from his mind, refusing to give in to his fears.

"Seth, please, don't do this. I'm not worth risking your life." Hannah's heartfelt words settled into Seth's soul.

"Darlin', I'm your night angel, remember? I'd do anything for you."

A sob burst from Hannah's lips before she clamped her mouth tight. Tears glistened in her eyes.

Marco tsked and dragged Hannah away from the crate. "Oh, how endearing. Now, drop your weapons."

Zain and Finn drew closer, flanking Seth on either side.

Seth stared at Marco for a long moment before glancing at Hannah.

She shook her head. "No, Seth, don't—"

He released his whip. The long leather weapon slithered to the floor.

"—they plan to torture and imprison you for eternity."

The muscles in Seth's shoulders tensed.

"Dagger, too." Marco sneered.

Seth said he'd do anything for Hannah, and he'd meant it. If spending eternity trapped in a dark cage was his future, then that was a small price to pay for Hannah's life. He ripped his dagger from his belt and tossed his last weapon onto the stone floor.

Hannah wanted to lunge at Seth and stop him from making the biggest mistake of his life, but the threatening cool steel of Marco's blade against her throat held her in place. She swallowed the sour pill of frustration and tried not to cry.

The muscles in Seth's shoulders bunched from tension, but resolve lined his features.

Hannah's lungs tightened as a wave of powerlessness swept over her.

"Come on, now. Walk into your new home." Marco raised his chin toward the crate.

Seth's attention traveled from Marco to the box before settling on her. She'd already pleaded for him not to do this, and she opened her mouth to try again, but his gaze held that burning determination she knew so well. She pursed her lips together.

Seth smiled at her. "Thank you, darlin'."

Confusion flooded her mind. She furrowed her brow. "For what?"

"For showing me the goodness in the world and reminding me what it is to love." His voice cracked on the last word.

Even as tears blurred her vision and spilled over her lashes, her heart swelled. Seth loved her. Unlike her father, her uncle, and her old boyfriend, Seth had kept his word. He hadn't treated her bad or abandoned her. Instead, he'd proven himself by coming for her.

She wouldn't lose him. There must be something she could do. Think, damn it.

Seth took a step toward the crate, then another. A tic pulsed to life in his jaw.

Zain and Finn closed the distance from behind.

"Gwawl will be so pleased with his new toy. I can't wait to give you to him." Marco smirked.

Seth strode up the stairs, the heels of his snakeskin boots clinking on the stone. He placed his hand on the doorjamb and stepped inside, his back now turned toward her. Blood trickled from the open wounds. Without his beautiful, majestic wings, Seth seemed so defeated.

Her heart ached for him and all he'd endured. He was a good soul and didn't deserve any of this.

"Belief in yourself and belief in others can accomplish great things..." Sasha's earlier comment echoed inside her head.

Determination to do something burned in Hannah's gut. She refused to let Seth suffer on her behalf.

Out of the corner of her eye, she peered at Marco. Mere inches from him, she got a good look at his features. Tension lines around his eyes displayed his unease. What did he fear?

Gwawl...

She'd noted the panic at the mention of his god not long ago.

"Gwawl is heartless. He likes things his way. As Rhiannon found out, don't ever cross him for his revenge is legendary." Seth's comments from the other night raced through her mind.

A tiny root of hope sprouted in her chest. She needed to use that information to her advantage, but how?

Memories of Uncle Frank and his abusive nature surfaced. Although she hadn't been physically strong, she'd stood up to him and used his fear of God to protect herself and Aunt Sally. An idea grew, along with her hope.

"Are you sure you want to anger Gwawl with this gift?" Hannah forced conviction into her voice.

Marco stiffened. The blade under her chin nicked her skin. Pain lanced from her throat and along her jawline to her ear.

He swiveled his head to face her and narrowed his gaze. "What do you know of Gwawl, human?"

"Hannah, don't." Seth's tight voice slid across the room.

She swallowed and refused to give in to her fear. "I've heard your God might be insulted if you gave him damaged goods."

"Damaged goods?" Marco laughed. "If you're referring to the gargoyle's back, the skin will heal within the hour."

Doubt threatened to creep through the cracks in her mental armor, but she held on to her conviction and her hope.

"Maybe Gwawl would've liked to toy with Seth's magical wings. Think of all the torture he could've inflicted. Instead, you cut them off. I wonder, would Gwawl take his frustration out on you?"

Marco's face reddened, and his features tightened into a scowl. "Don't push me or I'll—"

Hannah forced a laugh. "You're afraid—"

In the blink of an eye, Marco sheathed his blade and grabbed her by the neck. His sharp nails dug into her flesh.

Pain rippled all the way to her toes.

She pummeled her fists against his arms, his shoulders, his face, anyplace she could reach, but he only tightened his grip.

Lack of oxygen caught up with her, and as her vision dimmed, one thought echoed in her mind—Seth had taught her about love, but she'd never had the chance to thank him.

CHAPTER 25

*A*s Marco clasped Hannah's throat, Seth tightened his grip on the crate's doorframe. His need to protect her pulled strength from deep inside and propelled him forward at lightning speed. Before Zain or Finn could react, he leapt into the air, and with arms outstretched, reached for his love.

Marco tossed Hannah to the ground like a rag doll.

Seth crashed into Marco, and the fae landed on the stone steps.

A whoosh of air burst from his lungs.

With a rush of anger-fueled determination, Seth hardened his fist to stone and slammed Marco in the ribs. A cracking of bone echoed in the space between them.

"That's enough." Zain gripped Seth by the shoulder and yanked him to his feet. The fae sliced his claws down Seth's injured back. Pain rippled along the nerve endings and burned like fire.

Seth kicked the fae in the gut. Zain crashed into the wall and slumped to the floor.

"Seth, stop. Ya can't win." Finn strode forward, fingers flexing at his sides.

"No, you can't." Marco withdrew his sword from his cane, the distinct ting of metal on metal echoing in the chamber. He raised the blade over his head and aimed the tip at Hannah.

Hunched in a ball on the floor, she didn't move.

Ice formed in Seth's veins. No. Hannah couldn't die. Not like Emily. He had to save her.

Seth reached for his whip, but his hand clasped the empty casing on his belt. Shock rocked him to his core, stealing his breath.

Marco's attention turned to Seth, and he winked. "You shouldn't trust a fae. We lie, cheat, and steal. Now, I plan to finish the job, and I'll get a nice boost from all that goodness in Hannah's soul."

He tightened his grip on the handle and brought the blade down toward Hannah.

Seth launched himself in the air and prayed he'd get there in time.

"No!" Finn threw himself at Seth, knocking him off balance.

Finn landed in the blade's path, and the tip sank into Finn's eye.

He collapsed next to Hannah. Blood oozed from the wound, but a smile tugged at his lip.

A mixture of relief and sadness swept over Seth, nearly bringing him to his knees.

"Finn, you filthy liar. I knew I couldn't trust you." Marco seethed and yanked the blade free.

Seth wouldn't give Marco a second chance to end Hannah's life. He rushed at the evil fae, landed on the bastard, and took him down. The blade sliced across his forearm, cutting all the way to the bone.

He didn't feel the pain. Only the intense desire to protect Hannah registered in his mind as he slammed his fist into Marco's face.

Blood gushed from the fae's nose.

Seth rose to his feet, dragging Marco with him, and the fae's blade clattered to the ground.

Seth gripped the fae by the throat while Marco clawed at Seth's arm.

Movement to his left caught Seth's attention. Zain bolted toward him, fire in his eyes.

Seth threw Marco on the ground and braced for Zain's attack.

At the last second, Zain cut to the right and landed on Marco. A small dust storm burst to life and enveloped them along with Marco's sword.

"No!" Seth dove toward his enemies, but Marco and Zain disappeared in the churn.

Seth landed on empty ground, a few bits of debris pinging his skin.

"Seth?" Hannah's soft voice fluttered in the quiet room.

Seth's heart clenched. Tears stung his eyes.

He raced to Hannah's side, knelt on the floor, and wrapped her in his embrace.

"Are you all right?" He drew away enough to look at her.

She nodded and searched his features. "Are you?"

"Yeah..."

"Thank you for saving my life, again," she whispered.

Seth brushed his finger along her cheek and placed a stray strand of hair behind her ear. How had he ever compared her to Emily? She was stronger than his wife had ever been.

"Darlin', you used your smarts and riled Marco into a right fit, saving yourself and me in the process."

"I guess so. I thought about Uncle Frank and how I stood up to him, just like you'd said I did." She bit her lip.

Seth cupped her chin and stroked his thumb along her jawline. "You did great. You're strong. I never doubted that about you."

Her brow furrowed over those emerald green eyes he so adored. "I thought you had to stay in your gargoyle form for a week. How did you escape Drake's punishment?"

"I saw Finn carrying you through the quad and knew you were in trouble." The tension in his shoulders eased on a slow exhale. "I contacted Rhiannon, and by the grace of the goddess, she released me."

"I'm glad she did," Hannah whispered.

"Me, too. I don't know what I'd have done if—"

Finn's soft groan stopped Seth cold, and the hair on his scalp prickled.

His old buddy lay on the ground a few feet away. He held his palm over his eye socket, and blood dribbled between his fingers. With each breath, a rattled wheeze eased from his lips.

He grabbed his dagger from his belt, flipped the blade over in his palm, and extended the hilt to Seth. "Marco didn't shove the blade far enough in ta kill me. I can't stay here. It's not right. Finish the job, mate."

Seth stared at his friend. Indecision flitted through his mind.

Hannah placed her hand on top of Seth's and gave him a squeeze. "Rather you than someone else."

Respect for his woman made him seem ten feet tall. Mercy extended far beyond any kind of retribution.

He accepted the dagger and scooted next to Finn.

Finn lowered his hand. Blood dribbled from the wounded eye socket, down his cheek, and onto his shirt. With his good eye, he met Seth's gaze. "I never wanted ta kill anyone. Thank ya for allowing me ta right a wrong. Ya take care of the lass, now."

Memories of all the good times they'd shared on and off the battle-field swept through Seth. He'd miss his old friend, more than he could say. He swallowed past the lump in his throat and gave his friend one last nod. "I will."

Heart heavy, he leaned over Finn and plunged the dagger deep into the mangled opening. The blade sank into the flesh to the hilt. "May Rhiannon have mercy on your soul."

Dust and debris swirled around Finn. Instead of his soul disappearing into the Otherworld, the small whirlwind dissipated into the air, scattering Finn's spirit among the ether, the space between space. The ultimate death.

A somber shroud settled over Seth's shoulders. At least Finn had made amends.

"Seth." Hannah brushed her fingers down his arm.

His skin tingled at the contact. He grasped her fingers, ushered them both to their feet, and tugged her into his embrace. Her fresh scent wafted into his senses, and he inhaled a deep breath, enjoying everything that was Hannah.

"Seth, your back." She drew away enough to look at him. Her eyes glistened with unshed tears, but a smile tugged at her lips. "It's completely healed."

He blinked. Even with his preternatural healing ability, his skin shouldn't have healed that fast.

Hannah trailed her fingers over his biceps, along his shoulders, and over his chest.

She gasped. "And your spark stone. It's gone."

He gasped and touched the spot over his heart. Instead of the familiar bump of his stone, his fingers contacted smooth skin.

A tingle rippled over his shoulders and down his spine. He rubbed his chest again and glanced at the empty spot.

The ramifications swept through his mind. Had he passed his test? Was he human?

He grasped Hannah's hand and tried to dematerialize.

Nothing happened.

Hope fluttered deep inside.

He thought about his past—his need for freedom, his gambling, his inability to save his wife, his fear of dark, confined places.

"I think I passed my test." He grasped Hannah's hands in his palms. "I wasn't sure Marco would release you, but that was a gamble I had to take, and then, when I stepped into the container and sacrificed my freedom for you, I faced my biggest fears."

Hannah's brows furrowed over her pretty green eyes. "So, you're human now? You never have to go back to your post?"

A brilliant flash of light exploded in the room. Seth wrapped his arms around Hannah in a protective embrace and peered over his shoulder.

Rhiannon stood in the middle of the chamber. A long, silver gown flowed from her elegant shoulders, over her curves, and pooled at her feet. Dark hair fell around her shoulders, her trademark braids hanging loosely from either side of her temple.

Achos, her small dragon-like constant companion, sat on her left shoulder. He licked his front claws with his long tongue and smoke curled from his nostrils. His green scales shimmered in the subdued light.

Rhiannon glanced around the old derelict church until her gaze focused on the dome. A smile tugged at her lips, accentuating her beauty.

"Ah, Seth. It's fitting your test occurred under your favorite resting place." She turned to face him.

He bent to one knee and brought Hannah with him. "Rhiannon. My goddess."

"Rise, my warrior, and face me." Rhiannon strode toward him.

Seth rose with Hannah right alongside him. He met his goddess's gaze.

"Am I truly human?" He choked on the words.

Rhiannon extended her index finger. She tapped her nail, polished in silver to match her dress, on his chest right where his spark stone used to reside. "Yes, my warrior. When you faced your deepest fear and gave up your freedom to save another, you passed your test. Sometimes the soul reunites with a big bang. Other times, it slips in unannounced. I think yours was the latter. In either case, I love it when I can reunite a spirit with its host."

Happiness swelled deep inside his soul, along with a warm sense of worthiness. He wrapped his arm around Hannah and hugged her close. "Hannah, I don't have much, not a home or a job or even a penny to my name, but one thing I know for sure, I love you and want to learn and grow with you, marry you and raise children together, but I'm getting ahead of myself and babbling like an idiot."

He brought her fingers to his lips and pressed a kiss to her knuckles. "I'm a bit old-fashioned and set in my ways. Will you let me take my time and court you in every way imaginable?"

Hannah expelled a breath, part sob, part laugh, and nodded. "I love you, too. Thank you for teaching me what it is to love."

Seth grinned so wide his cheeks hurt. He unwrapped the cord at his wrist and held the braided leather in his palm. With shaky fingers, he offered it to Hannah. "Please accept this as my promise to you, always."

She nodded once again and held out her hand.

With tender care, he tied the braided cord around her wrist.

A single tear slipped over her lash and tracked down her cheek. Seth kissed the tear away then brought his lips to hers. He showered her with gentle kisses, but his passion erupted, hot and fiery, and he poured all his love for her into their connection, showing her just how much she meant to him.

Hannah relaxed into him, her curves melding against his body in all the right places. She was his sun for the rest of his life.

Rhiannon cleared her throat.

Seth broke the kiss and peered at his goddess.

"Well, it's time for me to go. I have a war to win, after all." Rhiannon stroked Achos's head, and the dragon purred. "Be sure to meet up with Beaumont. He'll give you the reintegration packet with your identification, bank account information, etcetera, so you can start your new life, and don't worry about the fae. Now that you're human again, they can't harm you. That's part of the agreement Gwawl and I have with Cernunnos. Gwawl hates it, but it's only fair that once a gargoyle passes his test, he deserves to spend the rest of his life in peace."

Seth had forgotten about that. His shoulders lightened. "Thank you, goddess."

"Good luck!" Rhiannon departed in a flash of light.

As Seth's eyes adjusted to the dimness once again, Hannah tugged on his arm.

"Let's go to my place." A twinkle lit in both of her eyes.

"Darlin', when did you say Beaumont and Sadie will return?"

A knowing smile crooked her adorable lips. "Day after tomorrow."

"You don't have to ask me twice." As if the hounds of the Other-world lapped at his heels, he grasped her hand and drew her toward the door. "That's not much time, but it'll have to do. I have plans for you, darlin', lots of plans."

Hannah raised an eyebrow. "Does it involve chocolate and whipped cream?"

Seth laughed. "If you want it to, darlin', if you want it to."

CHAPTER 26

*M*arco reformed in the Otherworld. His shoulder hit a stone floor, followed by his hip and one knee. Pain flared at the contact points, and a heavy weight pinned him to the ground. He struggled to breathe, but a few particles of air made it into his lungs, bringing Zain's scent along with them.

Anger flared at Marco's temple. How dare he take him out of the fight?

He flipped the guy onto his back, grabbed his sword from the floor, and pressed the blade against Zain's throat. "I should slaughter you right here, right now for what you've done."

Zain didn't flinch. Instead, he raised a dark eyebrow. "Don't like being indebted to anyone, do you?"

"What does that mean?" Marco pressed the blade tighter against Zain's neck. The skin puckered from the pressure.

"You and I both know I saved your life." Zain smirked. "But don't worry, I won't tell a soul."

A deep, familiar male chuckle echoed in the chamber.

Even beneath Marco's coat, the hair along his arms rose. In his effort to tackle Zain, Marco hadn't assessed their surroundings.

Instinctively, he'd known they were in the Otherworld, but the exact location hadn't sunk in until now.

He glanced toward the sound, catching sight of the fire burning in the familiar wall sconces. Seated in his elaborate throne, Gwawl toyed with the gold chain at his waist. An amused smile curled his thin lips, but his dark, black-as-ink eyes held a promise of retribution.

"My lord." Marco rose to his feet and sheathed his blade. He kept his gaze focused on Gwawl's sandaled feet.

One of the chair's human bones, a femur perhaps, slipped between the god's feet and rubbed along his calf before disappearing into the mass once again.

"Zain. Come stand before me." Gwawl's commanding voice reverberated off the stone walls.

Zain shuffled to his feet, strode across the room, and knelt in front of his master. His braid slipped over his shoulder and swayed from the movement.

Gwawl leaned forward and placed his palm against Zain's forehead. He glanced at Marco. The lines in his face hardened. He released Zain and motioned for him to step aside.

Zain complied, his head bowed in supplication.

"I didn't need to look into Zain's mind to know you'd failed yet again, but I hadn't realized you'd lost me a good fae in the process. In addition, it appears the gargoyle has been released from his servitude to Rhiannon. I can feel it."

Marco exhaled the frustration burning in his lungs. Not only had he lost his tribute, he'd missed his chance to drain Hannah's energy for himself. Protected by Cernunnos's rule, Marco couldn't go after either of them. Seems the god of the Otherworld thought gargoyles that passed their test deserved to live in the human realm without fear of retribution from a fae. The rule sucked, but so be it.

Gwawl crooked his finger at Marco. "Come here."

Drawn to Gwawl as if the god held marionette strings attached to Marco's muscles, Marco stepped forward. The scent of his own fear assailed his nostrils.

Gwawl rose from his chair of human suffering. The mass of bones swirled, filling in the vacant spot, and the soft, anguished cries of lost, forgotten souls echoed into the room. Would Marco join them?

A surge of panic rushed through him. He tried to resist, but the harder he fought against Gwawl's pull, the faster his feet moved.

He stood before the god, swallowed the bitter taste of bile, and met his gaze.

The god's nostrils quivered with rage. "I should banish you to the Isle of Tech Duinn, at the House of the Dark One, to leave your soul to rot. Instead, I have a much more fitting punishment."

He snapped his finger. A silver collar lined with sharp, pointed teeth rested in his palm. He rubbed his thumb over the tip of a particularly large fang. A drop of blood glistened on his abraded flesh.

He pressed his thumb to Marco's forehead and smeared the blood between Marco's eyes and down the length of his battered nose. As if his body had been invaded by ants, Marco's skin crawled.

"Fae, your craving for power and authority is only outdone by your incessant need for my praise. That is your downfall and your saving grace. For your retribution, I sanction you to wear this collar at all times, and you will report to Zain until I deem otherwise."

Gwawl snapped his fingers. The collar disappeared.

Something cold and hard rested around Marco's neck. Tiny pinpricks cut into his sensitive flesh. The collar tightened and the teeth sliced deeper into his skin.

Marco bit back a scream. He clamped his jaw so tight pain ricocheted through his cheek and up to his ear but didn't compare to the agony at his throat. Marco yanked at the binding. The collar melded to his skin as if it were a part of him.

"Marco, enjoy your new role." Gwawl laughed. The menacing sound reverberated off the walls, increasing in volume until shards of rock fell from the ceiling.

Marco dodged a rather large chunk and stared at Zain.

The fae met his gaze. Locked in a battle of wills, Marco refused to look away, but after a long moment, he buckled under the pressure and glanced at the floor.

Bile rose from his gut. He wanted to tear into Zain and shred him to pieces. Instead, he was at the guy's mercy. Gwawl was a malicious bastard, but Marco already knew that. The god was the leader of the fae, after all.

"I have a new task for the two of you." Gwawl reseated himself in his chair. The incessant wails of the bones picked up in fever and pitch as he settled into the seat.

Zain stepped forward and bowed. "How can we serve you?"

"Bring me the witch named Wynne Becknell." Light from the wall sconces flickered, casting a shadow over the god's features. He rubbed his chin. "I am in need of her services. Oh, and don't fail me, or I'll shred your soul into non-existence."

"It shall be done," Zain replied.

And I shall do everything in my power to see that you fail. Marco bent his head, not in supplication, but to hide his snide smile.

CHAPTER 27

"*H*urry, they're home. Did you cover it up?" Hannah released the drape from between her fingers. The material slid over the window, plunging the living room into darkness.

"Yeah. It's under the sheet." Seth's deep, familiar voice carried across the room.

"Everybody hide," Hannah whispered.

A sense of giddiness swept her from head to toe. Over the past two days, she and Seth had spent all their time together in this house, most of it in her bedroom except for the time she'd finished adding the pink touches to Sadie's picture and repairing the damage to the living room. Thank God for Wynne and her witch's magic.

Speaking of Wynne, the witch hid behind the clawfoot chair, and her sister, Sasha, slid under the sideboard table.

Hannah crept past the couch, careful not to make a sound and headed for the light switch. Sadie and Beaumont, returning from their trip, would open the door any—

The click of the door echoed through the room. A moment later, light from the streetlamp illuminated the entryway.

Hannah held her breath.

Seth wrapped his arm around her, and she leaned into his embrace, back to front. His breath tickled her ear.

"On the count of three," he whispered.

Sadie stepped over the threshold.

"One…"

She set her bag on the floor and let out a sigh.

"Two…"

Beaumont joined her, his massive frame blocking most of the light.

"Three."

Hannah snapped on the light.

"Surprise!" Hannah, Seth, Wynne, and Sasha shouted in unison and emerged from their hiding places.

Sadie jumped while Beaumont tensed.

"Welcome home, you two!" Hannah laughed.

Sadie dropped her carry-on luggage and her handbag. She hurried toward Hannah, a big smile on her face.

Hannah left Seth's side to meet her sister halfway. With all the love in her heart, she gave her sister a tight hug. After a long moment, Hannah drew away.

"Did you have a good time on your cruise?" Hannah grasped Sadie's hands. "What places did you see?"

"We had a great time…" Sadie's cheeks reddened, and she peered at Beaumont.

He laughed, his eyes sparking with mirth, and he wrapped his arm around Sadie's waist. "Can't say I remember any place other than the inside of our cabin, except for the buffet, but we won't talk about that. They stock the place for an army."

Sasha stepped forward. "Welcome back, lovebirds. Sounds like I need to take a trip like that. Just need to find the right guy first."

"Better you than me. I'll pass." Wynne fiddled with her yellow scarf at her neck. "You two look happy, glad to see it."

Seth cleared his throat and held out his palm to Beaumont. "Welcome home."

Beaumont gripped Seth's hand. His brow furrowed. "I wasn't expecting to see you here. Shouldn't you be on patrol?"

Seth released the handshake and shook his head, a sly smile forming on his lips. "I'm done with that, now."

He unclasped the first two buttons on his cotton shirt and tugged the material down enough to reveal the bare spot over his heart.

Beaumont audibly inhaled. "You're human."

"Yep, sure am."

Beaumont clapped his arm around Seth's shoulder and gave him a manly hug. "That's awesome. Way to go."

Sadie raised an eyebrow. "Does his becoming human have anything to do with you?"

Happiness flooded through Hannah, lifting her spirit so high she thought she might walk on air. She held up her palm, revealing Seth's braided cord at her wrist. "Everything."

A smile burst across Sadie's face. "Details. I want details."

"You'll get them along with some news about Finn, but first, I have something for you and Beaumont." Hannah guided Sadie toward the dining room. "C'mon everyone."

The group trailed behind Hannah and her sister. Her heart pounded so hard, she heard every beat in her ears. "I was going to wait until after your homecoming cake, but I just can't."

Hannah scooted past the long formal table, sidestepping a couple of chairs and stopped in front of the easel Seth had placed in the corner for her. A sheet covered the artwork, hiding Hannah's sketch from view.

Hannah held her palm toward the easel. "I never got a chance to give you two a wedding present. So, here it is. Happy belated best wishes. Whatever, you know what I mean."

Sadie laughed as Beaumont joined her. She peered at him, a smile on her face, before returning her attention to Hannah. "Do you want to unveil it?"

Seth wrapped his arms around Hannah's waist, his familiar warmth comforting and welcome. Hannah leaned into him once again.

"Why don't you and Beaumont do it together?" Hannah replied.

Sadie nodded and gripped a corner of the sheet. Beaumont clasped the other side.

"On the count of three." Sadie's attention focused on the sheet. "One, two, three."

Hannah's heart leapt into her throat as the sheet crumpled in a heap on the floor. Seth tightened his grip, holding her close.

Beaumont whistled.

"It's beautiful." Sadie gasped. "You captured Beaumont's happy expression just right."

The tension in Hannah's shoulders slipped away.

Beaumont nodded. "Yeah, and check out the pink in Sadie's hair. Nice touch, Hannah."

"I'm so glad you liked it." Hannah clapped her hands together.

"Of course I do. I love it, actually." Sadie turned to face Hannah. "I always loved the drawings you made for me."

Hannah opened her arms and welcomed her sister into her embrace. "I love you, sis."

"I love you, too," Sadie whispered.

"Hannah." Wynne's soft voice filled the air.

Hannah released her sister and glanced at her friend.

"Would you sketch a portrait for me of my family?" Wynne smiled. "We need to add Sasha, her girls, and myself alongside the pictures of our ancestors in my home. I'll gladly pay you."

"Really?" Hannah bounced on her toes. "I'd love to sketch for you, but you don't need to pay me."

Wynne held up her hand. "You are so talented. I insist."

Sasha sighed. "C'mon, Hannah. Let her do it. She'll be a crab for the rest of the day if you refuse."

A giggle escaped from Hannah before she could stop it. "All right. If you insist."

"I do." Wynne nodded, a smile tugging at her lip. "You know, maybe you should consider an art degree instead of business."

Hannah held her breath, her mind churning. After her experiences this past week, she'd grown in confidence and strength and wouldn't let her past dictate her future anymore. To follow her heart's desire instead of taking the safe route sounded fabulous. "You know, I might just do that."

"Seth." Beaumont smiled. "We need to take care of some business."

She glanced between Beaumont and Seth.

Seth rubbed Hannah's shoulder and stepped toward Beaumont. "What's on your mind?"

"Reintegration. As the Chicago representative of the Gargoyle Reintegration Guild, it's my job to set you up in your new life." Beaumont laughed. "I'll need a couple of days to finalize your identification and set up your bank account with your six-digit deposit. Just wanted to let you know that's coming."

Seth ran his palm over his face. "Six digits you say?"

Beaumont's lip quirked. "It's enough to settle down and figure out what you want to do with the rest of your life."

"What do you want to do, Seth?" Hannah placed her hand on his arm.

He wrapped her in his embrace, and she nestled into him, soaking up his warmth.

"I haven't figured it all out yet, but my first thought was to take flight lessons, become a pilot, and court Hannah along the way." He peered at her. "Would you fly with me?"

Like water on its endless flow from stream to river to ocean, Hannah rode the current of love swelling through her soul. She glanced at the portrait of Beaumont and Sadie and the love she'd captured between them.

I want to be loved like that.

Her birthday wish rang loud in her mind.

She glanced at Seth. The depths of his eyes reflected the love she longed for from a man all her life. He'd given her his trust, and she'd given him her heart in return.

She blinked back happy tears as she traced her finger over the braided infinity symbol at her wrist. "I'd fly with you anytime, day or night, my angel."

~

SNEAK PEEK - LOVE BEWITCHED

BOOK 3 IN THE GARGOYLE NIGHT GUARDIANS SERIES

Up next—*Love Bewitched*, book 3 in the *Gargoyle Night Guardians* series featuring Wynne Becknell, the wayward witch…

Be careful of gargoyles who can't commit…

Wynne's had enough of tall, dark, brooding males that aren't interested in her kind of love—the "until death do us part" kind. Attracted to unattainable men, she's in uncharted territory when not just one, but two males show an interest in her.

One's a gargoyle with muscles of steel and a deep, sensuous voice to match. The other, a dark, seductive fae with a smirk that can melt panties.

The problem? The men are on opposites sides of a war.

Caught between the two, who will she choose?

A love triangle romance that will leave you breathless and wanting more.

To purchase *Love Bewitched*, visit www.rosalieredd.com.

∾

Books in the *Gargoyle Night Guardians* series:
Heart Bandit - book #1
Night Angel - book #2
Love Bewitched - book #3
Books in the *Warriors of Lemuria* series:
Untouchable Lover - book #1
Untamable Lover - book #2
Unimaginable Lover - book #3
Undeniable Lover - book #4
Unforgivable Lover - book #5
Unforgettable Lover - novella
Marked by Love - novella
Other books by Rosalie Redd:
Concealed - A Blood Courtesans Vampire Romance
Clone Me a Lover - An Interstellar Lovers Romance

Reviews

Enjoyed *Night Angel?* The best gift you can give an author is an honest review. Please consider leaving a review on your favorite retailer to help spread the word and support an author.

Newsletter

Stay in touch with my new releases, special giveaways, and exclusive content by signing up for my newsletter. **For signing up, you'll receive a free gift!** Don't worry, your information won't be shared with anyone but my muse.

You can visit me at my website at www.rosalieredd.com or contact me at Rosalie@rosalieredd.com. I love to receive email from readers!

ABOUT ROSALIE

After finishing a rewarding career in finance and accounting, it was time for award-winning author Rosalie Redd to put away the spreadsheets and take out the word processor. She pens paranormal, science fiction, and fantasy romance in her office cave located in Oregon, where rain is just another excuse to keep writing.

www.ingramcontent.com/pod-product-compliance
Lightning Source LLC
Chambersburg PA
CBHW051503170626
46811CB00002B/614